NAUGHTY NAUGHTY

'Well?' she said. 'I hope you're sorry now.'

I nodded and she went on.

'I'm sure you are, but not nearly as sorry as you're going to be. Come here.'

She took my hand, and there was nothing I could do as she led me to the bed and sat down, quite clearly intending to put me across her knee and spank me. I was stammering as I spoke, thinking of how much it had hurt before, and the fuss I'd made.

'Not now, please, Sabina, not now!'

'I'll spank you when I please, young lady!' she answered.

'No, it's not that,' I blustered as I was drawn down into position. 'I'll scream, and everybody'll hear! You know I can't help it!'

It didn't stop her. I was laid across her lap, the huge puff of my nappy seat stuck up in the air and towards the three men. Only when she'd taken me firmly around the waist and pulled the rear of my nappy open to expose my cheeks, helpless and ready for punishment, did she speak.

'Do you really think it matters if the other guests hear you squalling?' she asked. 'What are they going to think? That some brat's getting her bottom warmed before bedtime? Big deal.'

Why not visit Penny's website at
www.pennybirch.com

NAUGHTY
NAUGHTY

Penny Birch

This book is a work of fiction.
In real life, make sure you practise safe, sane and consensual sex.

First published in 2005 by
Nexus
Thames Wharf Studios
Rainville Road
London W6 9HA

www.nexus-books.co.uk

Typeset by TW Typesetting, Plymouth, Devon

Printed and bound by
Clays Ltd, St Ives PLC

ISBN 0 352 33976 4

You'll notice that we have introduced a set of symbols onto our book jackets, so that you can tell at a glance what fetishes each of our brand new novels contains. Here's the key – enjoy!

cp (traditional)

cp (modern)

spanking

restraint/bondage

rope bondage/hojojutsu

latex/rubber/leather/enclosure

fem dom

willing captivity

medical

period setting

uniforms

sex rituals

One

What could set a girl up for the day better than having her bottom creamed and powdered before breakfast?

I lay on the changing table, completely naked, my thighs open to Poppy as she stood over me, in a red woolly jumper, faded jeans and disposable gloves, her face set in concentration as she applied the razor to the swell of my sex. She was nearly finished, my pussy mound scraped clean of the downy stubble I'd let grow over the weekend, and just the tricky bits to do.

'Roll up, Gabby,' she instructed, 'nice and wide too.'

My legs came up, right up, spreading my sex and bottom to her with my arms under my knees. It felt deliciously vulnerable, with my pussy and anus fully open to her, and as one rubber-clad finger slid in up my pussy I couldn't help but sigh. Poppy giggled.

'I suppose you expect me to bring you off?'

'Please, yes.'

She answered with a cluck of mock disapproval and went back to shaving me. I held very still as she manipulated my pussy, with one finger up my hole and her thumb stretching out my sex lips to let her get at every tiny crevice. My eyes were closed in sheer bliss, and my pussy hole had already begun to contract on her intruding finger by the time she began to dab the foam away with a warm flannel.

Only the skin around my bottom hole remained, and I pulled my legs higher still to show it to her. Her finger pulled from my pussy. Cool foam squirted between my cheeks, covering my bumhole. Her finger touched, rubbing the foam in and teasing me until I was wriggling with pleasure. The razor touched, scraping away those few tiny hairs that grow around my anus. The flannel touched, wiping my bottom and the last few flecks of foam around my pussy. I was ready.

'Lick me, please, *Bobonne*.'

Her answer was another little cluck of mock disapproval, making me feel more deliciously vulnerable than ever. She was fully clothed, completely in charge of me, and I was rolled up nude on the changing table, my pussy and bottom spread to her, begging for her attention. I got it too, one rubbery finger pushed in up my pussy hole, another applied to my anus, tickling, and her tongue, right on my clitoris.

The instant she touched, a shock of pleasure ran through me. My mouth came open and I tightened my grip on my legs, holding myself open for her. Her tickling finger burrowed into the mouth of my bumhole, just a little way; her licking grew firmer, and I was sighing and telling her how much I loved her as my body began to go tight.

I just came, utterly helpless, nude and surrendered to my lover as she worked on me so, so skilfully, bringing me off, so caring and yet so clinical, doing exactly what was needed. Her tongue continued to flick on my pussy, her fingers wiggling in my twin holes as I went into a gasping, shuddering climax, biting my lip to stop myself screaming the place down. When I was quite finished, she stopped and stood back, her pretty face set in a little, cool smile. 'There we are, is that better?'

It was all I could do to answer with a purr of satisfaction. She nodded, pulling off the glove with the finger which had been up my bottom, then the other. I knew to keep my legs up, because my orgasm had left me creamy and a little slippery, so I held my pose as she took a wet wipe from the box. She wiped my bottom, then my pussy, thoroughly and efficiently, her gentle fingers probing into every little crease and fold of my sex. A third wipe was used to shine up my newly shaved skin before she applied powder, shaking a little out over my open sex, and lower, between my bum cheeks and on to my anus. A few gentle pats to remove the excess powder, a little cream applied to the mouth of my bumhole and I was ready for the day.

'My turn tomorrow,' Poppy said firmly as she twisted the lid of the cream pot back on.

I kissed her as I climbed off the changing table, not needing to answer. Naturally it would be her turn tomorrow, with me as nurse. With both of us preferring to be on the receiving end, it was the only fair way to do it. Not that I minded, even when she wanted to be beaten with a strap or cane. It was her choice.

My clothes were in the other bedroom, the normal one, so I left Poppy to tidy up the playroom and began to dress, transforming myself from Poppy's naked adult baby-girl, Gabby, to Gabrielle Salinger, modern young woman and respected therapist. One of my appointments was with a new client, so I was particularly careful with my look, for him, and for the sake of my own head space.

White silk knickers and bra with a lace trim, stay-ups, a white silk blouse, a skirt suit of fine grey

3

wool, neat but plain black heels, my hair pinned up, a touch of make-up and my steel-rimmed glasses and I was ready. The mirror showed me as I like to look for the world, elegant, serious, thoughtful, not at all the sort of woman who likes to sleep in a nappy and gets her bottom spanked.

By the time I was ready Poppy was in the kitchen, munching a sausage sandwich heavily laced with ketchup. She spoke as I poured myself a bowl of cereal. 'What's up today?'

'Plenty. I have Monty at eleven, and somebody called Lyle Ranglin at ten, also three in the afternoon.'

'Monty Hartle? What's he been up to?'

'Voyeurism, according to the report. He was given a warning with the condition he comes to me, for a full year this time.'

'Dirty bastard,' she replied, serious, but with that telltale catch in her voice.

She was going to say more, but the buzzer went. It was Monty himself, his piping voice unmistakable. 'Hi, Gabs, let us up.'

'You're early, Monty.'

'Yeah, but I get the whole day off for this therapy lark.'

'Oh, OK, come up.'

I let him in, and opened the door, waiting as he climbed the stairs, wheezing with effort. He was the same as ever, his round face beaming at me over the top of a faded T-shirt advertising a rock band, his jeans held up around his enormous gut with a leather belt on its final notch. He kissed me and gave my bottom a familiar squeeze as he pushed into the flat, his nose wrinkling. 'Sausages! Got some spare?'

He waddled through into the kitchen, not waiting for a reply. I closed the door and followed, to find him propped against the work surface, finishing what was left of Poppy's sandwich. She'd begun to make coffee, and his little piggy eyes were lingering unashamedly on the well-filled seat of her jeans. I went back to my breakfast.

· 'So what have you done this time?' Poppy asked, chiding.

'Nothing,' Monty answered, his voice somewhat muffled as he pushed the last of the sandwich into his mouth.

'Really?' I queried.

'Yeah, really,' he answered, sounding slightly hurt. 'You know me, Gabs. I'm a reformed man.'

'So what did happen?' Poppy demanded.

'It was like this – I could well use another of those, as it goes, Pops?'

Poppy shook her head but bent to take the packet of sausages from the fridge, with Monty's eyes firmly glued to the seat of her jeans as she sank into a squat and rose again. Only when she'd begun to place them under the grill did he continue.

'It was like this. I was shopping in Croydon, just shopping, not even out for a peep. There's this café, just by some escalators, and I saw this guy playing the oldest trick in the book. He'd got a tiny mirror in with his credit cards, right, and he'd hang around, pretending he was window shopping, until he saw a girl in a short skirt going up to the next level. Then he'd go up behind her and drop the cards to get a peep of her panties in the mirror. He was going to get caught, 'cause you can only do that so many times in the same place, and the girls in the café were already whispering together. I went to warn him off and, would you fucking believe it, that's when the silly cows choose to call security, and who d'you think gets pinched!?'

'You, evidently,' I answered. 'And they wouldn't accept your explanation?'

'No,' he went on, thoroughly aggrieved. 'The guy legged it, and the bitches in the café tried to say I was his look-out, and that I'd been staring at every girl who went past!'

Poppy laughed.

'OK, so I had,' Monty admitted, 'but there's no law against that, not yet anyway. I didn't have any gear, and I hadn't been trying to get sneaky peeks, even, but they wouldn't believe a word I said! Both the café girls said they'd known I was up to something dirty the moment I'd sat down, and once we got to the station and they found I had a conviction for panty thieving . . .'

He shrugged and trailed off. I believed him, because he had no reason to lie to us, and for all the irony of the situation even felt sorry for him. Before the panty-stealing incident his attitude to women had been based on resentment, so he'd never really accepted that it was unreasonable to go peeping or to add to his collection of women's underwear, mostly stolen from washing lines rather than removed from the original owners. He had never been actually dangerous. More importantly, he knew about my own sexuality, and was as tolerant and as understanding as I could have hoped for. It was that which had allowed me to persuade him to alter his views on exactly what is meant by consent, although I'd never quite succeeded. Since then he'd behaved himself, more or less, and I'd occasionally provided for his needs in return for him indulging my own, although much less frequently since I'd been with Poppy.

Poppy soon had the sausages ready; she slit each lengthwise, put them between well-buttered slices of bread and smothered them with tomato ketchup before passing the result to Monty. He'd been watching the process hungrily, his tongue occasionally flicking out to moisten fat pink lips. I watched him eat in silence, sipping my coffee and trying to analyse my own reaction to him. Physically, he was repulsive by conventional standards and not exactly wonderful by my own, while men don't really appeal to me as such anyway.

Yet with Monty there were no boundaries. He was never shocked, never disapproving, never possessive, but he *was* dirty, and when it came to sex he could take control, completely. That appealed, and if it meant I had to compromise then the occasional sore bottom was worth it for the knowledge that I could surrender absolutely and still trust him, both to respect my limits and not to make my life difficult.

He was also quite easy as a client, because he listened, and spoke to me without the slightest trace of self-consciousness. Once he'd finished stuffing himself, we went out into my living-room-cum-consulting room, where he sprawled out on my black leather couch, still talking about voyeurism as if he'd been speaking to a fellow offender and not two young women.

'That's the thing, you see, you can't stop blokes looking at girls just because some PC pillocks find it offensive, any more than you can stop girls looking at blokes, or gay guys and lessie girls looking at each other – each other of the same sex, I mean. Sure, it's not on to give some girl you don't know a teaser flash –'

'What's a teaser flash?' Poppy queried.

'You know,' he answered, 'when two guys go up either side of a girl in a short skirt, to pretend to talk. They grab her, skirt up, knickers down and her bare bum's on show to the world, her pussy too if you've done it right, but you've got to get your hand in the side of her waistband –'

'What!? That's outrageous!' Poppy interrupted. 'And you're saying it's OK to do it to a girl you do know?'

'Yeah. I mean, it's a just a laugh, right? No harm done, and if she didn't want her bum flashed she –'

'No, Monty,' I cut in, 'that's really not acceptable.'

'Sure, like I said, not with a stranger, but when a girl's put a short skirt on just to tease the boys . . .'

'No, Monty –'

'Whatever. That's not the point I was trying to make. Give a girl a teaser flash, and you get arrested, but, if her skirt blows up and she's got no knickers, what's the difference?'

'The difference is that she hasn't been molested,' I pointed out.

'Yeah, sure, but she's still had her bum shown off,' he went on, 'and that's the real art of peeping. You've got to be where you're going to get an eyeful, without any consequences.'

'Why not just go to a club?' Poppy suggested.

Monty gave a snort of dismissal. 'It's not the same, is it? I mean, OK, it's nice watching a girl do a strip, but I tell you I'd rather see a girl's panties when she didn't mean to show them than her bare cunt when she did.'

I nodded, sipping my coffee. Psychologically it made sense, and especially for men, becoming more aroused by a hint than an open offer being a clear advantage for natural selection.

Monty went on. 'It's the same on a beach. I'd much rather see a girl in a wrap bend over and show her bum in her bikini than watch her sunbathe . . . hmm, maybe not if she goes nude, 'cause I know she wouldn't want me peeping.'

8

'You're a dirty bastard, Monty Hartle,' Poppy pointed out unnecessarily. 'More coffee?'

'And you're a dirty bitch,' he answered. 'Yeah, sure. Three sugars.'

She stuck her tongue out at him and made for the kitchen, collecting my cup on the way. He was sat in the centre of the sofa, his arms draped along the back, his legs wide, his cock and balls a substantial bulge beneath the overhang of his belly, with one testicle pushing out where his jeans had worn through, covered only by purple cotton underpants. I couldn't help but think of how it had felt to take those same oversized balls in my mouth as I tugged at his cock with his belly held up out of the way, or sucked on his erection with my freshly spanked bottom stuck out behind and my fingers on my pussy . . .

'So what else have you been doing, aside from looking up girls' skirts?' Poppy asked as she came back. 'We haven't seen you in ages.'

'I'm changing job,' he answered. 'Head of IT at this place in Morden. I start in three weeks. Serious money too.'

'Good for you.'

As she bent to put her coffee down he reached out to smack her bottom, just as the buzzer went. This time it was my client, whose voice was gravely East End with a touch of something else, perhaps Jamaica. I asked him to come up and quickly let go of the intercom button.

'That is Lyle Ranglin, you two, my ten o'clock. In the bedroom, quick, and be quiet.'

Monty gave Poppy's bottom another firm swat as they quickly made for the special bedroom, taking their coffees and locking it just in time for me to greet Mr Ranglin at the door. His appearance suited his voice: two metres tall at least, heavy set and with an easy power to him despite the evidence of age in his skin and greying hair. It took a conscious effort not to stare at his broken nose.

'Mr Ranglin. Do come in. I'm Gabrielle Salinger. Take a seat.'

I'd offered to shake his hand, but he didn't respond, simply lowering himself into one of my armchairs and glancing around the room as if he expected to find a collection of shrunken heads. As he spoke I realised why.

'You know Steve Stanbrook.'

It was a statement, not a question. Stephen Stanbrook had come to me to help him come to terms with his fantasies of male dominance. I'd done my best, but it had still ended in a messy and rather public divorce, in which Poppy and I had been cited as witnesses in Kate Stanbrook's claims of adultery. Fortunately it hadn't got into the papers, and rather to my surprise being known for handling clients with psychosexual 'problems' had done my career more good than harm. As I put on my most disarming smile and adjusted my glasses, I was wondering if the burly, down-to-earth Lyle Ranglin liked to have his bottom smacked or was worried about his propensity for tying girls up, or whatever.

'Yes,' I answered. 'Stephen was a client of mine for some time. How may I help?'

'You're supposed to be discreet?'

'Absolutely,' I assured him, with a twinge of guilt for Poppy and Monty, who undoubtedly had their ears glued to the far side of the bedroom door.

Ranglin hesitated, looking distinctly unhappy, so I went on. 'Please be assured, Mr Ranglin, that I will listen to whatever you wish to say without making a judgement. I consider that personal sexual proclivities –'

'No, no, not me,' he interrupted abruptly. 'I'm not into any of that shit, fuck no! Look, I – this bastard's taken my daughter, my little Sabina.'

'Taken her? Do you mean to say she's been kidnapped?'

'No – no, not like that. Well, yes, sort of. He's brainwashed her, the fucking little shit, and if I ever – it's all this filth, this stuff . . .'

He was twisting his hands together, quite violently, and his face was working in anger. It was more than a little unnerving, given his size, his manner and that he evidently associated me with whatever his daughter had got into. I reached for a tissue to wipe my glasses, allowing my breasts to loll forwards beneath my blouse, a gesture of submission that must go back to when we were apes. Stressing that I had glasses added to my apparent vulnerability, and he had calmed down a little as he went on. 'I'm sorry, but I'm out of my head here.'

'Please explain; take your time. Your daughter, Sabina, how old is she?'

'Twenty. Here.'

He delved into his inside pocket to pull out a somewhat crumpled photograph. It showed a girl posing by a plain white door. She was obviously tall, maybe taller than I am at one-hundred and seventy-four, and built not unlike her father, but in a very feminine way; long, shapely legs, full hips and a fuller bust that made her waist seem exaggeratedly narrow. Only her face really betrayed her age, with a pretty softness to her features, but there was also a certain awkwardness in her stance, as if she hadn't quite grown into herself. Her skin was honey coloured, much paler than her father's, and her shoulder-length hair was set into a multitude of tiny plaits.

All she had on was a white and red nurse's uniform, in rubber, with the zip pulled down to show

11

off the deep, golden-brown valley between her breasts, and a skirt so short that another inch less would have left her knickers on show. A matching hat, scarlet fishnets and black high-heeled boots completed the ensemble. In one hand she held a heavy leather strap, not unlike the one I sometimes used on Poppy, but she was having difficulty maintaining the look of cool dominance on her face, with one corner of her mouth threatening to twitch up into a smile.

I'd seldom seen a picture of anyone quite so obviously enjoying themselves, and it was hard to know what to say.

'And this was taken recently?' I ventured, keeping my voice carefully neutral.

'A couple of weeks ago,' he answered. 'He took her to some club, dressed like that! Like – like some sort of speciality whore. My daughter! He sent that to her by email, afterwards. That's how I found out.'

It was not the moment to point out that he shouldn't have been reading his daughter's private emails. He was still talking.

'Dressed her up like that. He's brainwashed her, corrupted her, turned her into a cheap tart, and now he's taken her –'

'Who has, Mr Ranglin?'

'David Anthony, of course.'

'I see. So, your daughter went to a club, a fetish club, with this David Anthony, and now she has left home, to live with him?'

'Not yet, no. They've gone to France together, to some perverted club in Paris, "La Belle Dame Sans Merci" it's called. Do you know it?'

'No.'

'There's an internet site for it, which ought to be banned. It's not natural what they do, and to think of my daughter being dragged into that.'

'How do I come into this?' I asked carefully. 'I can provide counselling, naturally –'

'No. Not that. I want you to go and get her back. She won't listen to me. She hasn't listened to me since she was about three. I've been too soft. I always spoilt her, and now – now . . .'

He stopped and shook his head. I was wondering exactly how much he did know about Stephen Stanbrook, and me, because if it was the full truth then I would have been the last person to ask to help him extract his daughter from a sadomasochistic relationship, when she was quite obviously willing. Not that it was my job anyway. I steeled myself to turn him down.

'I appreciate your situation, Mr Ranglin, but I am a therapist –'

'Exactly,' he interrupted. 'You understand these things. Stephen told me it was only you who stopped him going insane when things were falling apart with his wife. You've studied these perversions; you can make her see!'

I nodded. Now I knew how Stephen Stanbrook had explained away what he'd done, by pretending it was part of a mental illness, evidently the easier choice rather than defending his actions. Evidently I'd been painted as the one who'd brought him back from the edge, rather than the one who'd done her best to help him come to terms with his own sexuality. Mr Ranglin went on before I could compose a suitable response.

'I want you to talk to her, Miss Salinger,' he said earnestly, 'to talk to her and make her see reason. You know the downwards spiral this sort of thing leads to, the drink, the drugs, even prostitution. For all I know the bastard's paying her now!' He clenched his fists, the anger in his face hardening, then went on. 'Believe me, I know. All her life I've protected her, but I've seen it all, when I was a young man in the East End, the pieces of human jetsam. I dragged myself out of that, Miss Salinger, and I'm not having my daughter dragged back down by some lecherous little shit!'

'You are a boxer?' I hazarded a guess based on the state of his nose. 'I'm afraid I don't follow the sport.'

'I'm a promoter, now,' he answered, 'but, yes, I used to be in the game. Heavyweight. That's another thing. I can't risk the press getting hold of this. I'm divorced, and my two sons are still under age. My ex-wife . . .'

He trailed off, shaking his head. I gave what I hoped was an understanding nod, still wondering how best to let him down gently as he went on. 'I'll pay, of course,' he assured me. 'Five grand plus your expenses, that's if you bring her back to me with all this – this perverted filth washed out of her head. I'll pay you two just to go and talk to her. I know from Steve you'll do your best.'

'Mr Ranglin,' I replied, ignoring the irony of his claiming she'd been brainwashed and then asking me to do the same in reverse, 'it must be plain to you that at twenty years old Sabina has a right to behave in any way she pleases –'

'I know that,' he broke in, 'but the law is an ass. She's not grown up at all, not really. It's my fault, for being too protective and for spoiling her. She's just not ready for the world.'

'So you feel this man David Anthony has taken advantage of her naivety? What kind of man is he?'

'A piece of filthy scum, a dirty old bastard, a – He was a lecturer where she's doing a course in English Literature – and God alone knows what used to go on there – but he retired last month, then I get this photo, and the next thing I know she's gone off to France with him, and fuck knows what state she'll be in when they get back!'

As he'd spoken he'd made a wild gesture to the photograph, and I picked it up again. It was impossible not to feel sympathy for the state Mr Ranglin had worked himself into, and yet it was plain that Sabina was a grown woman exploring her sexuality, something I had no right to, or intention of, interfering with.

On the other hand, two thousand pounds simply to go and talk to her was very tempting, while at the least I could attempt to affect a reconciliation between father and daughter. Yet the ethics were tricky.

I steepled my fingers.

'Mr Ranglin, this is the situation. On the strict understanding that I have no right to do more than express your concern to Sabina, I will speak to her. However, I do feel that the situation might be better resolved were you to come to me for a few sessions.'

'Me? I'm just fine, except I want my little girl back.'

'Exactly. You are clearly a man of very strong character, but perhaps no stronger than your daughter. If you were to come together, to seek a middle ground, perhaps try to understand each other's viewpoints –'

'What are you saying? Sabina's been corrupted by a pervert, Miss Salinger. There is no middle ground.'

I nodded. Even to make him realise that his personal viewpoint didn't necessarily represent a moral absolute was going to be an uphill struggle.

He spoke again. 'The deal's simple. Go to France and talk her out of it, you get five grand. Try your best and –'

'Go to France?'

'Yes, of course.'

'Wouldn't it be easier to wait until they come back?'

'Are you mad? Fuck knows what he'll have done to her by then! She might be pregnant, hooked on heroin, dead!'

'I don't think –'

'You've got to do it, Miss Salinger. Who else can I turn to? She won't even speak to me, and I can't go to the authorities, and I daren't risk the press finding out. Steve swears by you. I'll pay three grand if you'll just go, how's that, six if you succeed? Say you'll do it, Miss Salinger, please?'

From the way he said 'please' I could tell it wasn't a word that came easily. I hesitated. He was staring at me. I began to extemporise.

'I have a great many commitments, Mr Ranglin. My schedule –'

'Just a weekend. The club's this Saturday.'

'I see. Still . . .'

'Six grand flat, up front.'

He began to pull notes from his pocket, grubby in rolls each restrained with two or three elastic bands.

I was not being rushed, and held a hand up. 'Please, Mr Ranglin, allow me to give the matter further consideration. I'll have a decision by tomorrow afternoon.'

He stopped piling the money on to the table and stood up, extending one huge hand. 'I knew I could count on you, Miss Salinger. Tomorrow then, and I know what your answer will be. God be with you, Miss Salinger.'

I shook his hand, and after loading his money back into his pockets he made his exit, leaving me feeling mentally bruised and in need of somebody to talk to. That at least was easy. Mr Ranglin's steps had barely faded on the stairs when Poppy and Monty emerged from the special bedroom.

'What was all that?' Poppy demanded, Monty making straight for the table where the photograph of Sabina still lay.

Poppy got there first, snatching it up to stare transfixed as Monty crowded in to look over her shoulder.

'Fuck me, look at the tits on her!' he drawled. 'That's his daughter?'

'Yes,' I admitted, trying to retrieve the picture.

'Hey, I want to look!' Poppy protested. 'Oh my! She is gorgeous! Oh but she's perfect! What a gorgeous nurse, maybe in a proper uniform, but oh my, just to be put across her knee and spanked and spanked and spanked, and then put to her chest and suckled, or to go down on her pussy and lick her out with my bum all warm and tingly behind . . .'

She finished with a little purring noise, to which Monty added a peculiar slobbering.

'Fucking great!' he agreed. 'Only I get to watch, yeah? I wish it showed her bum, 'cause I bet she's got a peach. A lot of them do, these mixed-race girls, like in Brazil, big fat tits and peachy arses! I'd stick my tongue right up –'

'Will you two shut up?' I said. 'This is a serious situation, and one I should do my best to resolve. Mr Ranglin is –'

'A silly old fart,' Monty cut in. 'Just look at her, she's well up for it! He's just one of these guys who won't let go, that's all. Boxing promoter he said, didn't he? Can't handle it when people won't do as he says, and religious too, by the sound of it, the worst sort . . .'

'Monty, shut up,' Poppy cut in, 'you're not helping. Look, Gabby, you're going to go, aren't you? Six grand, and I bet she'll give us both a scene at this French club. What was it called?'

17

' "La Belle Dame Sans Merci", from a poem by John Keats, I think.'

'Sounds like some sort of femdom outfit,' Monty put in, a little worried.

'That makes sense,' I responded, 'and I suspect that this David Anthony is submissive. True, that does not necessarily mean he has not manipulated her, but my guess would be that their relationship is equal, or roughly equal, in terms of power if not experience. After all, Sabina is young, beautiful and obviously has a very strong personality, while David Anthony really only has his wits, along with his maturity and any presence he may project. But look, Poppy, ethically, I am obliged to present myself as from her father and put his case, which is hardly –'

'I'm not. I can go straight up to her and ask for a spanking. I bet she would.'

'Silly cow if she wouldn't,' Monty agreed.

'What if she's straight?' Poppy queried. 'That would be a shame.'

'No way!' Monty countered. 'She probably prefers girls. They all do, these dominant types.'

'Not always.'

'Ninety-nine per cent of the time.'

'Just my luck to get the one in a hundred!'

'Nah. I'd put money on it.'

'You two!' I broke in. 'For heaven's sake! I cannot do that.'

'Why not?' Poppy demanded. 'Make a joke of it. Say her dad sent you but you only came because you fancy her.'

'Yeah, nice one,' Monty agreed. 'I bet she'd give you the spanking of a lifetime!'

'And then some! Maybe she'd threaten to cane you, Gabby, and I could offer to take your place, bent over a stool –'

'Or strung up by your hands,' Monty put in.

'Oh, yes, please! Or touching my toes –'

'Or holding your ankles, and extra if you let go.'

'Or even wiggle –'

'Or cry out.'

'No, she'd gag you, with your own panties.'

'My own wet panties, after she'd made me pee myself in front of everyone –'

'In a glass, and drink it!'

'No, when she'd beaten me she'd pour it all over me, on my head and on my hot bum –'

'You two!' I snapped. 'For goodness sake! This is a professional matter, and –'

'Gabby!'

'Come on, Gabs, it'll be a laugh. Don't tell me you don't fancy her.'

'She does, the dirty bitch,' Poppy confirmed. 'I can tell. Come on, Gabby, let's go and have some fun.'

'No, Poppy, I can't.'

'Yes, you can, Gabrielle.'

'No, I –'

'Yes, you can! Say it, or I am going to have Monty spank you until you do, hard. You know you hate that.'

'No. Look, Poppy, don't be silly. I'm going, but I'm going on my own.'

'No way!'

'Yes.'

'Hold her, Monty. I'll pull her knickers down!'

I'd seen the dirty leer on Monty's face before, and I dodged behind the sofa, struggling not to giggle and babbling desperately.

'Look, you two, no, not now. This is not funny.'

They were coming at me from either side, around the sofa. I jumped the table, caught my heel on the edge and went sprawling, across one of the armchairs.

Poppy grabbed me, too weak to hold me for more than a few seconds, which was just long enough for Monty to swing his leg over my back, settling his massive buttocks on to me. My breath came out in a rush and I'd been pinned to the arm of the chair, completely and utterly helpless beneath his twenty-odd stone. Poppy let go and scampered around the chair, giggling.

'Come on, you two, please?' I begged. 'This has gone beyond a joke!'

'All you have to do is say we're all going to France,' Poppy said reasonably.

'No! Poppy, listen –'

'Uh, uh, none of that, Gabby. Just say we can come and you won't be a spoilsport in the club. Or I'm going to turn your skirt up, Gabrielle, and pull down your knickers, and spank your bottom, until you do.'

'No, Poppy! I'm supposed to be working!'

'This is work. It's Monty's therapy. After all, why would he want to peep at other girls when he can have a good look at you, and a feel? Isn't that right, Monty?'

'Absolutely, one hundred per cent,' Monty agreed.

'No,' I tried, 'you said it was better if the girl didn't know what she was showing.'

'No, I didn't,' he replied. 'I said it was better if the girl didn't *want* to be showing it. Just like now.'

'Exactly,' Poppy agreed, 'you should listen more carefully to your clients, Gabrielle. Now, are we all going to France, or is your skirt coming up?'

'Poppy, please.'

I stopped as her fingers found the hem of my skirt and began to lift. My head was full of consternation, because I was so helpless, and at the way they were treating me, my lips pursed, determined to be angry as my skirt was lifted, all the way up over the seat of my lacy silk knickers.

'Cute panties, Gabs,' Monty remarked casually. 'I love the way your buns wriggle in them.'

I hadn't really been aware I was wriggling, but I had, and I stopped.

'Look, you two, please –'

Poppy's finger found the waistband of my knickers.

'No, Poppy!'

'Are we coming to France with you?'

'No! You know –'

'Oh yes we are! Say it, Gabby, or down they come!'

'No!'

Very slowly, she began to ease my knickers down over my bottom.

'Say it!'

'No!'

Monty made a slapping noise with his mouth as my knickers were taken a few inches lower, showing the top of my bum crease.

'Say it!'

'No!'

Poppy giggled and my knickers were halfway down. Despite myself I'd begun to wriggle again, in sheer frustration.

'Say it!'

'No!'

'Fair enough. You obviously want your knickers down, so down they come. Oops!'

My knickers were down, right down, not just off my bum but in a tangle around my knees, leaving me completely bare behind.

Monty smacked his chops in appreciation and Poppy spoke again. 'Right, Gabby, are you going to be sensible, or are you going to get spanked?'

'Look, Poppy, you know I can't – ow!'

She'd smacked me, hard, full across my cheeks. It stung dreadfully on my cool skin, and she didn't stop either. I can't take pain, and she knows it, but she was laughing as she spanked me, and so was Monty, because I'd started to squirm and kick and squeal.

It stopped.

'Well?'

'No, Poppy, really –'

'OK.'

My spanking began again, harder than before, and I was no more dignified, wriggling my body in a desperate and futile effort to escape the blows, but only succeeding in making myself look more ridiculous. Both of them were laughing louder, as Poppy began to spank harder still and I began to kick harder, spreading my pussy out, and my bouncing cheeks.

'I see she's been powdered,' Monty remarked.

'Powdered *and* creamed,' Poppy pointed out, the spanking stopped, and my bottom cheeks were pulled open.

They inspected my anus, Poppy holding my cheeks apart as Monty peered close. I knew my ring had started to twitch, but I couldn't stop it, but only stay put, my head hung in defeat, my cheeks stretched as wide as they would go. My stomach tightened as Monty's big, clammy hands touched me, cupping my buttocks as he took over. He had one cheek in each hand, his fingers down in my crease, just centimetres from my bottom hole.

'She is pretty below, isn't she?' Poppy said, and her finger touched my anus.

It went in, all the way in, slid up my creamy bumhole without difficulty, until her knuckles were pressed between my cheeks. I was shaking, helpless in more ways than one, with my girlfriend's finger in me and Monty Hartle leering down at my penetrated bumhole. Poppy began to bugger me with her finger, and I was gasping too.

'So, Gabby?' she asked. 'How about it, or maybe you'd prefer my finger to be replaced with Monty's big fat dirty cock?'

She clicked her tongue on the word "cock", in anticipation of what might be done to me, Monty's cock forced in up my bumhole, buggering me as I twitched and groaned on the load in my rectum, scarcely able to accommodate him.

'No. Do anything you like, but do not have me buggered, please?'

'Say you'll take us then,' she demanded.

'No, Poppy, you know I cannot do that.'

'Spoilsport.'

She smacked my leg with her free hand and Monty took the cue, his big hands lifting from my cheeks then coming down again, just playing pat-a-cake on my bottom, but hard enough to set me wriggling and kicking my feet, with Poppy easing her finger in and out of my slippery anus all the while. I was lost, and they knew it, the stinging slaps on my bum now warm and arousing, my bumhole open and receptive. Poppy sighed. 'Oh, all right then. Get your cock out, Monty.'

'What are you going to do to me?' I demanded.

Neither of them answered, but I felt Monty's weight shift. My clothes were pushed up, including the tails of my jacket and blouse, exposing my lower back. I heard the faint rasp of his zip, and felt the warm, squashy softness of his balls settle on my skin, just above my bottom cleft. He began to masturbate and Poppy gave a giggle of delight and disgust.

I could smell his cock, and imagine it, all too clearly, his big, hairy scrotum spread out on my pale flesh, his fat cock in his hand, the thick, greasy foreskin rolled back as he grew erect over the sight of my girlfriend fingering my bumhole. Maybe he would bugger me, and I wasn't sure if I could resist.

Poppy's finger pulled out of my bottom with a sticky noise, leaving me feeling open and vulnerable. Monty's balls had hardened up, his scrotum bouncing on my back as he wanked, so I knew his cock would be hard, hard and ready for my body, in my mouth, up my pussy hole, in my rectum.

'Lick her arsehole, Pops,' he grunted suddenly. 'I want to watch.'

'No!' She laughed. 'I – oh, what the hell!'

My mouth came wide as she gave in to his crude demand and her face pressed between my bottom cheeks. She was licking immediately, her little sharp tongue tip probing and dabbing at the crevices of my bumhole and licking in my cleft. I knew she was doing it to show off, as much as to pleasure me or herself, her face to my cheeks, but not hard, letting him watch as she tongued my anus.

'That's right, do her hole,' he rasped. 'Oh yeah, like that. There is nothing, but nothing, like watching one girl lick another's arsehole.'

Poppy didn't respond, too busy with my bottom to talk. I'd relaxed completely, trapped helpless under Monty's bulk as they amused themselves with my bottom, my head swimming with the delicious feeling of being completely under somebody else's control, somebody who'll do as they please with my body, taking absolute charge.

They could have done anything, introduced Monty's cock up my bumhole and anywhere else he pleased, made me give them both tongue service, taken me into the bathroom to be peed on, or worse. I'd have taken it, accepted it, just as long as I could keep that

24

glorious feeling of having no control whatsoever over what was done to me. Poppy's fingers curled under my leg, to find my pussy, rubbing in the slippery groove between my lips and my need grew stronger still.

'Tits out, Pops, I'm going to spunk soon,' Monty gasped.

Poppy pulled back, only for a second, and I knew she'd obeyed, lifting her jumper and bra to show him her big breasts. Monty gave a happy grunt and began to wank harder. Poppy's tongue was pushed back in up my bumhole, deeper this time, licking me in earnest, but clumsy as she wiggled her jeans and knickers down to get at herself. I could smell her sex, and hear the moist noises as she began to masturbate, and I relaxed my ring, letting her get deep in, now lost to everything but my own pleasure as her knuckles worked my clitoris. My bumhole began to pulse on her tongue; my pussy went into contraction and I was there, gasping out my ecstasy as Monty gave a last grunt and hot spunk spattered my spanked bum cheeks, and Poppy's face. She cried out in ecstasy, and for one moment all three of us were coming together, broken only when Poppy gave a sudden squeal of shock and surprise.

'You idiot, you've got it in my eye!'

Monty merely grunted, still milking his cock between my bum cheeks as she scampered off towards the bathroom, holding her lowered jeans and knickers one handed. I could do nothing anyway, only lie pinned as he finished off and caught his breath, with a trickle of thick, sticky spunk running down between my cheeks and into my open bumhole.

Two

I'd promised Lyle Ranglin an answer the next day, and I had one, after a fashion. The more I thought about my decision, the less satisfactory it seemed. After all, it would achieve nothing, and perhaps even make the situation worse. I owed it to Lyle Ranglin to attempt to resolve the crisis, but it was quite clear that simply hectoring Sabina was not going to work, and that would include sending people after her.

By lunchtime I was still vacillating: sure I should go but not sure what to do. To make matters worse, Poppy was sulking, despite what she and Monty had done with me. Her advice was that we should go to France, meet up with Sabina at La Belle Dame Sans Merci as if by accident, and thus give me an opportunity to advise her on how to make up with her father. It wasn't perfect, and it was far from ethical, but the more I thought about it the better it seemed.

We were at the Café Epernay, and by two o'clock a shared bottle of Riesling had helped me get over my scruples. I rang Lyle Ranglin to say I would accept his offer and that was that: I was going. Poppy was worse than ever as we made our way to Victoria, demanding to come and weakening my resolve by enthusing over Sabina's potential as a nurse. Back at the flat I decided to look at the club's website, and found it first go.

Just from the home page I could tell it wasn't my sort of thing at all. For me, sexual submission is something very private and very intense, giving myself up completely to another's control, so that I have no responsibility whatsoever. Trust is essential, and there are only a few girls, and really only two men, I feel comfortable with.

La Belle Dame Sans Merci was in many ways the opposite; strutting, exhibitionist sadomasochism with a strong emphasis on female domination. The home page showed a pair of flaming gates flanked by two whip-wielding women in skin-tight rubber, and the photos within showed a red-lit gloom crowded with black-clad women and near-naked men, all of it set to a throbbing, urgent music which was evidently what I could expect to be played on the night.

Their house rules were surprisingly strict, members only, with a rigid dress code of leather, rubber and fetish attire. It was made quite clear that dominant or merely curious males were unwelcome, with an obligatory ten of the cane from an in-house domina for each new arrival. Female submission was guardedly accepted, although it was clearly stated to be against the ethos of the club.

It didn't appeal to me at all, although Poppy, whose previous partner had made her living by dishing out deliberately harsh and unfeeling punishments to men, was more at home. I would have far preferred to simply catch Sabina somewhere else, preferably somewhere I'd actually be able to hear myself think, but it was hard to see how to do that. Also, I obviously needed to speak to her in the absence of David Anthony. Both things added fresh fuel to Poppy's argument.

'You've got to let me come, Gabby. I know what these places are like, and how people like David Anthony think. You don't.'

'I understand male submission.'

'Yeah, sure, you've read all the textbooks, most of them by psychologists who don't know what they're talking about anyway. How many sexually submissive men have you actually met?'

'Well, perhaps not –'

'None, not properly. I used to see the same men day in and day out with Anna. I could even distract David Anthony so you could talk to Sabina. Come on, Gabby, you're just not being fair!'

I changed the subject. 'Where is this club anyway. Let's see.'

There was a link showing how to get there, and the answer was Sarcelles, which I'd never heard of, despite my time at college in Paris. It proved to be a northern suburb, almost out in the country.

'You see,' Poppy said. 'If I come, we can hire a car, and think how much more convenient that will be. We can park close to the club, and we won't have to get dressed up in fetish gear at the hotel. Better still, we can let Monty come. He can drive.'

'Can you really see Monty behaving like that?' I asked, amused despite myself as I pointed to the picture we had open on the screen, of an elderly man in nothing but an abbreviated pink tutu, kneeling on all fours so that he could act as a footstool for a domina.

Poppy burst into giggles. 'Oh come on, Gabby, we've got to! Wouldn't you like to see his face? And think of all the things he's done to us! Come on, pretty please? How can you resist? Look, I promise I'll stay in the background and not interfere, and Monty'll do as he's told if we just pull his cock for him now and then; you know he will. Please, Gabrielle?'

She'd been standing behind my chair, but got down on her knees, her hands under her chin, curved down in her best imitation of a puppy begging. I was still going to say no, because after the Stephen Stanbrook affair I'd sworn to keep work and pleasure separate, but there was a lump in my throat so big the words wouldn't come. Instead, I found myself smiling and nodding.

Buying our outfits for the club felt as if we were getting into disguise, which I had to admit was fun. I don't even pretend to understand conventional female dominance, in the sadomasochistic sense, because even when I beat Poppy I'm taking care of her needs rather than satisfying my own. Yet with my height and figure it seemed to make sense for me to pretend to be Poppy's Mistress. Also, while the idea of revealing my submissive sexuality to several hundred dominant women absolutely terrified me, it made Poppy so wet I had to paddle her while she masturbated over the fantasy before we went out.

We went into Soho, after meeting Monty at a pub where none of our straight friends was likely to be, and after a period of wandering around to compare prices with mounting horror decided to keep things to a minimum. The choice was more or less between badly made and tacky but expensive, or well made and stylish but very expensive. It also seemed that all the designers were determined to be the ones catering for the most fashionable look, with just about everything designed for tall, slim women.

That at least made it relatively easy for me, and I selected a pair of tiny leather shorts with a matching bra top, a fishnet body to go underneath and a pair of black ankle boots with four-inch heels. Monty was drooling freely as I stepped out of the changing cubicle, which I took as a good sign. It was nearly two hundred pounds, and I could just imagine Lyle Ranglin's face if I tried to charge it to expenses, let alone Poppy's outfit, but given how much he was paying anyway it seemed a fair investment.

Poppy was harder, her full bottom, tiny waist and heavy chest not a figure which was at all well catered for. In the end we went to a perfectly respectable lingerie shop, for a matching set of lacy white knickers and a full-cupped bra, along with a suspender belt and stockings from the same line. We went back for ankle boots identical to my own but in white, which seemed a nice touch.

That left Monty, who by then had a rock solid erection which simply would not go down. When Poppy had come out in her fancy underwear, his eyes had been popping from his head, and he'd been unable to resist a squeeze of his crotch, drawing a look of deep disapproval from the girl who was helping us. It didn't get any better as we walked back down Wardour Street, his hands constantly wandering to our bottoms as we discussed what he should wear.

'Fair enough, I appreciate you want to keep fairly well covered, but the great majority of the men on their website were nearly naked, and some of them were as big as you.'

'It's not because I'm fat. I don't want to give some mad bitch with a whip ideas!'

'Who knows, you might enjoy it!' Poppy laughed. 'And maybe if you stopped fondling us and playing with yourself your cock would go down, yes?'

'Sorry, I can't help it. You two look so horny in those outfits. How about a quick toss, yeah?'

'Monty, we're in the middle of Soho!'

'Yeah, well, we could go in a pub bog or something?'

'No!'

'They'll be pretty empty now.'

'I am not taking you into a male lavatory, and that is final.'

'Go in the Ladies then.'

'No!'

'How about in a peep show? It's only a quid –'

'No! Look, if you really have to, do it in the cubicle. I've got some tissues.'

'Yeah, but . . .'

We'd reached a shop with a display of fetish clothing in the window, and he shut up as we went in. The male section had a very gay look, with straps and cuffs in a dense, oiled black leather with heavy-duty fittings, minuscule posing pouches, chaps, ripped jeans, heavy plaid shirts, peaked caps, and more. Monty examined them with an increasingly worried expression while Poppy walked over to a rack of spanking magazines, causing the three men who'd been browsing to make a hasty and embarrassed exit. The man behind the counter threw her an annoyed look, which she missed completely, calling out to me instead. 'Gabby, look, isn't she cute?'

She was holding the magazine open, at the centre spread, which showed a pretty young girl with shoulder-length blonde hair and a low fringe looking back over her shoulder with a worried expression as she took her knickers down for the attentions of an elderly janitor with a gym shoe in one hand. Poppy was right, but I found myself blushing and wishing Monty would hurry up. There was a complicated leather harness on a rack next to me, and I grabbed it, thrusting it towards him.

'Try this.'

He looked doubtful.

'Do you think it's me?'

'Just try it.'

He shrugged, took it and waddled across to the single changing cubicle. Poppy was still admiring her spanking magazine, and two men had already come in, taken one look at her and left. I was going to make some sort of apology to the assistant when Monty called out from the cubicle in an urgent hiss.

'Give us a hand, Gabs. I can't get the fucking thing done up!'

I shook my head and joined him, tugging the threadbare black curtain into place behind me. Monty occupied most of the cubicle, and he was nearly naked, with his top off and his trousers and underpants down to his ankles as he struggled to do the front of the harness up across the huge, pasty bulk of his belly. That was the least of it. The thing had no crotch piece, or, at least, only a large metal ring through which the wearer's cock and balls were supposed to fit, thrusting them forwards in a way that would have been provocative on any man, and on Monty, with his cock still close to full erection, was simply obscene.

'Breathe in!' I instructed. 'And hold the sides. I'll do the buckle up.'

He nodded, took a deep breath and pulled the sides of the harness as close as they would go. I took the buckle and strap, and just succeeded in doing it up, on the last notch. The second was easier, the third easier still, leaving him looking like an armoured bear, a grotesquely sexual armoured bear, with his gut held in and his cock hanging out beneath. A Hun in full battle dress would have looked more submissive.

32

Monty blew his breath out, then grinned. 'A bit tight, but my cock feels nice.'

'Sh!' I urged.

'Toss us off, Gabs.'

'No!'

'Oh come on, at least squeeze my balls. I've got to do it.'

'We'll get caught!'

'No way. He must be used to people getting off in here anyway.'

'Do you have to? Can't you just wait?'

'Come on, Gabs, with you in that leather gear and Pops in her frillies, I tell you, I'd shag a sheep. Anyway, I don't think I can get the ring off like this.'

'For goodness sake, Monty!' I answered, pulling some tissues from my bag.

He didn't take them, but began to tug rapidly at his cock. I was fidgeting with impatience, wishing he'd get a move on, but he didn't seem to be in any hurry, rolling his foreskin up and down over his helmet and stroking his balls, mumbling too.

'The way those shorts hug your bum, and Pops's boobs in that bra, like fucking melons, grapefruit maybe. God, I'd like to fuck her tits, and your arse, both at once –'

'Monty, sh!' I urged.

'Toss us off, then, come on, Gabs.'

'Oh, for goodness sake!'

I grabbed his cock, to tug rapidly at the shaft, his balls in my other hand, stroking his heavy sac. He'd shut his eyes in bliss, and one hand reached out to find my bottom, squeezing and stroking at me through my skirt. It was getting to me; I couldn't help it; but my main thought was to make him come as quickly as possible. Even when his hand pushed down the back of my skirt, I didn't stop him, letting him grope me on the seat of my panties, then down them, his fat fingers on the bare skin of my cheeks, and between them, burrowing in up my creamy bottom hole.

'Monty, no!'

'God, I love the way you cream your arsehole, Gabrielle –'

He came, spunk erupting from his cock in a high arch, at the exact instant Poppy tugged the curtain open. It went all over her front, from her breasts down to her belly, and on the spanking magazine she was carrying, open to show us a picture of a girl in school uniform being given the cane. She squealed in shock and jumped back, brushing at the spunk on her jumper. Her watch had caught the edge of the curtain, pulling it wide, for just an instant, but an instant too long. The man at the counter had looked up.

'Hey! What the fuck do you think you're doing!?'

I just ran, babbling apologies as I fled the shop, towing the protesting Poppy behind me and the man's voice floating after us. 'That's right, fuck off out of here, you bunch of perverts!'

Fortunately I still had the tissues in my hand, and made quick work of wiping her front as soon as we were around the corner. People were staring, and it was painfully embarrassing. I was still cleaning her up when Monty appeared, not looking best pleased.

'What happened?' Poppy demanded.

'Prat,' Monty responded. 'He expected me to pay!'

'Didn't you?'

'No way, it was too small.'

'Brilliant. Only you could get us thrown out of a sex shop.'

'What I meant,' Poppy insisted, 'was what were you doing pulling Monty's cock in the cubicle?'

All I could do was shrug, and as we turned into Soho Square Monty spoke again.

'It's fucking uncomfortable, this fetish gear, and I've got a better idea anyway. I'll go as a monk.'

'A monk?'

'Yeah, monks are well pervy. They whip themselves and that, don't they?'

'Only some of them, but yes, actually, that's a good idea. I think there's a theatrical shop just off the Charing Cross Road, isn't there?'

There was, and an hour later we were walking back towards Oxford Street Station, Poppy and I hurrying ahead to avoid being associated with the enormously fat monk walking behind us eating a chicken and mushroom pie with chips and giving out solemn benedictions to passers-by.

Monty seemed keen to organise the trip, and so I let him get on with it, contenting myself with checking that he hadn't done anything completely uncivilised. His idea was to take a night ferry from Dover to Calais, both cheaper and not crowded with booze cruisers, then to drive straight to Paris, so that we'd arrive before the traffic picked up and could spend the day taking our ease at the hotel, the Chez Jeanette. It made sense, especially as he didn't seem to mind Poppy and I sleeping during the journey.

He picked us up in his boxy little car at midnight on the Friday, and drove down to Dover at speed with Poppy asleep and myself dozing in the front and watching the sodium lights swing by overhead. Dover was empty, and the security system had been beefed up since the last time I'd been through, with armed police and customs men in a high shed. With nothing to hide, Monty drove blithely in.

We were asked to get out and show our documents, also to give our bags to an officer who passed them through an X-ray gate as his colleague asked us why we were going to France and how long we intended to stay. Beyond the X-ray gate was a table, and as a female officer slid open the zip on my biggest travel bag I was wondering if my leather outfit would be cause for question. To my relief she set it aside, on top of my cream angora jumper, without comment. My underwear followed, all clean and neatly folded, then a square pink parcel I recognised immediately, although I quite definitely had not packed it – my play nappies. I felt my face start to go red even as she peered curiously at it. A man was looking too.

I stepped forwards, hastening to explain. 'If you wouldn't mind, that's rather personal.'

'So I see,' she responded, and read out the all too painfully clear letters on the side. 'Extra snug – for naughty girls.'

I was blushing to the roots of my hair, and should have shut up, but went on, babbling. 'It – it's – they're the best make, that's all.'

'I bet they are,' she answered me, 'not that it's any of my business.'

'No, it isn't,' I answered, trying to sound haughty, but painfully aware that my face was the colour of a beetroot.

Poppy wasn't doing much better, and she was babbling apologies the moment we'd driven through, to a background of Monty's laughter.

'Sorry, Gabby, sorry. I didn't know they'd go through our bags, I really didn't.'

'Why in my bag?' I demanded. 'Why at all for that matter?'

'Your bag's bigger,' she answered, 'and, well, you know, I thought maybe for a bit of fun after the club?'

There was really no answer, and I held my peace as we joined a line of cars waiting to load up. We were over an hour early, but they let us on to the ferry without difficulty. I'd been working all day, and found a quiet corner to go to sleep in as soon as we'd left port, despite the bright lights and bustle.

Poppy woke me in time for us to get a coffee and climb up on to the observation deck to watch us come in. I hadn't realised just how big the ferry was, and we found ourselves looking down on Calais docks as if from the top of a fair-sized tower block, with the huge gantries and rows of cars and lorries bathed in orange-white light just fading with dawn, including one I recognised. It was unmistakable, a jeep, painted in camouflage colours with 'Razorback Paintball' on the side in brilliant scarlet and orange letters with yellow highlighting, along with a picture of a huge razorback boar pig, standing on his hind legs, his body criss-crossed with ammunition belts and a gun in his hands or, rather, his trotters. He was also wearing shades.

Razorback Paintball meant Gavin Bulmer, and in turn Monty's friend and fellow pervert Jeff Bellbird, perhaps others. They were not there by chance. Why Monty would have told them I couldn't imagine, but there was no question whatever in my mind that he had. We were already being called to our cars, and I lost no time, absolutely furious with Monty as we made our way down to the vehicle deck. He was already there, sitting complacently behind the wheel, munching on a double cheeseburger.

'Monty, why is the Razorback Paintball jeep on the docks?'

He looked up, and if his surprise wasn't genuine it was a very convincing act, especially as he had his mouth full of burger and hadn't even realised I was there until I spoke. When he'd managed to swallow his mouthful without choking he answered me. 'Jesus, Gabs, don't do that!'

'Monty, why is the Razorback Paintball jeep on the docks?'

'Oh shit. I'm sorry, Gabs, I only said it as a joke, honest, I didn't expect them to take me up on it.'

'Said what?'

'That they should come and help you sort out this kidnap business. I told Jeff in the pub, that's all. I –'

I took a deep breath. 'Monty, it is not a kidnap. Nobody has been kidnapped, and the last thing I need is Jeff Bellbird, or Gavin Bulmer –'

'Don't panic, yeah? All we have to do is drive straight off the ferry and head out of town.'

'Don't they know where we are going?'

'Well, yeah, but – but they're not going to go in a place like that, are they? It's guys getting whipped and boot licking and stuff, so no way.'

'No, but, still, I am going to have to talk to them. Idiot.'

He looked suitably abashed as Poppy and I got into the car, but went on with his burger, until the deck crew motioned us forwards and he was forced to cram what was left into his mouth so that he could steer. I could hardly bear to look, and he was still eating it as we came off the ferry and out on to the docks.

The sun was just pushing up over the horizon, striking long black shadows across the docks as we pulled out of line to where the Razorback jeep was parked, in a position we couldn't possibly have passed without being noticed. There was now a man leaning against it, Gavin Bulmer, with his arm resting on the open door and the sunrise striking red glints from the lenses of his shades. He was in combat fatigues.

38

As we drew up Fat Jeff climbed out of the car, his round, bearded face split by a lopsided grin as he saw us. Like Gavin he was dressed as if he was going off to play some sort of war game, right down to the sergeant's stripes on his sleeves. He gave us a thumbs up as I got out of the car. Gavin added a lazy salute.

'I do not know exactly what Monty has told you,' I began as I reached them, 'but I think there may be something of a misunderstanding. The thing is –'

Gavin raised a hand. 'Don't mind us, Gabs; we're just along for the ride, and, if the going gets tough, we're right behind you.'

'The going is not going to get tough,' I pointed out. 'This is not a game. I simply need to speak to Sabina Ranglin and do my best to bring about a reconciliation between her and her father.'

'What if the boyfriend cuts up rough?' Jeff asked. 'Like that arsehole with Tasha?'

'It's hardly the same,' I began, and paused.

Natasha had got herself into serious difficulty with a violent boyfriend, and they had come to her rescue. I couldn't see David Anthony, a retired academic and a submissive one at that, being a problem, but it was at least a possibility.

'I appreciate the thought,' I went on, 'but you really should not have gone to so much trouble. If we do get into difficulty, I will get in touch.'

He nodded. 'Sure thing, Gabs. Whatever you say. See you at the hotel then.'

'The hotel? You're staying at Chez Jeanette?'

'Sure.'

He gave me another casual salute and ducked down into the jeep. I turned, to find Monty grinning apologetically and starting into his explanation the instant I'd taken my seat.

'It's the nearest one to the club, you see, and seeing as –'

'Just shut up, Monty, and drive.'

He took the hint, staying quiet, as he negotiated the long concrete ramps leading out of the port and found his way to the Paris Autoroute. I relaxed, watching the sun come up over the hills in a blaze of pink and gold and thinking of when I'd first come over to England, younger than Sabina, determined to set up practice in London. Before I really knew it I was asleep.

By the time they woke me up, we were in Paris, and well past the turning for Sarcelles. Fortunately we weren't too far from one of the places I'd lived while at college, and I managed to direct him back out to the Peripherique and north again, until we eventually found it. By then he was getting tired and grumpy, so it was a relief to find that Chez Jeanette was neither a complete dump nor a brothel, both possibilities I'd considered, but a pleasant suburban auberge designed mainly for business people coming in at the airport.

He'd booked a double and a single, which caused a little confusion as the staff automatically assumed that he and Poppy were a couple rather than Poppy and I. When we'd finally sorted ourselves out, he went straight to bed, leaving us to look around. I'd hoped Sabina and David Anthony might have chosen the same hotel, but there was no sign of them, so we went out to walk around the district and locate the venue for La Belle Dame Sans Merci.

It wasn't far, just two streets away, a big, general purpose club and concert hall. The event was even advertised on posters, in a way I'd never seen in London, showing the same scene of burning gates and twin dominas we'd seen on their home page. There was a ticket booth open, so we bought three, along with two full memberships and a 'slave' one for Monty. Our tickets were printed with the same vivid scene and the club name on one side, with the details and house rules on the other.

Poppy was still tired, and I spent the rest of the afternoon reading on my bed, with a weak feeling in my stomach growing gradually stronger as my anticipation rose. By late afternoon the others had woken up, and we went down to eat, finding Gavin Bulmer and Fat Jeff already at a table. We joined them, sharing a bottle of Edelzwicker with a salad of Crottin de Chavingol while they washed down steak and chips with beer.

Inevitably Gavin and Jeff were curious about the club, but the house rules put them off so efficiently that they were soon teasing Monty about having to take the cane to get in. He was very casual about it, pointing out, quite correctly, that, if he could do it to Poppy and others, then it was only fair, and that he'd be able to handle it easily.

We left the Razorback boys drinking in the hotel bar and went upstairs to shower and change. We'd both brought long coats to go over our gear, and when we were ready we simply looked a little overdressed for the warm summer evening. Not so Monty, who didn't seem to care, and was waiting for us in the lobby in full monk's habit. I thought it best to run over what we were supposed to do on the way to the club.

'Now, Monty, remember, this is a femdom club, and a strict one too. You are my slave, so stick close; do not try and chat anyone up, and, above all, do not grope anyone.'

'Yeah, sure. I know the ropes, Gabs.'

'OK, and you are sure about taking the cane? It hurts a lot, believe me.'

41

'Yeah, but you're going to do it, right?'

'No. They have a house domina. Look, just go along with it, OK? After all, given the number of girls you've punished, or at least humiliated, you can hardly complain, can you?'

He shrugged. 'Yeah, but you're into it.'

'It still hurts,' Poppy put in, 'but, like you said, if I can take it, so can you.'

He nodded and I went on. 'From what I hear there will be more men than women, and most of them desperate for attention, so if you just stay out of the way you should be all right. If anyone does speak to you, just say you have to ask my permission.'

'How am I supposed to know what they're saying?'

'Don't you speak French? Not at all?'

'Not much.'

'Then just shrug and smile.'

He responded with a doubtful look. We'd reached the club. My stomach was fluttering as we went in, and yet more as we passed our coats over and were allowed through a second door into a square room of middling size hung with black drapes. A man in nothing but a rubber posing pouch and a collar gave myself and Poppy respectful bows and took our tickets, glancing at Monty's before ushering us through a side door.

There was another room, much the same, but with an upholstered whipping stool at the exact centre and a scattering of people around the walls, mostly near-naked men, many of whom were on their knees, and a few women, including one languid, black-clad girl with a straight, leather-handled cane in her hand. She immediately started towards us.

'He is new?' she asked, in French, and after so long it took me a moment to switch gear mentally and reply in my own language.

'Yes. He is new.'

'Is he collared?'

'No,' I answered, trying to sound confident as I had no idea what she meant.

My answer seemed to satisfy her, as she turned to snap a command to Monty, pointing one black-gloved finger at the whipping stool. He didn't need to know what she had said to understand, and went a trifle recalcitrant in manner, which earned him a rebuke and an award of two extra strokes.

Given the number of times Monty has taken charge of me, and made me do things purely for his own pleasure, I should really have enjoyed watching him get a dose of his own medicine. I didn't, far from it, feeling both guilty and sympathetic as his habit was lifted and his large grey underpants pulled down for a dozen hard cane strokes to be applied to his naked buttocks.

Poppy's reaction was very different, giggling behind her hand as he was exposed, and as he was beaten. She was a little nervous, but plainly enjoying the spectacle, at least until I pointed out that she presumably had to accept the same treatment. As the last stroke was delivered to poor Monty's now criss-crossed buttocks, she was pouting and fidgeting, but the woman merely waved us through into the main body of the club.

It was huge, and crowded, a far bigger event than I'd anticipated, yet a brief tour revealed that it was basically a single huge space with a stage at the end, on which various apparatus for punishment had been set up: whipping stools like the one in the outer room, padded benches in various designs, crosses, two great iron cages in both of which several naked or near-naked men already squatted uncomfortably, and a whole range of ropes and straps hanging from the lighting gantry.

I'd been right to think there would be more men than women, and that the girls would be getting plenty of attention. Before we'd reached the end of the room, no less than five men had propositioned me, some boldly, others merely kneeling in the hope that I'd notice as we passed, or meekly extending the leads which seemed to be almost as uniform as black leather collars.

What I hadn't expected was the amount of attention Poppy received, not only from men who seemed oblivious to the fact that she was in nothing but lacy underwear and white leather heels, but also from women. By the time we'd discovered that Sabina and therefore presumably David Anthony weren't there yet, three girls, all dressed to the nines in severe black, had approached us to ask if they could share her, or even borrow her. I was a little taken aback, and gave each the same reply, that we might be prepared to play later, but were waiting for friends.

It was only when we'd settled down at a table and Monty had bought us a round of drinks that I discovered our mistake. The very first woman who'd approached us had been a sharp-faced little virago whose high-pitched voice had been full of ill-concealed contempt as she suggested that I let her take Poppy on to the stage. She was shorter even than Poppy, and that in stack-heels, but clad in black leather from head to toe: thigh boots over trousers fitted snug to her slender hips, a corset laced back and front with inner plates so that not a millimetre of skin showed, a high collar that kept her chin up, and a hood fitted flush to her skull with her hair projecting from the top in a long braid. A catch at one hip supported a whip with a short wooden handle and a dozen or so square-cut leather thongs, also no less than three sets of collars and leads.

She approached as I took my first welcome sip of the cold white wine Monty had bought me, and took a seat without waiting to be asked. I smiled, not wishing to be unfriendly, and she responded with a nod, as if my reaction had confirmed some inner suspicion.

'You have not collared her,' she remarked, nodding towards Poppy, her accent pure, arrogant Parisienne.

'No,' I admitted, still unsure of the significance of the act. 'We're not really used to things being so formal. I live in London, at present, and –'

'I will tell you why you have not collared her,' she interrupted. 'It is because you yourself desire to be in a collar, perhaps my collar.'

I was more than a little taken aback, wondering how she'd seen through me so easily. Not that I had the slightest desire to be 'in her collar', or dominated by her in any way. There was simply no empathy, her manner wrong, her look wrong, stirring not desire, but resentment. Before I could find a suitable answer she went on.

'I thought so. It is in your eyes, your *soumission*.'

'Submission,' I corrected her.

'Mind your manners,' she answered. 'Is that not what you say, in England, to an impudent who needs to be whipped? What is your name?'

'Gabrielle,' I responded, 'this is Poppy, my girl-friend.'

'I am Martinette,' she replied, 'to you, perhaps, Mademoiselle Martinette.'

'Hi, I'm Monty,' Monty supplied, extending one bulky paw, which the girl ignored. 'Don't take this badly, or anything, but aren't you a bit – a bit short for this dominance lark? I mean –'

Up until then the woman's tone had been light, amused, but it changed instantly as she snapped an angry reply. 'Dominance has nothing to do with size.

It is in the heart that I am dominant, just as you, in your heart, you are a slave, even if your supposed Mistress lacks the strength to train you properly, or to put your fat neck in a collar!'

Monty had obviously touched a nerve, and as I caught his eye he mumbled a vague apology. She went on regardless, absolutely spitting fire as she turned on me.

'He needs to be taught respect, and you, Gabrielle, and you, Poppy, I suggest you benefit from learning the pleasure of my whip. Do you have the courage, either of you, to accept your true natures?'

Poppy was going to say something, but I was not having her getting into a scene with some little Parisian harpy.

I stood up, deliberately putting more than a touch of my father's Germanic accent into my voice as I responded. 'No. I shall whip her. Perhaps you will learn something.'

If Poppy has one complaint it's that I can't really put my heart into dominating her, and the expression on her face was of pure adoration as I twisted my hand into her curls and pulled her to her feet. Martinette also rose, her face set in a disdainful expression. I was looking down on top of her head as we made for the stage, and it was only then that I realised she already had an entourage, a group of males, all on their knees, keeping a respectful distance but creating a swirl in the crowd as we went.

As we climbed on to the stage I was wishing we'd brought an implement. Martinette had her eponymous whip, but to ask to borrow it would completely ruin my poise. Fortunately, the girl who'd caned Monty was there, standing talking next to a positive arsenal of instruments of punishment, which seemed to be available for general use.

The last thing I wanted was to be seen to hesitate, so I walked straight over, greeted the domina with a polite nod and reached out for the single school-style cane among the implements, always Poppy's favourite. If the club domina had objected, perhaps whipped me smartly across her knee for an impromptu spanking, I'd have been lost, completely. As it was, she simply acknowledged my choice with a quiet smile and went back to her conversation.

The nearest piece of furniture was a padded bench, as good as any other for bending a girl over for the cane. I nodded to it and Poppy scrambled up, all eagerness, to lay her body on the upper surface with her legs well spread at either side, the seat of her lacy knickers flaunted and taut over her meaty bottom cheeks and the chubby swell of her pussy.

Four cuffs allowed the bench's victim to be fastened into place, along with a belly strap to stop her – or him – wriggling too much. To leave them off was only going to provoke Martinette's contempt as she stood watching with a critical eye, and so I began to fasten Poppy into place, unhurriedly, fixing each strap as if I spent my whole time securing other girls for punishment.

We were already drawing a crowd, women particularly, while some of those men on their Mistresses' leads had hidden their faces, either by order, or perhaps simply because they couldn't bear to see a woman punished. That made me all the more determined to deal with Poppy properly, because the way they had badgered her to dominate them when that plainly wasn't her inclination had annoyed me. With her wrists still unfastened, I casually tugged her knickers down at the back, changing the fine sexual display of straining panty seat into an extremely sexual one of moist, spread pussy and winking pink anus between naked, fleshy bum cheeks.

Her response was a heartfelt sob, audible above the music, which was mercifully low volume. I gave her bottom a slap and paused to pull up her bra to leave her heavy breasts squashed out bare on the leather of the bench top before fastening one wrist. Having her naked, and so publicly, was exciting, and I was psyching myself up to enjoy her punishment as I walked around the table. There was certainly a good reason for it, without question, and as I fixed the last of the cuffs I couldn't resist whispering in her ear. 'While I'm caning you, Poppy, remember the customs shed.'

She let out a little whimper. I gave her nipple a pinch to bring it erect before kissing her and tugging the cuff tight to leave her completely and utterly helpless to my cane. As I stepped back I knew what I was going to do, or try to do, something I'd seen done to other girls and had done to myself, six of the best, English style, with five cuts laid parallel and the sixth across the others at a diagonal, a five-bar gate. It had to impress Martinette and, although I was sure it would be difficult, Poppy's full, fleshy bottom was the ideal target.

A few people had come close to the bench while I strapped Poppy up, but they made way as I got into position, tapping the cane to her bottom, flush with her skin and with the tip two-thirds of the way across her far cheek, the way I'd seen Natasha's boyfriend give her the same treatment. Only Martinette had stayed close, her arms folded across her corset front as she watched, and Monty, oblivious to the fact that every other male on the stage was on his knees as he drank in the glorious spread of Poppy's naked bottom.

I lifted the cane and brought it down, to land with a smart thwack against her flesh. She gave a little cry, no more, and I reached out to rub her first welt as it grew from white to an angry red. Again I measured up across her cheeks, and again I gave her a single, firm stroke, laying a second red line below the first. The third cut I put lower still, the fourth at the top and the fifth higher still, leaving her breathing deep and even and her eyes closed in pained ecstasy.

The sixth I gave her harder still, clean across the others, to leave the plump, pale orb of her bottom decorated with a near perfect five-bar gate and my darling whimpering softly into the leather with her pussy so wet she was dribbling juice down between her lips. I lowered the cane and gave a little bow to my audience, several of who began to clap, including one girl, the tallest there, big too, her more than ample chest and sleek lower body in tight fishnet with only a skimpy rubber skirt to cover her bottom and sex, but undeniably dominant.

It was Sabina, unmistakably, tall, golden brown and delightfully womanly. I was never going to have a better chance. Deliberately avoiding Martinette's eye, I pretending to look the crowd over, stopped at Sabina and stepped up to her. 'Would you like to continue with my girlfriend's punishment?'

She looked blank, unsurprisingly when I'd spoken in French. To first address her in English at a French club would have been a little suspicious. I repeated the question.

'You are German? Belgian? English? Yes? Then I'm sure you know how to use a cane. Would you like to punish my girlfriend?'

Her response was an enthusiastic nod as she took the cane from me, because she'd already caught on, and as she got behind Poppy she gave me a lead. I'd barely noticed the man at her feet; a late-middle-aged nondescript like a hundred others alone or at their Mistresses' heel. He could only be David Anthony.

'Take this, would you?'

I took it, pretending to ignore him but casting a surreptitious glance downwards. He was grey haired, of middling build, a little paunchy, with delicate, bony hands and the face of an intellectual. Already he was kneeling, his head hung low and his hands on his knees, motionless, and perhaps in submissive rapture.

Poppy glanced around, her eyes meeting mine, half-lidded in sleepy ecstasy, her mouth a little open. She blew me a kiss as Sabina tapped the cane on to her target, and I responded in kind. The cane lifted and was brought smacking down, sending a ripple of flesh through Poppy's bottom meat to leave a livid welt full across both cheeks and around the curve of her thigh. I winced, but Poppy merely gave a weak sob and Sabina appeared oblivious.

The caning continued, stroke after stroke, delivered with all the clumsy enthusiasm of somebody who had never had their technique criticised. Not that Poppy seemed to mind, taking the thrashing with growing pleasure, until she had begun to squirm her bottom about and push up in her straps. I didn't dare get behind her, not with Sabina waving the cane around so wildly, but gave David Anthony's lead to another girl at random and moved to Poppy's side instead, to take her around the waist with my hand curled in around her tummy to get at her sex.

Sabina gave me the most beautiful smile, compounded of excitement and just a little shock, but as I nodded for her to continue the cane came down across Poppy's bottom one more time and she was being masturbated as she was beaten. Her sex was soaking, the leather of the bench slippery with her juices, her skin prickly with sweat, her body stirring gently in my grip as I began to flick at her clitoris, with Sabina staring enraptured.

She wasn't the only one. Monty, inevitably, had the most revealing possible view, staring right up Poppy's bottom so that he could see every private detail between her cheeks and thighs in addition to the spread of her now well-whipped behind. As I masturbated her and she began to groan and wriggle, bucking her bottom each time the cane lashed down, his tongue was flicking in and out of his mouth, while I knew full well his cock would be rock hard beneath his habit.

The rest of the audience were fascinated too, the girls for the most part trying to look cool, the men with their faces hidden or staring in awe. Even Martinette was entranced. I rubbed faster, nodding to Sabina, and the cane was brought down harder than ever, and faster. Poppy cried out, not in pain but in raw, uncontrollable ecstasy, and again as her bottom cheeks, her anus and her pussy began to twitch, and then pulse, her flesh still bouncing and shaking to the now furious cane cuts.

She was coming, and noisily, screaming and begging Sabina to do it harder, by name. I could do nothing, only rub and pray, keeping Poppy on her high until at last her muscles went slack and I could raise a hand for the caning to stop. Sabina stood away, grinning, then came forwards to give Poppy a thank-you kiss, which had quickly turned into an open-mouthed snog. I watched indulgently until they broke apart, and only then began to undo Poppy's straps.

I was sure Sabina was going to ask how Poppy knew her name, but the question never came. Instead she began to chatter, full of mischief and enthusiasm as she complimented both Poppy and I, on our look, on what we'd done, on how uninhibited we were, and above all saying how nice it was to punish a girl.

By the time we were sat down with drinks in our hands once more and David Anthony, still not introduced, kneeling beside her chair, I knew that it was only her second club, and that the first had been one of Morris Rathwell's events in London. I knew Morris, and his wife Melody, and several of the other people involved, as did Poppy, better still, so in moments Sabina was looking at us with something approaching awe and starting to ask all the difficult little questions that plague any woman fighting to express her full sexuality. All that remained was to bring the conversation around to family and I'd be able to offer my advice, which she did not look like declining.

Poppy was talking to Monty. Sabina had sent David Anthony to fetch another round of drinks and I'd just mentioned that I'd left France to give myself room to explore my own needs fully when Martinette came to our table, taking the seat next to mine.

'So, it seems you have been well trained?

Her voice carried the same tone of amused contempt, and as she spoke she reached out to trace a slow line where my breasts rose above my leather top, her long, painted nail catching on each thread of my body stocking. David Anthony wasn't going to be in the queue for ever, and it was possibly my only chance with Sabina. I had to get rid of Martinette.

'Would you like to discipline my slave?' I offered, nodding to Monty. 'For his earlier insolence?'

She'd been after me, and hesitated, but stood up again. 'Yes. Why not?'

'Monty,' I instructed, 'you are to submit to Mademoiselle Martinette, for as long as she has use for you.'

Monty turned towards us, his face set in a look of obstinate refusal he was obviously about to put into words.

'Go with her,' I ordered as brusquely as I could manage, while trying to make urgent gestures towards Sabina without either girl noticing.

Monty rolled his eyes upwards but got to his feet.

'Now here is one who has not been well trained,' Martinette remarked. 'Don't you know to crawl to a Mistress, boy? On your knees, now!'

Monty got down, very slowly. Martinette detached a collar and lead from her hip, reaching down to fasten it around his neck. He was looking at me, and I knew it was going to cost me later, and dearly, but for the moment all that mattered was getting my time alone with Sabina. Unfortunately, she asked a new question just as Martinette was leading Monty away.

'So what are you doing in France?'

'We came over for the club. You?'

She nodded towards where David Anthony was still waiting at the bar in a press of other near-naked men.

'Oh, dog boy over there's taking me on the full tour. We're going to do Paris tomorrow, then drive out to the place where they make Champagne, to go round the cellars and that. I'm going to have him buy me some of that Crystal, the best stuff there is, and we're going to see round Moët, and . . .'

I glanced quickly to the side, where Martinette had led Monty out to a relatively open piece of floor on which various Mistresses were putting their slaves through their paces: one seated on a chair while her boots were licked, another standing with a man's head trapped between her booted ankles as she flicked his buttocks with a riding whip, two in fits of laughter, clutching bottles as they tried to ride their male mounts across the floor.

Monty was face down, his habit pulled up to expose his heavy, pasty body, Martinette's foot set in

53

the middle of his back. She seemed to be lecturing him, which seemed as harmless as it was pointless. I turned back to Sabina, who was still speaking.

'You ought to come with us; we'd have a great time! I tell you, he is crazy for me! He's bought me this ring, right, with a ruby like you wouldn't believe! I mean, my Dad's a rich guy, but –'

'Does he know that you like this sort of club, your dad?'

She laughed, loud and clear. 'You must be fucking joking! He'd flip! He'd fucking kill me! No way, girl, just no way.'

Evidently she didn't even know her father had seen the picture of her as a nurse. I needed to be very careful, choosing every word. 'Is he quite strict then?'

'Oh, yeah, he's –'

She didn't finish, looking around at a yell of pain very different from those which had been blending with the music ever since we'd arrived. I looked as well, to where Martinette was now sat on Monty's back, her face set in a sadistic sneer as she ground her heel into the flesh of his thigh. At that moment there was a lull in the music and I caught his voice, plain and clear.

'Bollocks to this.'

He just stood up. She tried to push him down again, and barked out a string of commands, in French, but she might as well have tried to restrain a rogue elephant. As he rose, she tumbled off his back, stumbling on her heels as she landed and off balance for a moment, a moment too long. Monty simply picked her up, under one arm, as if she weighed nothing.

'Right,' he announced, 'I'm going to give you a dose of your own medicine, a spanking.'

It took her an instant to understand, or perhaps for the sheer enormity of his statement to sink in, and then she was screaming and beating at him with her fists. He took three short steps to the nearest vacant chair, sat down and flipped her over his lap. I was already on my feet, trying to get around the table, but Monty didn't even pause, his thick habit providing ample protection from her raking claws, and he was indifferent to her screamed threats and orders, which were in French anyway.

His massive fist closed into the waistband of her trousers, and he gave one hard jerk; her zip burst and they were down, with her little pink bottom showing and the lips of her extremely hairy pussy peeping out from between her thighs. She'd been fighting before, but as she came bare she went completely and utterly berserk. Monty was in no mood for it, his face grim as he laid in, calling her a vicious bitch and worse as he spanked her.

'Monty, no!' I urged, grabbing his spanking arm as I reached them.

I got jerked forwards as the slap fell and I had to let go to stop myself going over on my heels. All around us people were yelling, two dominas already trying to pull Monty off, but his huge hand just kept rising and falling, smack, smack, smack, every firm blow squashing her little soft bottom out and wrenching a fresh squeal from her lips.

Men were closing in on us, and not submissive men, but club bouncers every bit as burly and pugnacious as their British counterparts. They grabbed his arms and he was forced to give up, but the job was done, with a vengeance. Martinette rolled off his lap with a final squeal, this time of surprise as he suddenly let go. She went face first, and for one second she was down on all fours, her naked, red bottom thrust high, hairy pussy and bottom cleft wide, as undignified as any spanked brat across the whole of history.

She jumped up, clutching at her trousers in a desperate effort to cover herself, but went over on her heels again, sprawling on the floor, still bare. Monty was being dragged towards the door, trying to explain to the stern-faced bouncers, and I followed, leaving Martinette still spitting curses behind us. Five minutes later we were in the street, Monty looking angry, and Poppy laughing so hard she had to steady herself on a lamppost.

'That was so funny!' she crowed. 'Did you see her face!? Oh well done, Monty, because if ever a girl needed spanking it was that one!'

Monty's expression softened a little, and more as she came to hug him, but I was less happy.

'Honestly, you two, I had Sabina eating out of the palm of my hand. Ten minutes more and I would have done it, or at least made a solid start.'

'Sorry,' Monty mumbled, 'but it was you who told me to go with the mad bitch.'

I nodded, too emotionally drained to argue.

'We could wait?' he suggested.

I shook my head. 'Don't worry, I know where they are staying. We will sort it out tomorrow. For now, I want to get back to the hotel.'

We set off, the streets now deserted. Monty still had on Martinette's collar and lead, which he took off but decided to keep as a trophy, only regretting it wasn't her panties. Poppy was full of life and mischief, with her bottom caned, and in public. The moment we were back in our room, she'd taken her coat off and was showing us the damage, with her bum stuck out and her knickers pushed down at the back.

'Cream?' she asked.

I nodded. Monty, who had followed us in and was sitting in the single armchair, stuck his tongue out and very deliberately licked his lips. Poppy just giggled and pushed her panties all the way down, stepping out of them as she made for the bathroom. When she came back her bra had gone too, and she paused to undo her heels, providing Monty with a prime rear view and leaving her in just stockings and suspenders as she bounced up on to the bed.

There was a bolster rather than pillows, and I rolled it down the bed, allowing her to lie over it. She gave a pleased little purr as she went face down, the bolster lifting her beaten bottom high enough to leave her pussy showing and let me get at every crevice. Monty already had his habit up and his cock and balls hanging out of the Y in his underpants as I retrieved a tube of cream from my bag. I let him get on with it, as it seemed the least we could do to allow him to watch after he'd been caned and then given to Martinette.

Poppy's bottom was a mess, my neat five-bar gate still visible but criss-crossed with harsher, longer welts from Sabina's wild thrashing. I couldn't have taken it at all, and as I twisted the lid of the cream free I leant forwards, to kiss her on the crest of each cheek, touching my lips gently to two of the worst welts. She sighed and gave her bottom a little wiggle as I sat back to apply the cream.

'So it was nice?' I asked, laying a long worm of cream out over the surface of one bum cheek.

'Gorgeous,' she purred, 'especially to be made to come like that, with all those girls watching, and Sabina caning me. She is so cute . . .'

She gave a little shiver as she trailed off. I laid a second cream worm on to her other cheek and began to rub it in, smoothing my hands gently over her skin. Her response was a long sigh as she settled her cheek against her hands, utterly content. For a while we were silent, the only noise the meaty slapping of Monty's cock in his hand as he brought himself to erection over the sight of Poppy's bare, creamy bottom.

I never tire of touching her; the feel of her flesh, the ivory smoothness of her skin, save for where the welts had roughened it, the wonderful way her cheeks swell and curve to create that perfect peach shape that for me is simply what sexual pleasure is all about. She lay still, her eyes closed, her mouth curved up into a lazy, contented smile, but I could smell her sex even through the tang of the cream, and she was provoking an inevitable reaction in my own pussy. Only when her whole bottom was shiny and moist, her skin glistening in the light, with cream rubbed well in to every welt and blemish, did she speak, her voice a sigh.

'That's so nice; do my bumhole too, please, and then frig me off.'

'Of course, but what about me?'

'What about me?' Monty demanded, and I turned my head to see him holding his erect cock out, the head so swollen with pressure it was glossy, and the tiny hole at the tip already moist with bubbles of pre-come.

'Do it in your hand,' I suggested. 'You look like you're nearly there anyway.'

'How about in her slit?'

Poppy gave a low, excited moan and pushed her bottom up, letting her cheeks come open to show the soft pink mouth of her anus. Monty stood up, one hand on his cock, the other holding up his belly.

'Wait,' I ordered him.

He stopped, watching with bulging eyes as I squeezed out some more cream, this time filling the shallow cavity of Poppy's bottom hole. She gave a little squeak as the cold cream was applied to her anal flesh, and a sob as I touched her, rubbing in circles around her little hole, and in, opening her slowly as my own excitement soared. Her bottom came higher, her cheeks flared, offering herself as she spoke.

'Put a finger in me, Gabby, right in.'

I didn't need to be asked. The top joint of my finger was already a little way in, deep enough to feel her ring pulsing as she squirmed in pleasure. I pushed deep, and felt my pussy tighten as my finger was enveloped in the warm, slippery flesh of her rectum. She was heavy, a little, and I wanted to taste her, to lick her, to hold my open mouth to her as my tongue pushed up, but held back, aware of Monty watching and not quite so abandoned I didn't care. I had to come though, without delay.

Monty stepped forwards as I rocked back on my heels to get myself bare. I didn't try to stop him, too busy with my body stocking. It was just too much effort to get out of it, and I simply tore it open at the back and pushed my leather shorts down beneath, to leave my bare bottom sticking out of a ragged hole. As Monty climbed on the bed, I reached back, to touch my own anus, and my pussy, teasing both the mouths into my body and thinking of all the delicious pleasures I might enjoy.

Poppy closed her legs as Monty straddled her, but her bum stayed well up, lifted by the bolster. Her cheeks had squashed together as he mounted her, but came apart with a sticky sound as she pushed up, leaving a tracery of moist white lines between. Monty put his cock in, pressing it down, and began to rub, smearing cream between her cheeks to soil the last few patches of clean flesh.

I had my pussy cupped in my hand, tickling myself, just gently, my lips and clitoris and the moist, open hole as I watched him rut in my girlfriend's bottom crease. His cock looked huge, for all her meaty bottom, and very ready, to be plunged up her pussy hole or into her slippery anus. I reached out to take him in my other hand, still teasing myself as I began to masturbate him, pulling at his shaft and rubbing his helmet between her cheeks.

Her bum came up higher still, and I pushed his cock down, his fat, glossy, cream-smeared helmet to her anus, with my own muscles jumping to the thought of my beautiful, sweet Poppy having his big, ugly cock up her bottom. Monty groaned, and pushed, spreading her ring on his cock head, to make her gasp and shake her curls even as she pushed her bottom higher still, in an agony of indecision.

I had to do it. His cock head just inside her, her anal ring loose and easy, thick with cream. I tugged harder at his shaft, guiding him up into the hot cavity of my girlfriend's rectum, only for him to grunt in sudden ecstasy. He came up her bottom, right in her open hole, then between her cheeks as he snatched his cock from me, mumbling obscene compliments on her bottom as his come spattered across her cheeks and between them.

He might have come. I hadn't, and nor had she. He'd left her bumhole an open pool of thick, white spunk, with bubbles in it where her ring was trying to close, and I knew just where I wanted my face as I brought myself to ecstasy. So did Monty. Even as I took my glasses off and leant forwards to kiss Poppy's bottom again, he had taken me firmly by the scruff of my neck. Before I could cry out, my face had been pushed into the slippery, spunk-stained cleft between her bum cheeks.

'Yeah, right in the slit!' he crowed. 'Lick it up, you dirty bitch!'

I was trying to, but he wouldn't let me, smearing my face in the blend of spunk and cream between her cheeks until I was blind with mess, my mouth and even my nose full of mixed soothing cream and his spunk. Only when he stopped rubbing did I manage to get my tongue where it belonged, well up Poppy's bottom, to lap up the spunk from her buggered ring. His hand cupped my pussy, rubbing me, one finger pushing in up my hole, and another leaving me free to finger my own bumhole, and as my ring gave, it all came together in a glorious, tight orgasm, my bumhole and pussy masturbated as I licked up a man's spunk from my girlfriend's anus, where his cock had just been, in the mouth of her sticky, gaping hole.

He didn't even let me stop, keeping my face well in as I came, and after, but pushed lower, to make me lick her pussy with my nose pressed into the spunk-filled cavity of her bumhole. She was moaning and rubbing her bottom in my face, Monty laughing, still masturbating me, and talking.

'That's it, swallow it down, a good mouthful of spunk while your nose gets brown, you dirty bitch, Gabrielle, you filthy, dirty little fuck pig!'

I was helpless, utterly, held by my neck and by my pussy, my body completely under his control, used to bring my girlfriend off after he'd rubbed in her bottom, in her bum slit, the way he'd said it, and put his cock up her bottom, and spunked in her hole, and made me lick it, swallow it, eat it.

Poppy cried out my name in ecstasy, and, as she came, so did I, for the second time, rubbed off under Monty's fat, probing, loitering fingers, as my nose got brown up my girlfriend's bumhole, again his own, dirty words, helpless, soiled and used, to bring me to a peak that set me screaming and left me weak and limp in his grip.

Three

Sabina and David Anthony were staying at the Tour d'Amboise, in the centre of Paris. We'd left the club before them, and it seemed safe to assume they wouldn't be getting up early. It was eleven o'clock before we'd managed to rouse Monty in any case, and noon before he was ready for the road. We took a bus and the Metro in, bringing back plenty of memories for me, and with Poppy and Monty admiring the sights. The hotel was easy to find, one of the finest among those fronting the Seine in Issy, but Sabina and David Anthony weren't. Not only had they left, but also shortly before ten o'clock.

Sabina had told me she intended to go sight-seeing, and Poppy and Monty wanted to anyway, so there was nothing for it but to allow myself to be dragged around for the rest of the afternoon, up and down the Eiffel Tower, through the Arc de Triomphe, around Notre Dame, and even through the Bois de Bologne to see if they could tell the difference between the real girls and the transsexuals.

By the time we got back to Sarcelles my feet were in agony, and it was time to go. Only I didn't want to. I'd come so close. It wasn't difficult to arrange myself an extra day in France, and I knew where Sabina and David Anthony were going to be. After a quick shower and a cuddle on the bed with Poppy, we came down to the dining room, where Monty and the Razorback boys were already happily scanning the menu, and made my suggestion. Not surprisingly it was taken up with enthusiasm.

'You've got to do it,' Gavin asserted, 'no two ways about it. So what's the plan?'

'Probably nothing you need worry about,' I replied cautiously. 'I need a chance to speak to Sabina alone, that much is obvious. We know they have left the hotel, and that they are visiting the cellars at Moët et Chandon tomorrow, so presumably they have gone straight to Epernay –'

'Cool,' he broke in. 'What we need here is surveillance. No way can we find where they're staying, so we need teams in the street from when this place opens.'

'It is in the Avenue de Champagne,' I pointed out, 'so it will be easy to see when they arrive, but I do not think you need to –'

'We're here to help,' he insisted. 'Do you have a photo of the target?'

I drew a sigh as I dug in my bag for the picture of Sabina in her nurse's uniform, but he was right, and if somebody had to spend maybe the best part of a day hanging around in the street I preferred it not to be me. He took the picture, Jeff also leaning close.

'Fuck me! That is nice!'

'Told you so,' Monty put in. 'Fucking gorgeous, eh?'

'And then some,' Gavin agreed, with Jeff nodding vigorously as he tried to get a better look. 'Easy to spot too. Not many of you French fillies with a rack like that, eh, Gabs?'

'She is distinctive, yes,' I admitted. 'He is about the same height, grey haired, with a rather lean face, sixty-five I believe.'

'Sixty-five?' Gavin queried.

'I think so. He's just retired.'

'And *she*'s gone off with him?' he said, tapping the picture. 'Weird!'

'She sees the relationship as a liberating experience,' I told him.

'She didn't seem too bothered with him, last night,' Poppy added, 'more into us.'

'Who'd blame her,' Jeff responded, 'but I'm not surprised her old man's pissed off.'

'His real concern is what he sees as the corrupting influence of his fetishism,' I pointed out.

'Nah, I don't reckon it's the fetish stuff,' Gavin suggested, 'more that she's gone off with an old bloke. My cousin Mandy, she was with this older bloke, only about forty, mind, and Uncle Ted nearly fucking lost it. Calling the guy every bastard under the sun, a dirty paed, the lot, even though she was nineteen. Then when she dumps him for this younger guy it's all roses. They were both shagging her, much the same. What you want to do, right, Gabs, is sort it so she gets off with some young guy, good looking, bit of money in the bank. Then the old man won't mind, take it from me.'

'Younger, good looking, money in the bank?' Poppy echoed. 'Like you, perhaps, Gavin?'

'You said it,' he answered. 'Seriously, though, that's your solution, and that way the old man doesn't have to worry about the fetish stuff, either.'

'You have a point,' I admitted, 'but you are assuming she is not devoted to David Anthony.'

'I don't think so,' Poppy put in. 'She pretty well ignored him last night.'

'This is what he wants, I suspect,' I countered her. 'He did not speak to us, after all, except to ask what we wanted to drink, and even then he addressed us both as Mistress.'

'Yeah, and me with a caned bum.' Poppy laughed. 'Prat.'

'In any case,' I pointed out, 'it would be unethical, and frankly wrong, of me to attempt to bring their relationship to an end.'

'Why?' Poppy asked. 'He's just some old goat getting his jollies with a younger girl.'

I was going to reply, but the waiter appeared and I turned my attention to the menu. One thing was clear. We were going not to Calais, but to Epernay.

We booked a second night at Chez Jeanette, and Poppy and I went up soon after dinner, both very glad to be sleeping in a bed again instead of Monty's car. The excesses of the night before, and the day, had caught up with us. She wanted to play, despite being half-asleep, and insisted on putting me in a nappy for the night, but we simply went to sleep in each other's arms, too tired even to lick each other to orgasm. It was only ten, and I was awake shortly after six, making a nuisance of myself by rousing the others and demanding an early breakfast in case Sabina and David Anthony chose to visit the Avenue de Champagne first thing and then managed to lose themselves.

For once I was glad of Gavin Bulmer's pseudomilitary behaviour. He agreed we ought to hurry, and we were on the road before the rush hour had really picked up. Poppy and I went in the jeep, leaving Jeff to map read for Monty, and we'd lost them even before we'd got to the autoroute. Gavin was explaining his ideas about what we should do, but I wasn't really paying attention, preferring to make my own decisions.

I had him take the exit for Château Thierry and drive up the Marne Valley, which had the effect of switching his conversation to the German advance of 1918 and allowed me to have my thoughts entirely to myself. From Sabina's viewpoint, I was a slightly older, much more experienced practitioner of something for which she was full of new-found enthusiasm. Evidently David Anthony fascinated her, perhaps because he was undoubtedly very different to the men she was used to, who quite likely bored her. She also thought of me as dominant.

What I didn't know was whether she was herself naturally dominant, or if she had simply allowed her growing appreciation of sadomasochism to be channelled by David Anthony. She'd enjoyed caning Poppy, probably more than I had myself, so there had to be at least an element of dominance in her make-up, or sadism at the very least, but that only told me so much about what actually went on in her head.

She had explained about collaring, a relatively new idea whereby a submissive gave themselves up to a dominant in a specific ceremony, after which the one became the other's property, at least within the conventions employed by that particular set of sadomasochists. It was exactly the sort of attitude Poppy's ex had taken, so by no means new to me, but far too rigid for my personal tastes.

Sabina had collared David Anthony, so it was obviously a line she took, although perhaps not very seriously. Nevertheless, it might well reduce my glamour in her eyes if I told her that, in fact, I only really took a dominant role to please Poppy and certainly didn't see domination and submission as immutable opposites. For the time being at least it was best to maintain my false role.

One thing I could be fairly sure of was that she enjoyed forbidden fruit, presumably that forbidden by her father most of all. Unfortunately, Gavin's suggestion of luring her away from David Anthony really was unethical, because it seemed practical, only with me, or more probably Poppy, as the bait. That way Sabina would be able to indulge in yet more strictly forbidden fruit, not only kinky sex but also with another girl, or even two other girls. We could then return with her to England, with David Anthony safely out of the picture, and her father in blissful ignorance of how we'd achieved our end.

Unfortunately, it was out of the question, and I was going to have to take the more sensible option of setting myself up to advise her on how best to cope with her sexuality, as I'd been about to do at the club when Monty had decided to turn the tables on Martinette. Yet even that was far from ideal, and I was still seeking alternatives when we reached Epernay and I had to help Poppy with the map reading.

I'd visited the Avenue de Champagne just once before, and had only a vague impression of a wide, arrow-straight avenue lined with the huge and ornate mansions of the great Champagne Houses. We still spotted Moët easily, a four-storey façade of pale brick and cream-coloured paint topped with a row of flags, the company name and founding date picked out in black letters over a metre tall.

We managed to park easily enough, and I went in to discover they'd only been open an hour. There seemed to be every chance Sabina and David Anthony had yet to arrive, and, when I enquired after my English friends, with loose descriptions of them, nobody could remember either. As Gavin had pointed out, they were pretty distinctive. The tour began in an older and finer part of the building, the front of which we could see clearly from where Gavin was parked. We only had to wait.

I volunteered to go first, as neither of them had ever been there, and settled down to watch as they went off to explore. There was no sign of Monty and Jeff, but that could only be a matter of time, and probably just as well. Poppy and Gavin couldn't have been gone more than a quarter of an hour, and I was idly contemplating the statue of Dom Perignon when I saw Sabina and David Anthony. They were coming from behind me, visible in the wing mirror, and they looked very different to the last time I'd seen them.

She was in low-rise jeans, worn with a studded belt angled across her hips and her golden-brown tummy a soft, bare swell below a scarlet crop top several sizes too small for her, so that she gave the impression of having two footballs painted on to her chest. Not for the first time I wondered how it would feel to have her delightful breasts lying soft and heavy on my back as I was held down over her knee for a thorough spanking. She was in heels too, which made her a little taller than him.

He looked like an elderly academic taking his niece to see the sights, which, after all, wasn't far from the truth. Dark trousers, a plaid shirt in muted colours and a herringbone twill jacket went with his build and features to give an impression of other-worldliness, and perhaps slight embarrassment, as if everybody knew what he got up to with his ebulliently sexual companion.

They hadn't seen me, and I was hoping to catch some interesting snippet of conversation as they stopped by the gate, just feet away from the car, David Anthony inspecting the contents of his wallet with a rueful expression, Sabina gazing up at the statue.

'Who was he?' she asked.

'Dom Perignon,' he replied, 'the man who invented the modern method of making Champagne.'

I resisted the temptation to correct him, wishing they'd say something more relevant as he began an explanation of the technique. After a moment they moved on, in through the high, black iron gates. I waited, not wishing to turn up too soon after they'd gone in, so that my arrival would look at least plausibly coincidental. Five minutes seemed about right, as there was no point in waiting for Poppy and Gavin, who weren't due to relieve me for nearly two hours. Once I'd made contact it would be easy anyway, as at the very least I was sure to have an opportunity to visit the loos in Sabina's company.

After locking the jeep and putting Gavin's keys into my bag, I strolled casually into the courtyard and up a flight of steps to where a door opened into a high-ceilinged room with a reception desk, various people, both staff and tourist, and no sign whatsoever of Sabina or David Anthony.

I enquired at the desk, to find that a tour had just left, undoubtedly the one they were with. It took a moment to listen to the receptionist's explanation of the different ticket prices and which tasting went with which, and I was pointed in the right direction to catch up with the party. They proved to be in a sort of lecture theatre, with the lights already dimmed. I couldn't see a thing, and had no choice but to take my seat and wait. As soon as the little film on the glories of Moët et Chandon was over, we were ushered downstairs, a group of at least twenty, but which did not include either Sabina or David Anthony.

By then we were in the cellar, and all I could do was stick with the group as we were shown around the maze of arched passageways and enormous stacks of bottles. The commentary was entirely in French, but it was only when another tour guide with a Union

Jack lapel badge passed by that I realised my mistake. I'd joined the wrong group, and Sabina was either ahead, or behind.

It was pointless to wander off on my own through the cellars, with several kilometres of interconnecting tunnels to choose from, which was also discouraged if not forbidden. So I stuck with my group, hoping to catch up with them in the shop, where I knew Sabina was determined to have David Anthony buy her an expensive present.

The price of my ticket included two glasses of vintage Champagne, Brut and Rosé, which I made the best of, allowing the guide to refill my glass as well. Up in the shop there was still no sign of my quarry, but they had to be somewhere around, so I waited and tried to look interested in what was for sale. Still they didn't come, and when the next English-speaking group came up from the cellars without them I was forced to conclude that they'd gone down before me.

Feeling thoroughly fed up, I bought a bottle of White Star, a brand made for the US market I'd never tasted before, and left, not a little embarrassed and seething quietly. The jeep was as before, and I began to walk disconsolately up and down the road, wondering what to do and how to explain that I'd managed to lose them to the others.

Half-an-hour passed, and an hour, before I was passing the gates of the Perrier-Jouet Domaine as Monty called out to me. 'There you are, Gabs. Have we got news for you!'

He was coming across the courtyard, with Jeff in tow, both grinning hugely.

'We,' he stated proudly as they reached the gate, 'have just spent a happy half-hour drinking fine Champagne with the gorgeous Sabina Ranglin, and, I might add, at her boyfriend's expense.'

'I thought they were at Moët?' I managed.

'They were,' he told me, 'then they came here.'

'Where are they now?'

'This guy they met said they ought to try a private grower.'

'They've gone?' I demanded.

'Relax, Gabs,' Jeff urged. 'We've sorted it for you, every last detail.'

'How do you mean?'

'You'll love this. You know what Gavin was saying about her going with him, right? Good idea, sure, but not half as good as what we thought up.'

'Not by a long way,' Jeff took over. 'We reckon it would be far better if she went with you.'

''Cause she obviously fancies you.'

'And you're into her.'

'So it's perfect!'

'Hold on!' I demanded. 'What have you actually done?'

'Just this,' Monty said, immensely pleased with himself. 'She was asking all these questions about you, but I said we couldn't answer in front of him –'

'So she sent him away!' Jeff said. 'And we told her what you're really like.'

'You are joking!?' I broke in, the blood rushing to my cheeks.

'Not the adult-baby-girl stuff!' Monty laughed. 'Just that you're sub and fancied a good spanking from her. Jeff nearly fucked it up though, said you liked to feel helpless.'

'But it's OK,' Jeff put in quickly. 'I said you liked kidnap fantasies, and bondage and that. If she doesn't come on to you the next time you meet, I'll eat my fucking hat, and I mean that.'

I drew a heavy sigh, my carefully guarded ethical standards in tatters.

'We've fixed that too,' Monty went on with pride. 'We're all meeting up at this private place, and going tasting.'

We'd just come out of our sixth Champagne domaine. The man the others had met at Perrier Jouet had recommended one, pointing out that his vineyards were exclusively Grand Cru, which was not true of any of the big houses. He was right, and the Champagne was exquisite. So was the next one, which we went to for the sake of comparison, and the next. Monty noticed that the next village along was called Bouzy, which he found so funny that nothing would do but we drive over and buy some of their famous red Champagne. We'd visited three domaines before we made our decision, and in all three the proprietors insisted we taste the Brut, the Sec, the Demi-Sec and the Rosé, then the red. Something about Poppy in particular seemed to encourage them to generosity, probably that she was getting drunker by the minute and every time she giggled her breasts quivered under her thin top. Not that Sabina and I were short of attention.

I'd been using spittoons all afternoon. The others hadn't, all except David Anthony. He was very much the skeleton at the feast, dry and disapproving, perhaps because he didn't have Sabina's full attention, although his curt answers to the boys' frank questions about his sexuality suggested a heavy burden of guilt. Not that it made much difference to the rest of us, and even I couldn't help laughing at Monty's attempts to order fruit tarts in the patisserie.

Gavin and Monty were in no state to drive. David was, fortunately, because there was neither a restaurant nor a hotel in Bouzy. There was in Ambonnay, the next village along the slope, and he was persuaded to run us there in his large, old Volvo estate. With seven of us he was going to have to make two trips, which set him grumbling, so I volunteered to walk. Sabina and Gavin were going to come with me, and at that David really showed his jealousy, positively shrewish as he claimed he needed her to read the map.

It was only a couple of kilometres, and impossible to go wrong, but she went with him, rather sulky, showing a very different side to their relationship. Poppy, Monty and Jeff piled into the back, leaving me standing in the street with Gavin. He spoke the moment the car had pulled away. 'You're well in there, Gabs, no problem.'

I knew Jeff had explained things to him, and I didn't try and contradict him. David Anthony's attitude had been wearing my patience thin, and as we moved from domaine to domaine the idea that it had been taken out of my hands and that therefore my professional ethics were no longer an issue had become ever more appealing. So had Sabina, her beauty, her bold, playful manner, and the fact that being told I was submissive hadn't changed her attitude in the slightest, along with the wine, all combined to make me want her, badly.

Despite myself, the idea of her dominating Poppy and I had been building in my head all afternoon. She was a little inexperienced, perhaps a little rough, which added a touch of fear to my desire, yet with every glass of Champagne that fear had grown a little closer to the sort of frightened anticipation that turned Poppy on so much. Maybe Sabina would cane me, as hard as she'd caned Poppy, and with me tied, and perhaps gagged, so I'd be thoroughly helpless. It would hurt like anything, and I knew I'd cry, but afterwards, when she cuddled me against the full, soft pillows of her chest, I would be able to melt into her, giving myself up completely.

'Penny for your thoughts, Gabs,' Gavin remarked as we came to the last of the houses in the village, with pale-green vineyards on both sides of the road.

'Sorry,' I replied. 'I was miles away.'

'So, er, looks like you'll be going off with Sabina then?'

I merely shrugged, unwilling to deny what I wanted so badly.

'Do you want us to dump that Anthony bloke somewhere?' he asked, completely earnest.

'No!' I insisted, even as he went on.

'It's no problem, and he is a miserable cunt, isn't he?'

'Maybe, but just leave him alone, OK?'

'Your call.'

He stopped, looking out towards where the slope rose to distant woods and a background of small white clouds on blue. I walked on to the top of a gentle rise from which I could see the yellow-stone houses and peaked red roofs of what was obviously Ambonnay.

Gavin hurried to catch up, speaking as he reached me. 'So, er, you won't be needing us, yeah?'

'I wouldn't think so, no, but thank you anyway.'

'Oh, right – so, er, what's the chances of squeezing a blowjob out of you then? You know, just to say thank you properly.'

'What? I do not believe what I am hearing! How can –'

'Aw, come on, Gabs. I know you suck Monty's cock.'

'That is between Monty and I,' I answered, already blushing, and wondering just how much he knew.

'He says you're dead good,' Gavin persisted.

I walked on, quite fast, hoping he'd give up. There was something about him, what Poppy called creepy, and always had been, but I was trying to fight down an irritating little voice in my head telling me it was only fair to give him what he wanted, and another that it might be rather nice to take a cock in my mouth as I imagined Sabina ordering me to do it.

'It won't take a moment,' he protested, whining, as he caught up with me.

I turned on him. 'It is a completely unreasonable thing to ask, Gavin, especially to a woman you hardly know, and who is in a stable, lesbian relationship.'

'We don't have to tell Pops, or anyone. Come on, love, just a quick suck?'

'No!'

'Aw, Gabs! You're fucking gorgeous, you are. I have fantasies, just about your tight little arse.'

I forced a laugh. 'And that is supposed to make me give in to you?'

'Yeah. Shows I don't think you're just any slut with a handy hole, doesn't it?'

'A slut with a handy hole!?'

'No, no, you're not, that's what I said; you're not. You're something else, so cool, like some queen or something, but what you do to Monty – fuck me, that's dirty!'

'I wish Monty would keep things to himself.' I was walking faster, tight-lipped and determined not to give in, but I had to ask, thinking of nappies. 'What has Monty been saying, exactly?'

'About what you and Pops let him do, titty fuck you, spunk in your slits and that, spank your bottoms . . .'

'Is that all?'

'All!? Fuck me, you mean there's more!?'

'No.'

I was blushing furiously, but glad Monty had had the decency to at least keep my most private thing to himself. We walked a few metres in silence before Gavin spoke again. 'How about it then?'

'No!'

'Aw, come on!'

'No. Where would we do it anyway?' I spread my hands, taking in the great green and yellow expanse of vineyard and cornfield that stretched in every direction, broken only by the occasional village and distant, wooded hilltops. Gavin merely jerked his head to one side.

'In among the plants. Who'd see?'

'In the vineyard? But –'

He was right. There was so much leaf on the vines I couldn't see more than a few metres down between the rows. Nobody was working within view.

'So yeah?' he asked eagerly.

'I did not say that.'

'You said there was nowhere to do it. That has to imply you'd be up for it if there was.'

'No it has not.'

'Yes it has. Come on.' He crooked his finger, beckoning, and stepped in quickly between two rows of vines. The leaves closed behind him, and as he turned around only his head and shoulder were visible. He looked down, then up, at me. 'Come on, Gabs, I've got it out. Sucky, sucky!'

'No!'

'Spoilsport. I'm going to toss off then, 'cause I've got to. At least give us a flash of your bum, yeah? You know I put a lot out for you.'

I felt seriously put upon, but there was a high tractor coming out of Bouzy, and he was going to see me as he passed. Shaking my head, I nipped in among the vines and ducked down.

'Nice one.' He chuckled. 'I knew you'd be up for something dirty!'

'Sh! Somebody is coming, in a tractor, the sort they work with in the vines.'

'Deep in then. Stay down.'

He moved in deeper, at a crouching run, stopping only when there was no chance whatsoever of being seen from the road. I'd stayed close, and as he turned and sank into a squat I saw that his cock and balls were still hanging out of his fly. I caught the smell of him even as he took himself in hand, showing himself off to me.

'Sure you don't want a piece of the action?'

I shook my head.

'Just your bum then. Turn around, and stick it out.'

'OK, if you have to, but be quick!'

'I'm not going to be slow, love, not with that cute little arse to toss myself over!'

I turned around, steadying myself on the chalky soil with my finger as I pushed out my bottom.

'Good girl,' Gavin sighed. 'Boy, do I love the sight of a well-filled pair of blue jeans, nice and tight across a cute little arse.'

The cock smell had grown stronger, and I could hear the slapping noise as he tugged himself erect. I closed my eyes, fighting down my rising humiliation by thinking of Sabina ordering me to pose, just as I was, my bottom stuck out, flaunting myself for a man to get excited over, my cheeks bulging in my jeans.

He gave a soft moan, then spoke. 'I could spunk right now, Gabs, all over that gorgeous little bum.'

'Don't you dare!'

'Pull 'em down then; show it bare. I'd like that.'

'I bet you would! Do not come on my clothes, Gavin.'

'Show us some skin then; you've got tissues, ain't you?'

'You are a filthy pig, Gavin Bulmer.'

'And you're a filthy piglet, Gabrielle. What did you do? Let Monty spank you and spunk in your slit? Go on, show me what you've got.'

'OK. Bastard.'

My fingers were shaking as they went to the button of my jeans, but I was going to do it. He spoke again as I pulled my zip down.

'That's it, now just ease those blue jeans down, nice and slow, with it stuck well out, yeah? Then your panties . . .'

I thought of Sabina as I pushed my thumbs into the waistband of my jeans, how it would be to have her standing over me, giving me orders, telling me to pull down my jeans for his satisfaction, so that she could give me a lovely, warming spanking in front of him, let him come on my hot bottom and hold me tight as the spunk trickled slowly down my flushed skin.

My jeans were down, eased off my bum just the way he'd told me to, very slowly, to show off my knickers and the swell of my cheeks. I had on pale-yellow ones, with a slight frill, simple and comfortable, and just by good luck not a babyish design.

His response was a low moan, then a set of queer little gulping noises before he began to talk once more. 'Oh yeah, that is nice, Gabs, fucking gorgeous! You know what I could do right now? I could pull out your panties and spunk down the back, right in your slit.'

'No.'

'Or rub off in your crease with them still up, but I want to see it; I want to see everything. Pull 'em down, Gabs; pull those darling little panties down. Show Willy your cunt, yeah?'

I shook my head, but my thumbs were already in the waistband of my panties, and they were coming down. He was grunting and gulping as I exposed myself, and I just had to look back, in case he took it into his head to fuck me. His face was red, his eyes fixed on my bottom as I came bare, my waistband slid down, showing the top of my cleft, the swell of my cheeks, the full bare width of my rear view, my bumhole, pink and glistening with cream, and my smooth, powdered pussy.

Gavin sighed. 'You shave, you gorgeous fucking little tart! I might have guessed it, and such a pretty cunt, such a pretty little cunt. One day I'm going to fuck you, Gabrielle, fuck you hard, and make Pops suck the cunt cream off my cock. I know what you do with Monty, Gabs; I know what you've done with Jeff. I want a piece of the action, Gabs. I want to fuck your cunt, or maybe I'd stick it up that little pink arsehole, good and deep. Ever been fucked up the arse, Gabs, ever been –'

'Yes,' I managed, fighting to contain my feelings of mingled disgust and arousal but unable to hold back the truth. 'Monty – Monty did it.'

'Oh you filthy bitch!' he gasped. 'I'm coming, Gabs, I can't help it. I'm coming. Hold 'em down, right down, like that, show me it all, cunt and arsehole . . . oh, yeah, I'm there. You like the feel of spunk in your bum slit, don't you? Monty said. Well, here's a portion.'

He shuffled forwards, jerking furiously at his cock, and if he'd just grabbed me and fucked me I couldn't have stopped him. It was only fair that I should be his, and everyone's, to be made to lick pussy and suck cock, to have my pussy and my bumhole used, to be stripped and spanked and treated as their property, held and helpless.

As Gavin's come spattered hot and wet on to the cool, bare skin of my bottom, I had already stuck a hand back between my legs. I didn't care any more; I just had to come, and I went forwards, on to my knees in the chalky mud, rubbing my pussy with my bum stuck high as he milked his spunk into the cleft of my bottom, right in the little puckered hole he should have driven his cock up to the hilt.

I wanted to abandon myself completely, giving in to my deepest needs, to pee on my fingers as I rubbed, even in my knickers, and I just let go, gasping in ecstasy as hot piddle squirted out from my sex, all over my hand. Gavin gave a gasp of shock and disgust, but I barely heard. I was nearly there, held back only because my bladder was running, with piddle squirting and dribbling over my busy hand as I masturbated in helpless, wanton joy.

When it hit me I screamed out loud, rubbing hard at myself as I pictured Sabina standing over me, looking down in delight as I wet myself, my bottom spanked, my pussy fucked, my bumhole buggered, and spunk squeezing out of my twin holes as I masturbated. At least I had the spunk, and I snatched it up, smearing it over my bumhole and sex lips, as I gasped and shook in orgasm, hardly aware of the man who'd teased me up squatting behind me, staring at what I was doing in numb surprise.

I'd wet my panties a little, and Gavin's leg rather badly. He didn't seem to mind too much, only grumbling occasionally as we walked on towards Ambonnay, and he quickly went up to the room Jeff had booked for him when we got to the hotel. I was suffering from more than a little chagrin, with one more man to add to the list of those who know what I'm really like. Given how friendly he was with Jeff, and Jeff in turn with Monty, it was plain he'd known a fair bit anyway, but there's a big difference between being into a little SM, which is really quite fashionable, and peeing myself, which is something most people can't handle at all. Why, I've never been sure, when bondage and corporal punishment are painful and symptomatic of violence, consent notwithstanding, but a little pee never hurt anyone. Unfortunately, that is in the nature of taboos and sexual fashion.

I also went to my room, a comfortable, airy chamber wallpapered pale blue and decorated with Champagne advertisements from the twenties and a Matisse print. Poppy was on the bed in her knickers and bra, fast asleep. I wouldn't have minded a nap myself, as I was feeling drunk and tired too, but it was only a hour until dinner and I needed to get out of my wet knickers and into the shower.

The shower did wonders for me, with the water set cool to wake me up, and by the time I was towelling myself down I was smiling at my own behaviour. I suppose it comes of liking my partners to take charge of me, and perhaps because I'm too kind hearted for my own good, but if people are pushy with me they tend to get what they want. Not aggressive, which just puts my back up, but pushy, in the way Gavin had been, determined and openly sexual. Monty knows, and it did occur to me they might have compared notes, but I didn't mind.

I'd wrapped a towel around my head and was sitting on the bed in the nude when Poppy woke up, smiling sleepily at me before staggering into the bathroom. She went straight to the loo, and I caught the tinkle of pee as she relieved herself, setting me smiling again at the memory of how often she'd done exactly the same all over me, even in my mouth. I had to tell her.

'Gavin pushed me into letting him masturbate while I showed him my bottom, on the way over.'

'You lucky cow!' she answered. 'Monty and Jeff wanted to see the village war memorial of all things, and I had to put up with David Anthony whingeing at Sabina. I got fed up in the end and came up here.'

'What is the matter with him?'

'Oh, he's just pissed off because we're around and he can't have his way with her.'

'We're not stopping him.'

'No, I mean he likes to keep her to himself, ideas wise. I reckon he's trying to mould her into his perfect domina and thinks we're polluting her.'

'There is probably some truth in that. Our opinions are hardly in accord with conventional SM practices.'

'Sabina seems to like it our way.'

'Sabina is still finding her way.'

She stood up, pulling her knickers up as she came into view, only to take them down again and step into the shower. They were left on the floor, her bra dumped on top of them, and as the hiss of water began I could no longer hear what she was saying.

It was a warm evening, and I wanted something cool and light to wear, also pretty and not too casual as we were all dining together in what had looked like an extremely smart restaurant. The best bet was a strapless summer dress I'd brought, light cotton, but dense enough to let me go without a bra underneath. Big, comfortable panties also seemed sensible, along with red court shoes. Other than a plentiful supply of knickers, the dress was also my last clean outfit, so it was just as well we were returning the next day.

I still needed my chat with Sabina, unless Monty and Jeff's plan came to fruition and she decided to come home with us. Ethics or no ethics, it was an enticing prospect, and I made a point of applying a little make-up to soften my eyes and make my lips seem fuller. I was still ready before Poppy, but only just, and we went down together. Monty and Jeff were back, dressed as they had been all day, in sloppy jeans and tops. Gavin was there too, in his combat fatigues. All three were drinking beer and studying the big, art deco menus.

'No Sabina and David?' I asked, as neither was about.

'I don't think so.' Jeff laughed. 'Apparently we're not suitable company.'

'We don't have the right attitude,' Gavin added.

'We make a mockery of SM practice,' Monty put in.

'Did they have an argument then?'

'You could say that,' Monty went on. 'He's a miserable cunt, isn't he?'

I put my finger to my lips, glancing at the very genteel couple who were the only other occupants of the little well-furnished bar they'd settled into. They seemed to be Belgian, to guess from their accents, and took no notice. Monty changed the subject, pushing a menu towards me.

'They do some serious stuff here. We're having the *gastronomique*.'

I nodded, opening it to find an impressive selection of both local and national specialities, including several things I hadn't had for years. The *gastronomique* was six courses, including choices of oysters, fresh foi gras, tornedos with morelles and roast saddle of hare. I could see why they were so rapt, but I still needed my chance to talk to Sabina.

'Do you know where they are?' I asked.

'In their room,' Gavin answered, 'but don't worry about it. We've got it covered.'

'I need to speak to Sabina.'

'You'll get a chance to speak to Sabina, don't worry,' Jeff assured me.

'Yes, but –'

'Relax, will you?' Gavin urged. 'Just enjoy the meal. We've sorted it so you get to speak to her afterwards, OK?'

'OK,' I agreed, somewhat reluctantly, as the proprietor was hovering to guide us through to the restaurant.

The meal was wonderful, served in a quiet, comfortable room with the same twenties feel as the rest of the hotel, with attentive waiters, excellent food and still more excellent wine. As the nearest thing we had to an expert, I was given the list, and selected only Grand Cru wines from the village itself, a Blancs de Blancs first, a magnum of Blancs de Noirs, and lastly a demi-sec. A single smoked oyster served in a tiny silver dish was followed by two dozen fresh oysters between the five of us, then for me a leg of chicken in a reduced wine sauce, a huge slab of fresh foi gras served with chilled grapes, the Tornedos aux Morilles, a large slice of Epoisse, and a huge slice of delicious, sticky chocolate cake. Even when I'd finished they brought pink biscuits and I was left leaning back in my seat, my tummy a hard, round bulge beneath my dress, and extremely grateful I wasn't in polite company.

The boys ordered a bottle of Fine de Champagne brought to the table, and I poured myself a small glass, sipping as I listened to them discussing adventure role-playing games, a subject so foreign to me I could barely follow it at all. It didn't matter, my tummy too full, my senses too mellow, so that the sound of their voices just seemed to wash over me. Poppy was the same, sat back, her eyes half-closed, her mouth set in a gentle smile.

Sabina and David Anthony had sat across the room, and didn't appear to have enjoyed their meal at all, he looking stuffy, she with a sulky scowl on her face. Perhaps it would have happened anyway, without us, perhaps not, but it occurred to me that her father need not really have worried. When it came down to it, they simply didn't have enough in common for more than a brief fling. Once she'd found out that his submission was purely sexual, and that he was as jealous and controlling as any other boyfriend, the glamour had quickly faded.

Possibly I didn't even need to speak to her, but I wanted to, and as the boys had evidently gone to a lot of effort to set something up for me it was only polite to go along with it. Maybe it would be fun. Maybe I'd be taken up to the woods on the hill and put on my knees to lick her pussy, or be taken across her knee for a spanking while the others watched, or even be made to kneel at her feet while she peed all over me, soaking my pretty red dress, the cotton plastered to my breasts, my mouth full as I drank straight from her sex and rubbed myself to ecstasy with my hand pushed down my own soggy knickers.

Across the room, David Anthony had stood up. Sabina followed, still looking sulky, but as she caught my eye she winked. I didn't dare respond, or he'd have seen, but raised my glass to my lips in salute. On their table, a half-bottle of Champagne stood upside down in the ice bucket, empty yet still barely a couple of glasses each.

As they left the room, Gavin spoke. 'OK, men, this is how it works, and we need to keep it tight. We're zero minus forty-five. By zero minus twenty, Sabina will have her mark in a scene, tied on the bed. He'll think he's going to be left for a while. If he won't play, she'll pretend to lose it and storm out. Either way, she's scheduled to leave the building at zero minus fifteen, take his car and move north on the D26 Trépail Road; that's the right-hand fork at the fountain, got it?'

I nodded, shaking my head to try and clear away the Champagne.

He went on. 'You, Gabs, and Pops, will already have left, at zero minus forty, taking the same route, north towards Trépail. Monty, Jeff and I will be sitting on the fountain, so if he does come out we can misdirect him. Gabs, by zero minus ten you should be where the woods come down close to the Trépail Road. There's a war memorial. Stop there, and Sabina should be with you at zero hour. All clear?'

Again I nodded.

'Then go, go, go.'

I stood up, not particularly steady on my feet and a little taken aback by his sudden burst of energy and enthusiasm. At the least I'd hoped for a chance to digest, but an evening stroll was a nice idea anyway, so I didn't protest but followed his orders, leaving the hotel and linking arms with Poppy as we started down the road. She was a little nervous, talking about nothing very much rather fast and with an edge to her voice. So was I, wondering if it would be just a conversation with Sabina, or something more.

It was dark, with a bright moon already up and the sky a glittering field of stars as we left the lights of the village. My tummy was getting tighter, and I was wishing I hadn't eaten quite so much, especially if she was going to want to spank me. I knew I'd give in though, because it was simply too good an opportunity to miss. Whatever happened, if the consequences were that she got rid of David Anthony, I knew I'd feel bad, but not that bad. He was cold, controlling, aloof, and if she wanted me . . .

We reached the war memorial, a black spike against the dull, roughened silver surface of the moonlit vineyard. There was a bench, and I sat down, trying to think of sex instead of dead soldiers. Poppy stayed on her feet, looking back down the road and fidgeting. When she spoke her voice was more nervous than ever.

'I need to pee, do you?'

'I could, yes, but – but maybe Sabina would like to make us wet, or something? Or not, it might turn her off?'

'I don't know, but I do know she's going to spank us, both, and I don't think she'd be best pleased if I did it down her leg during my punishment. I can't wait anyway.'

She was already making little treading motions with her feet, and immediately disappeared in among the vines, where she wouldn't be seen from the road. I nipped in after her, pulling up my dress and pushing down my panties as quickly as I could. Poppy sighed as her pee came, splashing on the ground beneath her, and as I too let go I was thinking of my coming spanking, and what a pity it was the pee trickling from my pussy wasn't running down Sabina's thigh as she dealt with my bottom, an exquisite piece of surrender I always enjoy. Poppy was right though: Sabina almost certainly wasn't ready for anything quite so liberated, and it would have been such a shame to spoil our spankings.

I let it all out, gave my bottom a little wiggle to shake the last drops free and patted myself dry with a tissue. Poppy was already finished, and was adjusting her panties under her dress. I hastened to follow suit, wanting to retain at least a little elegance before I was put across Sabina's knee and my knickers taken down. Not that the indignity of a spanking gets to me as much as some, but I wanted to feel that wonderful come down from poised woman to squalling brat. I do squall too, because I really can't handle the pain, and Sabina was a big girl . . .

She was also coming along the road, or somebody was – white, English headlights approaching, the car slowing, then stopping. The lights died, leaving after them green and purple images dancing in the back of my eyes. There had to be at least a faint chance it would not be her, but David Anthony, and I briefly steeled myself for the confrontation. A single figure climbed from the car and I heard the click of heels on tarmac in the darkness, unmistakable. I took Poppy's hand, my stomach fluttering dreadfully as she approached, until we could see it was her, still in the black two-piece she'd worn at dinner. Not that I could make out more than an outline, but I could still imagine the wonderfully motherly look it had given her, just right to spank me until I was crying in her arms.

'Gabrielle? Poppy?' she asked, with a deliberate and wonderfully stern lilt in her voice. 'I understand you two would like to have your bottoms spanked?'

'Yes, please,' Poppy answered immediately.

'Yes,' I managed, any last thoughts of serious conversation gone on the instant.

'Yes, what?' Sabina demanded.

'Yes, Mistress Sabina,' Poppy answered promptly.

I didn't. I wasn't used to it, but managed to follow on. 'Yes, Mistress Sabina.'

'That's better,' she replied coolly. 'I'm really going to enjoy this. I think I'll do Poppy first, and you can watch, Gabrielle. Come on, into the car, both of you.'

She turned on her heel and we followed the staccato clicks back towards where the Volvo was parked beside the vines. Sabina opened the back door

and the interior light came on, revealing her clearly
for the first time, tall and dominant in her black suit,
her hair pinned up, her blouse a little undone, to
show the first swell of her big, golden-brown breasts,
her face set in an expression of tolerant amusement.

'In the front, Gabrielle,' she ordered, and I obeyed,
climbing in to kneel on the passenger seat, looking
back.

Sabina sat down, at the exact centre of the rear
seat, her lap flat and her knees together. Poppy came
behind, crawling in, to lie down over Sabina's legs
without having to be told. Her bottom was lifted, her
legs up to let Sabina close the door, which plunged us
once more into utter darkness.

'Light, Gabrielle,' Sabina ordered. 'I think you
ought to see this, for your own good.'

I fumbled for the light and once again the little
scene was revealed in a yellow glow, now with
Sabina's arm curled around Poppy's waist, holding
her down, over the knee, the standard way to spank
a naughty girl, and the best. Poppy looked around,
her eyes wide with anticipation and excitement, then
closed in sheer bliss as Sabina very slowly began to
ease up her dress. The big, pastel-blue panties she'd
chosen that evening were exposed, tight across her
fleshy cheeks and caught a little in her crease to make
her bottom seem fuller still.

'Very pretty,' Sabina said, and gave Poppy a pat on
the panty seat, 'but I still think they'd better come
down, don't you?'

Poppy nodded urgently.

'Slut,' Sabina remarked, 'this is supposed to be a
punishment. Oh, well, I suppose I'll just have to make
it nice and hard then, won't I?'

Again Poppy nodded, but with a little less enthusiasm. Sabina took hold of Poppy's waistband, her

smile cool and haughty as she peeled down the big blue panties, all the way, into a tangle at ankle level. Poppy hung her head and gave a little sob. I knew exactly how she felt, her bottom bare as she lay across a fully dressed woman's lap, ready for spanking, complete surrender.

Sabina gave a little purr and laid a hand on to the crest of Poppy's bottom, golden-brown skin against pale cream, save where the blemishes still showed from the cane. I already wanted my hand down my panties, but held back, knowing it would be all the better if I did as I was told until I could simply no longer help myself.

'Beautiful,' Sabina sighed, still stroking Poppy's bottom. 'I do love a girl with a nice, plump bottom.'

Poppy was purring, her bottom lifted to Sabina's caresses, her cheeks a little open, her thighs parted, to hint at the swell of her pussy. I could smell her excitement too, and my own, a rich, feminine tang, filling my head with all sorts of delicious thoughts of what Sabina might do with us once our bottoms were warm.

First came the pain, and, as Sabina abruptly stopped stroking Poppy's bottom and started spanking it, I was immediately biting my lip. She was hard, really laying in, with Poppy held tight to stop her from struggling as her bottom bounced and wobbled to the slaps. Poppy was kicking her feet, too, and shaking her head, her dark curls hiding her face as she fought to cope with the sudden, stinging pain.

In moments she was better, as her cheeks started to warm and the pleasure kicked in. Her frantic kicking stopped, her thighs came a little apart and her legs went limp, making her sex available. She'd had her fists clenched, but her fingers came open as she propped herself on one elbow, to stroke at the heavy swell of one breast as her punishment continued.

'A cheeky one, are we?' Sabina said as she saw, and began to spank all the harder, her face set in determination.

Poppy winced in pain, once, and then she lifted her hips, her hand was down between her thighs and she was masturbating, rubbing her sex as she was spanked with her face set in delirious pleasure. Her bottom was pushed high, her fingers busy in the wet groove of her pussy, her cheeks spreading to the now furious slaps to show off the soft pink hole of her anus.

'Harder, Sabina,' she gasped, 'as hard as you can!'

Sabina shook her head, but she did try, spanking faster than ever to send Poppy's bottom into a jiggling, squirming frenzy. I reached out to stroke Poppy's cheek, and lower, down the front of her dress and into her bra, pulling out her big breasts to add to the sense of exposure she loved. With that she cried out in ecstasy and she was coming, shivering and gasping her way through orgasm as she was beaten, until at last it was over.

For her, maybe. Not for me. I swallowed the lump in my throat as Poppy sat up, dishevelled and bleary eyed, but smiling. By the time she'd come, her bottom had been reduced to a ball of hot red flesh, and she winced a little as she sat on it. Her panties had come off when she'd been kicking in pain, but she didn't bother to retrieve them, or cover her chest, instead beckoning to me as I clambered between the seats.

'Let me suckle her while she's beaten,' Poppy advised. 'She'll like that.'

I felt my cheeks start to colour at the suggestion, but Sabina merely patted her lap. Poppy was right, though, I needed a cuddle, badly, because I'd seldom been so scared before a punishment, because the way Sabina spanked was punishment, and not the sort of

91

gentle affirmation of who's in charge Poppy gives me. It was going to hurt, and I knew I could never take it as well as she had. What makes Poppy purr and sigh leaves me blubbering, but I wanted it; I had to have it, and my stomach was tying itself in knots.

When I'd managed to get over the seats I was already half on top of them, and I laid myself down as Poppy had done, across Sabina's lap with my legs kicked up. Poppy took me in her arms immediately, holding me tightly against the warm softness of her chest and feeding a nipple into my mouth. Sabina had me around the waist, holding me helpless, to make my bottom feel deliciously vulnerable as her hand settled on the seat of my dress.

'Not so plump,' she remarked, 'but nice and cheeky all the same. Now, we'd better have you bare, I think, so, up comes your dress.'

I closed my eyes, suckling urgently at Poppy's breast as my dress was lifted to unveil my bottom. It was what I'd wanted from the instant I'd seen her picture, for all that I'd tried to put my work first. She was so lovely, so big, and strong, and firm, yet utterly feminine, the perfect person to punish me, to have me.

'And down come your panties.'

My dress was on my back, the full seat of my big white panties showing. Her fingers took hold of my waistband and I was shivering in blissful reaction as my knickers were taken down, baring my bottom in a wonderfully matter-of-fact way, just because I needed to be bare for my spanking.

I thought she'd pull them off, but she left them inverted around my thighs; always wise the way I kick, and perhaps Poppy had told her. Again her hand settled on my bottom, now skin to skin, stroking my cheeks, tickling in my cleft, just centimetres from the urgent bud of my anus, to set me wriggling in her grip and sucking at Poppy's teat in desperate need.

'Bad girl.' Sabina laughed, and began to spank me.

From the moment the first, hard swat landed on my naked bottom I was completely lost. It stung so much I just went wild, kicking in my panties and thrashing my whole body, holding tight on to Poppy, my mouth off her breast and open, gasping and squealing in my pain. They held me down, keeping me firmly in place as my poor bottom was turned to a blazing, aching ball of pain.

Again, Poppy had told her. It's the best way to do me, just to hold me down and spank me the way I should be spanked, because I can't control myself: I never could. In just moments I'd burst into tears; my glasses had fallen off and I was screaming so loudly that Poppy had to gag me, laughing as she wadded her discarded panties into my mouth. Being gagged shut me up, but it didn't stop the pain, and still Sabina spanked, the smacks of her hand on my bare bottom echoing around the car as they reduced me to a blubbering, tear-stained mess.

I was fighting even to breathe, my nose snotty with my crying and my eyes blind with tears. It hurt so much, and I couldn't stop it, and the stinging was driving me crazy, and it was so right, exactly what should be done to me, taken in charge and just spanked, with my panties down, always, spanked and spanked and spanked, and held and cuddled and stroked, my pussy so hot and so wet and so ready, until I could be brought off under Sabina's firm and purposeful fingers.

'OK, put the cuffs on her.'

The spanking stopped. Poppy had spoken, her words coming to me through the dizzy haze of my spanking pain. Sabina stopped, leaving me snuffling pathetically over their laps as I fought for air. My nose was running badly, and my vision was a blur, but my bottom was ablaze and my pussy in urgent need of a hand, so if they wanted to cuff me they could, or anything, just as long as I was thoroughly taken care of.

I hate to be spanked, but it takes me somewhere no other treatment can. As Sabina reached into the back of the car I was limp, my mouth back on Poppy's teat, trying to suckle through my panty gag, with my mingled tears and the snot from my nose running down over the plump swell of her breast. She was stroking my hair as my arms were taken up behind my back and put in soft leather cuffs joined by a metal chain that lay cold against my skin. A second pair of cuffs were applied to my ankles, Sabina took me by the hair and pulled me off Poppy's chest, to apply a single leather strap around my head, holding the panties in place.

My sense of helplessness was soaring, unable to move, unable to speak, unable to see more than a blur, and they were going to have me, to use me as they pleased. I was squirming my bottom, a slut begging for a caress, which was what I got.

'I'm going to rub her off, it's only fair,' Poppy said casually. 'Spank her bum, would you?'

She'd taken me in hand again as she spoke, now with one arm pushed down under my front, her hand on my pussy. Her fingers burrowed into the wet crease between my sex lips as Sabina cocked one knee up to get my bottom high, and the spanking had begun again.

It still hurt, every stinging slap, to set me kicking and wriggling in my bonds with even less dignity than before. That wasn't going to stop me coming, not with Poppy's expert fingers working my sex to bring me higher, and higher still, until at last I was sticking my bottom up to the smacks, my cheeks well apart, showing off my bumhole and my open pussy, as lewd and urgent as could be. It hit me, my whole body jerking, my cuffs and my lowered panties taut against my skin as Sabina spanked and Poppy frigged, and had my mouth not been plugged with my girlfriend's now soggy knickers I would have screamed loud enough to be heard at the hotel.

I almost fainted, it was so intense. My vision had gone and I couldn't breathe properly, snorting bubbles of mucus through my nose. Poppy had a tissue, and wiped my face and her chest, giggling, as Sabina pulled up my panties. As my senses slowly came back, I began to fill with a deep sense of gratitude, and wanted nothing more than to be allowed to cuddle them both, held trembling in their arms, or put on my knees to lick them to a well-deserved ecstasy if that was what they wanted.

It wasn't. They didn't even release me. Instead, I was lifted between them and bundled into the back, still completely helpless. The cover was pulled over me; I was plunged into darkness and left, squirming weakly in my straps and wondering what they were going to do to me, because Sabina had quite obviously taken Monty and Jeff at their word, and kidnapped me.

Four

I knew why Poppy had wanted me to pee before we met Sabina. She hadn't wanted me to disgrace myself in the back of the car. Unfortunately, it was going to happen anyway, unless they let me out soon.

It had all been too much for me: the drink, the huge dinner, the spanking and being brought to orgasm in bondage. Despite the situation I was in, I'd gone to sleep, or maybe passed out, in moments. I was safe, after all.

When I awoke the car was moving and I was in absolute blackness. My body was stiff, but because I was in chained cuffs a little wiggling had my circulation flowing again. All I could hear was the steady grumble of the Volvo's engine and the occasional swish as another vehicle passed by, at speed. We were on a motorway, presumably heading back for Calais, but I could be absolutely certain they hadn't kidnapped me simply to take me home.

I was going to be used, maybe made Sabina's slave, somewhere safe, where I could be put through my paces without danger of interference. The thought had me shivering with expectation as soon as I was fully awake. I knew how it would start too, with the humiliation of being helped from the car, my panties taken down and held in a squat while I peed in front of them. Poppy would do it, for certain, because it was just the sort of thing that turned her on. At least, she would do it if I didn't wet my panties first, because the strain was already beginning to tell.

They weren't talking, so either Poppy was asleep or I was alone with Sabina, which was a little scary, adding to my already strong sense of erotic apprehension. Not that it mattered about my feelings. I had given myself over to her, and she could do just as she pleased, which was what held me on a steady level of excitement and longing and fear as we drove on through the night. Sabina also seemed to have stolen David Anthony's car.

I think I slept again, a little, because suddenly I could see light around the edges of the cover, bright, blurry lines, but definitely daylight. We were no longer going fast either, or straight, but slowly, and on bendy roads, with frequent stops for turning. We had to be approaching our destination, and my apprehension rose higher still, but cut with relief at the thought of finally being able to empty my bladder, however humiliating.

At last we stopped, and the engine died to leave absolute silence, save for a twitter of birdsong. Every sound was suddenly sharp: the click of the car key or the door catch, Sabina as she yawned and blew out her breath, the dull thud of one door behind shut and the hiss of another being opened, the back. I wriggled round as bright light flooded my compartment, to see the middle part of Sabina's body, her neat black skirt and stockinged legs. The cover was pulled off and she was standing over me, her face set in a wicked smile as she gazed down on my bound and helpless body.

'Are you OK?' she asked.

I shook my head, making muffled noises through Poppy's panties and nodding down to try and show her I needed a pee. My dress was still up, my panties showing, so I clenched my cheeks, hoping she'd understand. She did, her smile growing more wicked still.

'Oh, you need a piss, do you? Or are you just trying to escape?'

I shook my head again, urgently.

She chuckled. 'OK, but you needn't think you're getting off. Come on.'

She took hold of my ankles, pulling my body forwards, before setting my feet carefully on the ground. I was starting to shake as my dress was pulled up and my panties lowered, feeling as helpless as I'd ever been, even in nappies. Still supporting me in her arms, she let me squat down, my bare bottom just inches from the ground. I let go, my eyes closed as my pee gushed out, such a relief, and so intense because it was under her control, yet so humiliating because she didn't know what she was doing to me.

When I'd finished she stood me up, and even used a tissue to pat my pussy dry before pulling up my panties. I was getting a little stubbly, and it tickled as the cotton was pulled snug around my sex, making me tighten my cheeks. Her response was a gentle pat to my bum before she let my dress fall.

'None of that, bad girl. Believe me, you'll get plenty later.'

She took my arm, both leading me and supporting me as we moved away from the car. We were in woodland, very dense, with young trees growing on uneven ground beside a track mettled with worn concrete, all rather blurred without my glasses. Ahead was a squat, concrete building with a rusting metal doorframe and a single square window. She steered me towards it, and inside, as I walked with tiny, jerky steps in my ankle cuffs. A dark passage led away inside, with a door to the right, through which

I was led into a bare room, the floor green with algae and lit bright with pale, morning sunlight from the window.

'Kneel down,' she instructed.

I obeyed, supported as I sank to my knees on the smooth, cool concrete. Helpless and ready, I looked up to find her smiling down at me, her beautiful face full of amusement and mischief. As she stepped away I gave her a quizzical look, hoping she wasn't going to leave me, but she merely put her finger to her lips.

'Sh! Everything's going to be OK.'

She left, and returned immediately with the collar and lead Martinette had put on Monty and a long piece of twine. The collar was attached to my neck; the twine passed through the eye of the lead and tied off to an ancient, rusting light fitting directly above my head. More helpless than ever, I was shivering with reaction, but surprised only that I'd been allowed to keep my clothes on. Again Sabina stood back, speaking as she reached the door.

'There we are, darling, now be a good girl and stay still, while I fetch Poppy and the boys. Then we're going to have some fun with you.'

Again I threw her a look of alarm, and tried to speak through my panty gag, but too late: she was already gone. I thought she was teasing, until I caught the sound of the Volvo's engine and the crunch of tyres among twigs and leaves. She'd gone, leaving me to the mercy of anyone who happened to stumble across what was obviously an old bunker. Maybe it would be a man, or several men, hunters or woodsmen who might be tempted to make use of a helpless girl, in my mouth, between my breasts, up my pussy, in my anus . . .

Only of course they wouldn't. Poppy would never have let her do anything that left me in real danger.

She and the boys would be nearby, intent on waiting until I'd worked myself into a real state before they came in and made use of me. Then I would get it, in every hole, perhaps three at once, mounted on Monty's cock, while I sucked on Jeff's and Gavin eased his in up my bumhole, all the while with Sabina standing over us, directing what was done to me in her cruel, laughing voice.

I hung my head, as low as my lead would permit me, my eyes closed, thinking of how I might be used. Sabina would be in control, presumably, but I didn't know her, if she'd be a stern Mistress, or a gentle one, if she'd take charge of everything and keep the men under control, or if she'd simply let them have me, to do with as they pleased. If she did give them to me, I was in trouble. It was hard to think of three men who would be dirtier with me, especially after I'd been difficult with Gavin in the vineyard.

They'd fuck me, no question at all, but that was the least of it. I'd be made to suck their cocks, all three, maybe take their balls in my mouth, even kiss or lick their bottom holes, a thought that wrung a sob from my throat. They were sure to want to bugger me, too, and the fact that I can barely take it wasn't going to matter. I'd just get my bumhole well lubricated before their cocks were put up. Maybe they'd spunk up my bottom too, and make me suck them clean when they'd done it, or one might give me a good buggering and pop his cock in my mouth to come while another took over in my rectum.

Sabina would watch as I gradually lost control, until I was begging for more, as I had when she spanked me. Only this time it would be worse, far worse, my utter degradation the subject of my pleasure, and hers, or maybe disgust if it went too far. Even then she might be amused, and I couldn't see her stopping it. It didn't matter anyway. I was hers to give, to use, and what happened was what happened, not my responsibility. Maybe she was as bad as they were, deep down, and might pee in my mouth and all down my dress before making me lick her to ecstasy.

A strong shiver ran through me at the thought. The crotch of my panties was already sticky and wet, and both my nipples were rock hard, painfully sensitive even against the light cotton of my dress. It was all very well making me wait, but I was getting frustrated and uncomfortable. That was the point, of course, even if I wasn't afraid. I was worried, though, because they were certainly taking their time.

I knew they were just playing mind games, rationally, but rationality doesn't mean much when you're chained on your knees in an abandoned place. Maybe something had gone wrong, after all? It wasn't impossible. Maybe Sabina had stopped to rest and gone to sleep before she could tell the others I was ready? After all, she'd been driving all night. Maybe she'd got lost? Maybe she'd crashed the car?

No, the others would be nearby, maybe even deeper in the building, trying to stifle their laughter at my plight. Soon they'd come, and the only thing I'd have to worry about would be satisfying all five in whatever way they wanted. Even then there was going to be an added discomfort, or humiliation, to my choice, because my rectum was feeling distinctly heavy from the huge meal I'd had the night before. Either I had to ask to go first, or suffer.

It was best to ask, and hope Sabina was sympathetic, because that sort of thing was sure to be far beyond her limits. It nearly always is, even with people who'll happily whip a girl until she's screaming. Yet if they didn't get a move on her limits weren't going to make any difference, because I'd already have done it, in my panties. It was unthinkable, to be caught like that, by her.

Another thought occurred to me. Perhaps they were waiting for me to try and escape. It had to be possible, because the light fitting I was tied to was almost rusted through, while I could just about get my hands to my ankle cuffs. Yes, that would be it: they'd let me escape, just so they could hunt me down through the woods. It would be Gavin's idea, or Jeff's, just the sort of thing they were into. Perhaps they even had their paintball guns?

Real fear gripped me, so strong I had to clench my bum cheeks to prevent a disaster. Jeff had shot me before, and it hurt like hell. Maybe if I stayed put after all, refused to run? If I did, I was going to fill my panties, any moment. Maybe I could escape and move deeper into the bunker to relieve the now sullen, bruising weight in my rectum? Yet it was dark and there might be holes in the floor, all sorts of obstacles.

I was starting to panic, and I forced myself to calm down. The sensible thing to do was release myself, get Poppy's panties out of my mouth, go outside and call out 'Red', the stop word all my friends would understand, except Sabina. It would spoil things, but there was really no choice, and doubtless they would take it out on me later. Besides, even Gavin and Fat Jeff weren't mad enough to shoot me without giving me a pair of protective goggles.

My first thought was to get Poppy's panties out of my mouth, but I couldn't. The strap was too tight, while the light fitting proved stronger than I'd thought, my jerks only showering my body with rust. Nor could I get my wrists free, and reaching down behind my back really hurt my bloated tummy. Wriggling about made my tummy worse, too, and the pressure was starting to come in waves, each one a little harder to contain than the last, also more painful, until every time one came I had to stop struggling and close my eyes, concentrating on holding myself until it had passed.

Before long I was shaking my head in raw consternation and tugging in futile effort at my cuffs. My body was prickly with sweat, and the sheer, awful helplessness of my situation was making my pussy juice more and more. A fresh spasm came, so painful it left my jaws clamped tight on my mouthful of soggy cotton. I held on, but it left me feeling weak and I knew I couldn't do it again, or maybe once, or twice, and then I'd fill my knickers . . . unless I got them down with my toes.

I tried, fighting to get my feet high enough to push my big toes into my waistband. My dress was in the way, filling me with a frustration so strong I started to cry, and to panic, kicking stupidly at myself as once again the pressure started to build. I stopped struggling, the tears squeezing from beneath my tightly shut eyes, telling myself I could do it, but I couldn't.

It was too late. For all my desperate clenching, my bumhole had started to open, spreading on the hard, heavy load inside, wider, and I was sobbing in bitter defeat as my ring began to pout. Out it came, my anus no longer under my control as I felt what Monty so obscenely referred to as the turtle's head start to emerge, squeezing out between my cheeks despite my furious efforts to pull it back. With my bumhole agape and my whole body wracked with my sobbing, out it came, on to the taut, clean white cotton of my panties, and I was dirty.

At that I gave in, completely. My bumhole was wide open; my panties were soiled, and I couldn't bear the pain of trying to hold on any more, or of defying my own emotions. Still I held it, a last spark of dignity refusing to allow me to break my toilet training, until, with the next wave of pain, I broke completely. A final, choking sob came up from deep in my throat and I let go, my body shaking hard, my eyes now tightly closed, the tears still streaming down my face, but now in a state of bliss, my dignity forgotten.

Surrendered, a long sigh escaped my lips as I gave in to the pressure, releasing what was already halfway out of my bumhole into my panties, pushing out the cotton into a tent-shaped bulge beneath me. It was huge, and heavy, hanging in my pouch, a sensation that left me shaking my head in reaction and wishing my hands weren't cuffed behind my back so that I could stuff one down my panties and bring myself off then and there.

Nothing of the sort was possible, my bondage too tight to allow me to do anything but kneel there in hopeless, blubbering submission as I emptied my dirt into my clean white panties. With the first lump now in my panty pouch the pressure had died, and I might have tried to break free once more. It was pointless. A soiled girl is a soiled girl, regardless of whether she's done a little, or a lot. They'd know.

Besides, I wanted to do it, despite myself, as much as possible, so that the glorious sensation of being unable to stop it would go on for ever, the weight in my panties grow so great it pulled them down. It was going to be a lot too, the full consequences of my huge meal the night before; oysters, chicken, foi gras, tornedos, cheese and cake, all of it out in my panties, to bring me all those awful, glorious feelings that come no other way.

So out it came, with my head hanging on my lead, hot tears streaming down my cheeks to wet my dress across my breasts, my toes wiggling, my wrists and ankles jerking a little in my cuffs, my bumhole working, open and closed, open and closed, squeezing my dirt into the seat of my gradually expanding panties, piece by piece, to make my bulge grow fatter and heavier, until the need to rub myself off had grown to a physical pain.

I was still scared of the others coming, except Poppy. Poppy would have known what to do, teasing me as she slid a hand down the front of my panties, telling me off as she masturbated me, perhaps pulling out my waistband to show what I'd done, perhaps holding my bulge as it grew, or spanking the sides of my cheeks to make my load wobble as she brought me to ecstasy. When I'd come she'd have held me shivering in her arms, kissing my tears away and stroking me to calm me down; then she would clean me up without a word of condemnation.

She wasn't there, not to frig me, not to release me, not to clean me, and my frustration and need was still growing with the weight in my knickers. At last I stopped, so full of raw emotion that my jaw was trembling on the soggy panties in my mouth. I thought I was done, but no. Again came the pressure inside me, and this time I pushed, my head thrown back in ecstasy as I squeezed my dirt out of my bumhole, to squash between my cheeks and push my overloaded panty seat into a fat dome under my bottom.

A little pee came too, soaking my crotch and dripping from the underside of my bulge to make a yellow pool on the floor beneath me. With that, it stopped, my full load now in my heavily distended panties, my chest wet with tears and the snot running from my nose, my face slippery wet, my vision a blur. I stayed still, not wanting to soil my pussy, as my emotions slowly came back under control.

Still I had to get free, no matter what, and I had to come. I could picture just how I'd look from the rear, with my panties swollen beneath the taut seat of my dress, showing off what I'd done in them. They'd know, immediately.

What I needed was Poppy, but I could hardly wait. It might be Gavin, or Jeff, who would laugh their heads off at the state I was in, or Monty, who was quite capable of buggering me in my own mess. Worst of all was the thought of Sabina's uncomprehending disgust. A new idea came to me.

Very, very carefully, I stood up, bringing my lead to a new angle, so that I could exert pressure on the light fitting with the back of my neck instead of my throat. As I came upright the load in my knickers shifted, allowing me to feel the full weight of my dirt, at least a kilo, enough to pull them a little way down at the back. The top of my bum crease came bare and I froze, terrified my panties would fall right down, because with my ankle cuffs on I wouldn't be able to step out of them. Nor could I pull them up, and even if I did escape I'd be left waddling about in an even more agonisingly embarrassing condition, with my soiled panties around my ankles.

They stayed up, my load wobbling jellylike slightly under my bum as I moved, and as I pulled the fitting broke at the first tug, showering me with rust. I'd done it. My shaking was so hard I could barely stand, and my breathing was coming in little ragged gasps, but I was free. I drew a sigh, or rather a snivel, thinking of how I might have been well out in the woods before my accident happened, perhaps even managed to free my wrists and get my knickers down in time, but also what a waste that would have been.

A little effort and I was free of the ankle cuffs too. I moved cautiously to the door and peered out, half-expecting to find a ring of grinning faces. No-body was there, the track empty, the wood still and hot after the cool of the bunker. Without my glasses it was all rather blurred, but I knew what I needed, water, and that meant going downhill, into the wood, where with luck I could find a stream and wash my filthy bottom.

The woods were better than the track anyway, because the thought of being caught in the state I was in was unbearable. The ground was rough, forcing me to go painfully slowly, while brambles and twigs kept catching in my dress, ripping the hem, and all the while with what I'd done in my panties bobbing and wobbling beneath me. Soon I was wet with sweat, and shaking harder than ever, but there was nothing I could do but push on.

Maybe a hundred metres had passed, though it seemed like a thousand, when the slope changed abruptly. I found myself on the lip of a wooded gorge, with a glittering stream a good hundred metres below me. Better still, no more than twenty metres to my side a cluster of rusting iron spikes thrust up from the ground, each ugly, jagged tip the most wonderful sight I could have imagined.

I hurried over, my load swinging heavy in my panties as I moved. I turned round, and very carefully put the chain of my wrist cuffs into the top of a spike, and twisted. Five minutes later I was running sweat, my fringe plastered to my face and my dress to my chest and belly, but my arms were free. Ten minutes later I was stretching in the sunlight, my mouth no longer clogged with Poppy's panties, my limbs stiff and sore, but loose.

Being free changed my whole perspective, but I still had to clean up, and that meant the river, so I scrambled down the steep slope, in an elation that maybe verged on hysteria, but I didn't care. Every movement kept me aware of the huge load in my panties as it jiggled and swung. When I had to jump, they'd get tugged a little lower down my bum, until I was half-bare and had to pull them up. Then, when I had to bend, it created a delicious squashy feeling between my legs. Each sensation brought me that little bit higher.

It was going to get better too. Long before I'd got to the river my exertion had brought what remained inside me down into my rectum. I let the feeling build, now thoroughly enjoying myself, until when I reached the bank I could barely hold myself. There was a little copse of young beeches – perfect concealment. My dress came up, and off; I kicked my shoes away, leaving me in nothing but my cuffs, collar and my already well-soiled panties.

I took hold of a tree, hugging the trunk as I slid to my knees in the moist leaf mould. My thighs came wide; a hand went down my panty crotch and I was sighing in ecstasy as my fingers found the slippery crease of my sex. As I began to masturbate I gave a little shimmy, making my huge load wobble in my panties. It felt so wonderfully heavy, and it was about to get heavier. I closed my eyes and my mouth came wide as I gave in to the pressure in my rectum, letting my bumhole open one more time as I rubbed at myself in truly filthy bliss.

Out it came, and again I felt my panties swell, just as they had when I'd been in bondage, tied and helpless as I hung on my lead. I'd been unable to stop it then, and I was unable to stop it now, loading my knickers as I masturbated, piece after piece of dirt oozing out into my already straining underwear, until at last it could hold no more. My waistband was already halfway down over my bum, and as I pushed the last lump out my knickers began to slide lower, pulled down by the sheer weight of what I'd done in them.

With that glorious feeling I started to come, and the last fragile strand of my reserve snapped. I reached back, to take my bulge in my hand, holding what I'd done, the heavy, squashy bulk of my own dirt, which I'd done in my panties because I'd been tied up, helpless, unable to stop it as I soiled myself; as I shit in my clean, white knickers.

I screamed the wood down as I came; I just couldn't stop myself, the unbearable shame of being caught masturbating with a good kilo of dung in my panties irrelevant beside my need. I was wiggling my bum too, to make my panties fall down and show myself behind, still holding my load, and at the supreme moment, when I was so high my vision had gone red and my muscles were jerking in uncontrollable spasms, I squeezed.

Five

Only when I came down from my blinding climax did the reality of my situation sink in. Even once I'd cleaned up and taken off the broken cuffs and my collar I'd be left in nothing but a torn party dress and a pair of court shoes. I had no bag, no phone, not even my glasses. Nor did I have any idea of where I was, or what had happened to the others.

If they found me gone, they'd search the woods, which was another good reason for cleaning up as fast as possible. After stripping off my collar and cuffs, I waded into the shallow stream, and squatted down to pull off my panties. They were beyond hope of rescue, and I hid them under a heavy rock before washing myself thoroughly, all the while with a rueful smile for my own filthy behaviour.

My dress was better than I'd expected, torn but not enough to show anything, and soon clean. It wasn't going to take long to dry in the hot sun, but I had to stay stark naked while it did. Not that I minded, as nudity means nothing to me as such, only when combined with some taboo sexual practice. I was also confident in my ability to be able to browbeat anyone who came across me into stammering apologies in a matter of seconds.

I'd screamed with all the power of my lungs as I came, so I half-expected somebody to turn up, hopefully my friends. Nobody did, the gorge and the surrounding ridges remaining in a silence some would have found eerie. I wasn't even sure where I was, beyond the fact that it was almost certainly nowhere near Calais. The landscape was completely wrong.

When my dress had stopped actually dripping I put it on and started back up the slope. I felt very tired, physically drained from spending so long in bondage and mentally drained from what I'd done, and I hadn't dared doze while my dress dried off. Only my increasing worry kept me going as I climbed back up the long slope to the lip of the gorge.

The bunker stood as before, the track empty but for a pair of Speckled Wood butterflies dancing in a patch of sunlight. With no watch, I had no idea how long it had been since Sabina left me, but the sun was close to the zenith. I was supposed to be getting back, but before anything else I had to find my friends. My passport, my money, everything I needed was in my bag, maybe with Sabina, maybe with Monty, maybe still in the hotel in Ambonnay.

After a while I called out, thinking that the entire thing might have been set up for me. There was no response, either to their names, or my stop word, which would have indicated that the game was over. Taking a piece of rusting wire from among the leaf litter, I took a moment to scratch a message into the algae-encrusted wall in the chamber where I'd been imprisoned, left an arrow of twigs pointing at the bunker door and started down the track, counting my paces.

A kilometre passed, and a second, before the track turned; the woodland gave way on my right and I was looking out across low downland as far as I could see to a blur of green and yellow and blue. A second track joined the one I was on, just a few metres away, and down it was coming a vehicle, too blurred to make out. I waved as I ran forwards, determined to stop it, and could have cried with relief when it came to a halt, a battered van with a man in scruffy *bleu de travail* seated behind the wheel.

'What's going on?' he demanded as I reached the car. 'Been out to a party?'

'Something of the sort,' I answered. 'Can you tell me where we are?'

'Where we are? That was some party you had. We are near Vienne-la-Ville.'

'Which is a town?'

'A village, my village. The nearest town is Saint Menehould.'

'Saint Menehould, in the Argonne!? Shit!'

I'd sworn in English, and he gave me a slightly puzzled look before speaking again. 'So, party girl, would you like a lift?'

I hesitated, not particularly keen on the way his gaze was directed to where my breasts were quite clearly bare under my dress, or at all sure where I wanted to go. Sabina had run into difficulty; there could no longer be any doubt.

'I am not sure. Have you passed a British car at all, a dark-green Volvo, estate model?'

'No.'

I bit my lip. The whole plan smacked of Gavin and Jeff, not Sabina. They'd have been supposed to meet up, surely, and most probably at the nearest village to the woods where I was to be dealt with. It was better than standing around in the road, and if the worst came to the worst I could ring my parents or go to the police.

'Yes, thank you. Where are you going?'

He shrugged. 'Moiremont, Saint Menehould, perhaps. It is ten kilometres.'

'Moiremont, please, if we're north of Saint Menehould.'

'You are truly lost, party girl. So what will you pay me?' He was grinning. He was not thinking of money.

I drew a heavy sigh. 'Never mind. I'll walk.'

He shrugged. 'You are foolish, party girl. Here you are, lost, but you would refuse me a moment of pleasure for my help? Get in the car, suck my cock and you will have my gratitude and my help. Perhaps you are hungry? I will buy you lunch. Perhaps you are thirsty? A beer in the first bar we find, my promise. Why not? You are no nun for certain, but you are very beautiful, naked under your dress. Come on, can it be so bad?'

It made sense, in a way, and I was thinking of the times I'd taken men in my mouth, sometimes just out of sympathy, Monty for instance. This was different, my pride too strong to allow it. I shook my head. He gave another shrug and moved on, disappearing down the chalky track in a blur of dust. I walked on, feeling angry and abused despite the fact I hadn't given in.

I counted a thousand paces and a second thousand, until my throat was parched dry and my legs were aching. The sun was hotter than ever, beating down out of a cloudless blue sky, with the heat haze over the track so strong I could see it even without my glasses. I gave up counting, unable to bear the thought of the remaining eight kilometres and just putting one leaden leg in front of another. No more vehicles passed, but when I finally came to where a little quarry had been cut beside the track the same man was there, seated on the bonnet of his van with a piece of well-filled baguette in one hand and an open bottle of beer in the other, the brown glass glittering with droplets where the cool fluid within had caused condensation, blurred, but quite clear enough.

That beer bottle was too much. I had never been so thirsty and there were still at least six kilometres of dusty, baking track to walk. As he gave me a salute, at once mocking and friendly, my pride seemed a very small thing indeed. I left the track and leant gratefully on the roof of his van, which was parked in the shade of the quarry wall.

'OK, you win. I'll do it. Get your dirty cock out.'

He looked a little surprised, but gave another of his shrugs and got into the car, placing his baguette on the other seat and his beer on the floor before hunching his *bleu de travail* down from his shoulders. I walked around the car, arriving at the opposite door to find him with it, and a pair of badly worn underpants, around his knees. A heavily hooded, rather greasy-looking cock and a set of bulging testicles lay in his lap. My gorge rose a little at the sight, and smell, leaving my thirst worse than ever.

'Might I have a little beer first, please?' I asked.

'What, and then you run off into the woods? Make me hard, then you have a little beer.'

I nodded weakly, and began to lean down, only to have him shake a finger at me.

'No, no. First your dress comes off. I like my girls naked.'

'Look,' I began, and thought better of it. 'OK, but if I strip you let me have some beer? I'm going to run off in the nude, am I?'

He simply laughed and picked up the beer bottle. I took it, and drained the entire contents down my throat, barely touching the sides.

'Thirsty, eh? Well, it is a hot day,' he said happily, and eased himself a little forwards to make it easier for me to get him in my mouth. 'You can suck my balls first, OK?'

I'd have nodded if my dress hadn't already been up, and a moment later it was off, leaving me stark naked and feeling extremely vulnerable. His eyes drank me in, and he gave a grunt of appreciation. I went down, determined to get it over with as fast as possible, lifting his cock and opening my mouth across the hairy, wrinkled bulk of his scrotum. He gave another grunt as I took his balls into my mouth, sucking as best I could with my mouth full of the acrid tang of his skin. A hand went under my chest, to stroke my breasts, and I didn't stop him, but began to tug on his cock.

He seemed to take forever, his thick-skinned, greasy penis expanding only slowly in my hand as I jerked at him and bumped his balls over my tongue. His groping grew more urgent, bringing my nipples to erection despite myself, and he'd begun to mumble about how good it felt, and how I was better at sucking his balls than his favourite prostitute in Reims.

Maybe it was because of what I'd done earlier, maybe it was because I was nude and felt so helpless, but by the time his cock was hard and I'd transferred it to my mouth I was getting horny. Not that I was going to give him the benefit of my reaction, but I wanted to come, and preferably with my mouth still full of cock. I might have given in, maybe, but, if he'd taken a long time to get hard, he didn't take long at all to come once he was there.

It took me completely by surprise. He'd begun to pull at my nipples, and I was going to tell him it was hurting me, but as I lifted my mouth he just erupted, full in my face, and the next instant I'd been forced back down, with my eyes popping and my cheeks bulging with spunk as he used my throat to fuck in and called me a 'little whore party girl' over and over.

I had to swallow, or I'd have choked, but taking my mouthful of salty, slimy spunk down very nearly made me throw up. When he finally let go, I was left gagging, with two tendrils of snotty come hanging out of my nose and both my eyes blinded with clots of it. When I asked for a rag, he told me to use my dress, and I had no choice but to comply, wiping myself with the torn hem.

Still naked, and feeling very horny, I think I'd have masturbated then and there if I also hadn't felt quite so used. I pulled my dress on instead, speaking as I adjusted my front. 'OK, satisfied? Now take me to Moiremont. Do you have any water, or some more beer?'

'Neither,' he answered. 'You drank all I had, and I have done my business in Moiremont.'

'You said you'd take me there, if I – if I sucked you!'

'From here? Yes, if you wish, but it's only just there.'

He nodded down the track, to where it disappeared over the brow of the low hill into which the quarry had been cut. For a moment I was speechless.

'You said ten kilometres!'

'But no. Saint Menehould was ten kilometres. Moiremont was four. Where do you think I bought my lunch?'

'But you – you let me . . . you made me –'

He shrugged, smiling. 'Such is life.'

I got out of the car, because if I hadn't I'd have hit him. Boiling with humiliation I set off, as he did, in the opposite direction. Sure enough, as I breasted the rise there was the village of Moiremont, the first house just a few metres below the crest. I walked on, ignoring the curious looks from those few locals about at lunchtime, too angry to even think of what

I needed to do, until I reached the little square in the centre. There, outside a tiny police station, stood a box-shaped car against which, eating a large loaf filled to overflowing with meat and salad, was Monty. He'd seen me first, and raised a hand in casual salute. 'Hi, Gabs, we were wondering when you'd turn up. How come you've got spunk in your hair?'

I might, just might, have taken Monty back to the quarry and sucked him off while I masturbated, naked and carefree, perhaps even with fingers up my pussy and bottom, just to deny the pig of a Frenchman the pleasure of my response, however abstract the revenge. I didn't, because what had been happening in my absence pushed everything from my mind but how lucky I'd been to be lost in the woods.

Sabina had been alone, and left me tied up in the bunker to see how worked up I got, as I'd supposed. Unfortunately, things hadn't gone entirely to plan, as Monty explained while I washed iced buns down with strong coffee in a café near the square.

'He reckoned we might have been sent over by her dad to fetch her back – he's not stupid, old Anthony – and so when he found out she'd gone –'

'I thought she left him tied up?'

'Oh yeah, that was a right laugh. She'd got him in a skirt and frilly pink knickers, fixed to the bed end with a pair of handcuffs. The owner's wife found him!'

I had to smile at the image as Monty went on.

'And was he furious, or what!? Only she's not there, and of course he can't get his head round the fact that his precious Mistress has fucked off with another woman, so he starts going on about how we've kidnapped her, which is when the owner rousts us up from where we're drinking in the bar. Course we don't know anything about it, and our cars are in Bouzy anyway, but no sign of Sabina, or Pops, or you, so he goes out to check the car –'

'Which is missing.'

'Yeah, and then he really flips. He's calling us kidnappers and abductors and every bastard under the sun, until in the end the owner rings the gendarmes. All hell's going to break loose, so Gav runs off to warn you lot, only it's too late. He meets Pops on the road and she tells him we're all meeting up here, in Moiremont, today. They figure we have to tell the truth, 'cause that way it's none of the gendarmes' business and old Anthony'll never get to Moiremont before us. We try, only Anthony won't have it. He says we're lying, and in any case his car's been stolen, so they put the word out to look for it.'

'And Sabina parks where you are, outside the police station.'

'You got it. So they want to know what's going on. She says she and Anthony had a row and she took the car but dropped you in Saint Menehould to catch the train.'

'As opposed to leaving me bound and gagged in a disused bunker?'

'Oh, right, found a good place, did she? Brainy girl, Sabina. Anyway, the gendarmes were well pissed off, and they drove Anthony here to sort it out. When she wouldn't go off with him and called him a boring old fart, boy, did he blow his stack! Tried to hit her, he did, and the gendarmes have stuck him in a cell to cool off. Jeff and Gavin were here by then, and have to give witness statements and that. Pops is in there too. They should be out soon.'

'I see. You don't know where the Volvo is, do you? Only my glasses were on the back seat.'

Monty shook his head and extracted them from the pocket of the blue anorak he had over the back of his chair. I took them and put them on, my eyesight returning to normal with a sense of relief not that much less than when I'd finally filled my knickers in the bunker. I swallowed the rest of my coffee and ordered another, Monty speaking just as the others pushed in at the door.

'So how did you – oh, hi, Jeff, hi, Gav, hi, girls. All sorted?'

'Sorted,' Gavin confirmed. 'What an arsehole! Would you believe the bullshit he tried . . .'

I wasn't listening. Poppy was in my arms, cuddling tight, with Sabina standing behind babbling apologies and thanks that I was OK. In no mood for recriminations, I waved away her remarks, pointing out that if it was anyone's fault it was David Anthony's. He was apparently still in the cells, and likely to stay there for some time, having managed to get on the wrong side of both the gendarmes and the local police, first by trying to hit her, and then by his high-handed attitude.

'We'd still better leave,' I suggested. 'I'd rather not see him again.'

'Bollocks to him,' Sabina answered. 'So you got out OK, then?'

'I managed to break off the light fitting,' I explained, deciding to keep the details of my ordeal to a minimum. 'Eventually, that is. You see, I thought you lot would be waiting outside until I freed myself, maybe so you could hunt me.'

'Nice one!' Jeff answered. 'Wish we'd thought of that, eh, Gav?'

'For all I knew you have your paintballs guns.' I laughed. 'And you must admit, it is the sort of thing you might do.'

'Fucking right!' Jeff agreed happily. 'We haven't got any gear, but if you're up for it I reckon we could buy some in Reims.'

'I have to get back,' I protested, 'and besides –'

'What's this?' Sabina queried.

'We play this ace game, right,' Jeff explained, 'at the Razorback place in Hertfordshire. The girls go in just bikinis and goggles –'

'Kinky gear sometimes,' Gavin added.

'Or panties and bras,' Monty put in, licking his lips, 'topless sometimes. Boy, you want to see those tits and arses jiggle.'

'And we hunt them,' Gavin went on, 'with paint-balls, and the girl who takes the most hits has to do whatever the guy who's scored the most wants. It can get well dirty.'

'How about the girls doing the shooting?' Sabina asked, slightly affronted, or maybe just shocked.

'Yeah, whatever,' Gavin responded. 'The four of us could hunt down Gabs and Pops, Pig Sticking rules – that's where the girls wear these rubber snouts and curly tails, like pigs, and it's one –'

'Snouts and tails!?' Sabina echoed.

'Sure,' Gavin went on, 'it's ace. You'd need a strap-on, obviously, so you could give 'em a decent fucking –'

'Hold on, all of you,' I cut in. 'This is all very well, but I need to be back in England.'

'Don't sweat it,' Jeff answered. 'Now we're over here, let's have some fun. The woods round here are perfect.'

'No, they're not,' I answered. 'I only realised it when this man who, er, gave me a lift said where we were, but we're only just outside the Red Zone.'

'Red Zone?' Sabina queried.

'The old trench line, from World War One,' Gavin explained.

'It would be disrespectful to play here,' I added.

'A lot of old munitions too,' Jeff pointed out. 'Five shells per square metre in places, never mind grenades and shit. Not safe. That's why we told you to stay south of Moiremont, Sabina.'

'Plenty of safe wood, though,' Gavin pointed out. 'You've just got to be careful. Come on, Gabs, Pops, how about it?'

'Not near here,' I insisted. 'My great-grandfather fought at Vauquois.'

'Cool! Did he kill many Krauts?'

'He was a Kr– a German, you idiot,' I answered. 'Alsace was part of Germany.'

'Oh, right. Did he kill many Frogs?'

I just shook my head, desperate to change the subject. 'Not here, OK, but maybe, something, some-where, now I've got rid of the David Anthony problem.'

I stopped, realising what I'd said. Maybe if I'd just carried on, she wouldn't have noticed. Maybe if I hadn't had quite such a stressful day and then had to put up with Gavin Bulmer's mind-numbing insensi-tivity on top of it, I wouldn't have said anything so stupid in the first place. But I had, and Sabina was looking at me with her mouth coming slowly open.

I was going to be punished. Maybe I didn't deserve it, but I was extremely grateful Sabina had decided to do it rather than lose her temper.

The full truth had come out in the café in Moiremont. As David Anthony had already planted the seeds of doubt in Sabina's mind, there was no use denying it. All I could do was be absolutely honest, admitting I'd promised her father I would speak to her, but that everything that had happened after-wards had been beyond my power to stop, including the fact that I, and Poppy, found her so desirable.

She'd been angry, at first, and stormed out of the café. I followed, and Poppy, both babbling apologies while the men trundled sheepishly behind. Finally Sabina had stopped, right on the peak of the hill, and told us we had a choice. Either we could go our separate ways and never meet again, or she could punish us both in whatever way she saw fit. Poppy had answered immediately, her head hung in very real remorse, promising Sabina she'd accept whatever was chosen. I'd hesitated, then gave a single, shamefaced nod.

The gesture was typical of an enthusiastic beginner at sadomasochistic sex, but, if it was what Sabina wanted, then I could only accept. I wanted her, as she wanted me, and, if my punishment was what it took to restore her hurt feelings, then so be it. The boys accepted the idea with enthusiasm, not surprisingly, until she pointed out that they shared a portion of my guilt, and that if they wanted to stay with us, let alone watch as Poppy and I were dealt with, then they'd have to take their medicine.

Unfortunately Monty and Gavin owned the cars, so after a little hard bargaining the three of them got off with having to kneel in the road and kiss Sabina's boots. Poppy and I were not going to get off so lightly, and as we rearranged our gear between the cars she was already asking their advice on how to get the most out of each of us. I had to speak up, and moved as casually as possible to behind Sabina, so that Monty and Jeff could see me, before providing an urgent and distinctly embarrassing pantomime in my efforts to get them not to mention nappies.

Jeff saw, making a puzzled face as Sabina bent down to push a bag further into the boot. I made frantic signals, indicating a bulge around my hips and between my legs, which drew extremely strange looks from a passing French couple. Monty had caught on too, and, as I stuck my thumb in my mouth and began to suck, both nodded in comprehension. I shook my head, making the gesture a negative, too late.

'I'll tell you what she really, really hates,' Monty said blithely. 'Put her in nappies.'

I hid my head in my hands as Sabina straightened up.

'You what? Nappies!?'

'Yeah, nappies,' Jeff answered, warming to the theme. 'She hates it, really hates it, but it gets her off. She can't help it.'

I was bright red, and must have been beetroot by the time Sabina had turned to me, her expression wavering between doubt, amusement and disgust.

'It's what Pops does to her, when she's really bad,' Monty supplied.

'Well?' Sabina asked, turning to Poppy, who shook her head.

'No, they're just playing the fool, trying to embarrass Gabrielle and get a laugh.'

'I'm not quite sure I believe you,' Sabina answered slowly, looking from Poppy to me.

Monty had finally caught on. 'Pops is right, we're only joking.'

Jeff hadn't. 'No, seriously, Sabina, make her go around in a nappy for a bit; she'll hate it, but she'll cream for you.'

'OK,' Sabina went on. 'Somebody's lying, so let me see. Gabrielle, what if I were to give you, say, thirty strokes of the cane?'

I winced; I couldn't help it, but that was all.

She gave a little chuckle, openly pleased by my apprehension at the prospect of pain, and went on. 'And if I were to make you go in nappies for a while?'

I was blushing hotter than before, I couldn't help it, and shaking, the mixture of embarrassment and excitement at the prospect of having her put me in nappies far too strong to let me hold back my emotions. Even my chest had gone pink, prickly heat rising between my breasts and up my neck.

Sabina gave a little smile, and laughed. 'Yeah, you're right, Jeff. I mean, what in the world could be worse than a grown woman being made to go in nappies! Nappies it is then, and you, Poppy, get extra for lying.'

Returning to England was plainly impractical. If Monty had left Moiremont straight for Calais and we'd taken an evening ferry I could have been ready for my appointment with Jo Warren at nine o'clock on the Wednesday morning. It wasn't going to happen.

Before leaving Moiremont, Poppy had rung Natasha back in London, to say that I'd been taken ill in France and couldn't possibly be back until the weekend. Even my girlfriend was in on the scheme to keep me there and to have me well and truly dealt with, and I had no choice but to follow my heart and surrender myself.

Poppy was determined to build up our relationship with Sabina, if possible to the point where she'd nurse us. Second, there was Sabina herself, now determined to exert her dominance and punish both Poppy and myself. Third, there were the boys, who were our drivers and made it quite clear that they would go anywhere in France except Calais. I'd effectively been kidnapped again, and, if I was willing, the prospects of what might happen to me had my stomach fluttering as we drove south.

My first ordeal was to buy nappies, because we could hardly admit I already had some in my bag, not when wearing them was supposed to be a rare and hated punishment. Then there was wearing them in front of Sabina, and trying to pretend I was feeling deeply humiliated. Not that I'd have much trouble, when she was sure to laugh at me. After that came whatever bizarre schemes they hatched, which Poppy was determined to go through with for the sake of our relationship with Sabina. I agreed with her, except that, while there's nothing she likes better than being whipped or shot with paintballs, I can't bear it.

We drove south from Moiremont, turning east on to the A4 at Saint Menehould and then south again along the Voie Sacrée, which the boys wanted to see and led us deep into rural France, where there was no chance whatsoever of David Anthony following. I went with Monty, Poppy and Sabina, and was made to explain the full truth of our expedition as we went. Sabina took it well, other than the occasional meaningful nod or lift of her eyebrows.

Apparently she had resented being mollycoddled by her father for as long as she could remember. Her teenage years had been a series of rebellions, but he'd never once changed his attitude, treating her as a child, and a pretty stupid child at that, as she put it. He had been in the habit of collecting her from teenage parties at her ten o'clock curfew, a source of ever-increasing embarrassment, and later had called the police to report her missing when she stayed out late, five times.

It came as no surprise to her to learn that he'd managed to access her computer log-in and discover what had been going on with David Anthony, nor that I'd been sent to France, while my refusal to do more than talk to her was appreciated. Not that she was going to reduce my punishment, because the more we talked the more determined she was to punish me effectively. I could tell that there was something personal to it, underneath. Not simply that she fancied me, but a desire to be cruel to me for who I was.

I could see how she was thinking. With Monty, Poppy and I all swapping stories of our experiences, she was inevitably left feeling very much the junior one. Yet she was also the dominant, and so she was determined to prove that she could handle us, both to Poppy and I, and to herself. I would rather have trained her, but it was impossible. If we were to get anything close to what was possible out of our relationship, she had to be left to make the decisions, and at least think she was in charge. It's never the same if you're tied up, or across somebody's knee, or in nappies, and you keep having to give instructions to the person who's supposed to be in charge.

By late afternoon we were in the Marne Valley. We stopped in Chaumont for coffee and to decide where to go for the night. I'd slept a little in the car, and that, combined with my sense of apprehension, had restored my energy. It had become a game, with Poppy and I doing our best to keep the trouble we were in to a minimum, and yet completely acquiescent to Sabina's orders.

Directly opposite the café where we'd stopped for coffee was a large chemist. I was simultaneously praying they wouldn't notice, or not realise what the big green crosses meant, and hoping they would. Sabina and Monty had their backs to the street. Jeff and Gavin entirely failed to notice. Not Poppy, who was thoroughly enjoying my discomfort.

She waited until we'd finished our coffee before speaking up. 'Sabina, if you turn around you'll see a shop marked with green crosses. It's a chemist.'

Sabina turned. 'So it is.'

'Big one too,' Monty supplied helpfully. 'They might well have adult nappies.'

'No,' I asserted. 'You'd need a specialist for that.'

'No harm in asking, is there?' Jeff pointed out.

I could feel myself going pink. 'They won't, really, they –'

'Maybe not,' Sabina cut me off, 'but it will do you good to ask. In fact, that can be the first part of your punishment, and, if you don't ask properly, you get six with my cane, in front of the boys, this evening.'

I winced, as before, remembering the mess she'd made of Poppy's bottom. If she did want to cane me, I'd have to at least try and take it, but it was something I genuinely wanted to avoid. Next to the pain and frustration of a caning, trying to buy adult nappies in an ordinary chemist didn't seem so bad after all. Besides, all I had to do was go in.

'Monty,' Sabina instructed, 'go with her. See that she behaves.'

Monty nodded, quite happy for her to tell him what to do so long as it involved pain and humiliation for Poppy and I. I got up, trying to tell myself it was nothing to worry about as we crossed the road. I'd bought adult nappies before, even in a sleazy sex shop with the owner leering at me as I chose the right size. This was different, because Sabina had ordered me, and I was blushing furiously even as I walked in at the door.

The assistants were at least female, but there were four of them. I was going to do it, but as I approached the counter I realised there was a way out. The assistants were hardly going to speak English, and Monty's French wasn't up to much. I could ask for something obscure, which they would tell me they didn't have, and that would be that. Besides, he was looking at the shelves. The only question was what to ask for, a specific product, an English one.

'Good morning,' I began, 'do you stock Boots own-brand conditioner?'

'No, I don't think so,' the nearest assistant answered. 'Perhaps an alternative product?'

'No, thank you, it has to be that. Thank you anyway.'

'I'm sorry we cannot help you, Madame.'

'That is quite OK. I realise it was unlikely.' I smiled.

She smiled.

Monty loomed up at my left shoulder. 'How about these ones? Do you think they'll be big enough?'

I turned to find him holding out an immense pack of nappies. They were marked extra-large, for girls, eighteen kilograms plus, but quite clearly for babies. I felt myself going scarlet.

'No, don't be stupid!' I hissed, but the assistant had already leant forwards, examining the pack.

'These are the largest of our range, Madame, Monsieur. They will be sufficient, I think.'

'Maybe with a bit of tape at the sides?' Monty suggested.

'Tape, at the sides?' the assistant responded, in perfect English.

'To hold them on,' Monty supplied, and pointed his finger to my hip.

'This is not good for your daughter's skin,' the girl answered. 'We have, er, towel nappies, larger? How old is she?'

'Eh? What are you, Gabs, twenty-eight? I'd have thought hip size was more important, and you're pretty skinny, so –'

'Monty, shut up!' I managed, my face burning as I fought to get out the words I had to say. 'The nappies are for me, please.'

'For you? This we do not stock. Towel nappies . . .'

I was wishing, urgently, I'd just asked in the first place, instead of trying to be clever, and was stammering an apologetic thanks as I turned for the door.

Monty wasn't finished. 'Give us a pack of the towelling ones then, the biggest you've got. She likes them. Oh, and some of those huge safety pins, with pink tops if you've got them.'

I fled, my face, my neck, my chest, all flushed burning hot. Normally I can cope, easily, but not now, not with Monty, and Sabina, never mind the others. I was shaking as I took my seat at the café, and could barely get my words out as Sabina asked what had happened.

'Monty's got them,' I managed. 'He's coming over.'

He was, holding a huge, pink plastic sack clearly marked with the legend '*Couches Grandes*', which he put down on our table. Poppy immediately tugged it open, to extract not what I'd expected, an awkwardly small towelling nappy, but a monstrous thing, made of thick, cream-coloured material and designed to fit a woman of truly impressive dimensions.

'Are you nuts?' she demanded, holding it up for inspection. 'These are vast! They'd fit you, Monty!'

'Take them back and exchange them,' Jeff suggested, sniggering.

'They'll do,' I sighed. 'Come on, let's find a hotel.'

'Yeah,' Gavin agreed, looking up from the Michelin he'd been reading. 'There's this great place outside Dijon, La Maison des Vignes. We can make it if we step on it.'

La Maison des Vignes was everything Gavin had promised. It was also expensive, so much so that we had to club together to pay for Sabina, who had been relying on David Anthony's largesse to support her in France. It was also magnificent, a converted château above the village of Fixin, looking out over the slope of the vineyard, the city and the plain of the Saône.

We'd chosen a suite with two large beds, for Poppy, Sabina and I, the most cost-effective choice, and one that opened up a world of delicious possibilities. The boys had their own three-bed suite, and I was looking forward to the night with no more than a trace of unease. Perhaps Sabina would want to spank me before bed, but I could cope, just as long as I got a cuddle afterwards.

I also hoped for a quick shower and a little peace before we went down for dinner. The first I managed, by stripping off and climbing in under the water as soon as I'd dumped my bags on the floor. It was immensely refreshing, but also noisy, so I got quite a surprise when I stepped out, in nothing but a towel on my head and another held loosely in my hand, to find Monty, Jeff and Gavin all seated in front of the TV.

'You need a shave, love,' Gavin remarked, glancing meaningfully at my stubble-covered pubic mound.

'I know,' I admitted. 'I don't suppose you three would go to your own room while we wash?'

'What, and miss the sight of you getting put in a nappy?' he answered. 'No way!'

'A nappy, now?' I queried.

'Now,' Sabina stated as she emerged from the bedroom, holding one of the huge towelling nappies in her hand, 'and perhaps it might be an idea to give you that shave, too?'

I hesitated, then hung my head. It would be a lot easier to pretend I hated it with the boys there.

'Yes, Miss Sabina.'

'Can I shave her, please?' Poppy chirped up.

130

'We've got razors, and powder, and cream, and everything.'

'Yes, why not,' Sabina answered. 'On the bed with you, Gabrielle.'

It wasn't difficult to put a rueful expression on my face as I laid a towel out on the bed. With the men watching, it genuinely reflected my feelings. They were evidently intent on a good view too, pulling their chairs into a ring around the end of the bed, so that I'd be spread open to them as I was shaved. I climbed on, telling myself that nudity was nothing to be concerned about, only not very successfully, not with the three of them out to enjoy such an intensely intimate moment.

I lay down anyway, feigning nonchalance as I lifted my legs and let my thighs come wide, showing off every single private detail of my sex and even my bottom hole. Monty gave his cock an appreciative squeeze at the sight, but it was Gavin who really brought the blushes to my cheeks.

'Gorgeous, right up her fuck hole!'

'Silence!' Sabina snapped. 'Or you're out.'

'Sorry,' Gavin answered quickly, 'but you have to admit, that's a lovely view.'

'Yes,' Sabina replied, reaching out to stroke a slow finger down my belly and on to my pubic mound, 'a view any man should be privileged to see, so mind your manners.'

Gavin made a face, but shut up. I closed my eyes, trying to imagine it was just Poppy and Sabina shaving me to put me in nappies, and that Sabina understood how I felt. I heard Poppy come in, and felt her sit down on the bed.

'A little wider, please,' she said, in her best nurse's voice.

I obeyed, spreading my thighs to stretch my pussy wide, fully open, and unable not to think of the three sets of prying, masculine eyes drinking in every detail of me. Poppy's hand brushed my leg and I felt my muscle tighten in response, then again as the cool cream was laid out on top of my pussy mound.

'Cunt like a cream cake!' Monty hissed, and sniggered.

'Shut up, final warning!' Sabina answered him.

He might have meant the way Poppy had topped my pussy mound with a whirl of shaving cream, or he might have been referring to the state of my sex, because I was so wet I could already feel my juice trickling down between my bum cheeks to wet my anus. Already I was fighting to keep my feelings in check, and as Poppy began to rub the cream into my sex it grew harder still. She was a real bitch about it, deliberately teasing me by not only coating my stubbly skin, but also brushing the crease of my sex, and my clitoris.

By the time she'd finished, my pussy had begun to make slow, even contractions, which I could do nothing whatsoever about. I kept waiting for one of the men to make some dirty remark, or to hear the meaty slapping of a cock being tugged to erection for my body. Neither came, but my feelings grew stronger anyway, as Poppy squeezed fresh cream out, between my bum cheeks.

'Roll up, right up,' she ordered. 'I need to do your bumhole properly.'

My answer was a sob, but I did it, taking myself under my knees and pulling my legs up to my chest, still well parted so as not to smear the cream on my sex. Again Poppy's finger touched, right next to my bumhole, and I felt my ring tighten by instinct, responding to all those times that same finger had been pushed inside me. This time she didn't, but rubbed the cream in around my anal star, not touching, but leaving my hole a wet pink target at the centre.

I heard one of the boys snigger at the sight, but I held my ridiculous pose, wide open, smeared white with cream, save for the moist pink shapes of my pussy and bumhole, standing like an absurd exclamation mark to show where I could be fucked – here's where you put your cocks in, boys . . .

Poppy seemed to take for ever getting the razor ready, but at last it touched, scraping the fine stubble from my pussy mound. My breathing was getting hard to control as my fur was removed, the sheer intensity of being made to hold such a vulnerable position with three men watching almost too much. Yet I didn't dare break position, not with the razor working on the most sensitive areas of my body, not to mention my fear of the cane. So I stayed still, trying not to imagine being held down while the three men took turns up my pussy or bumhole by choice.

My pussy mound was scraped clean, my sex lips, between my bum cheeks, once, and a second time to make sure I was left absolutely spick and span, as smooth as a baby, with every last hair gone. Only then did Poppy go into the bathroom for more warm water and a flannel to clean off the cream and pat my pussy down, again teasing my clitoris until I was biting my lip in frustration. A little more and I'd have given in, begging to be fucked in turn as Sabina sat on my face, to let me lick her pussy and bottom as cock after cock was fed into my freshly shaved pussy or jammed well in up my slippery bottom hole.

She stopped just in time, applied powder, patted my pussy down a second time, applied more powder between my bum cheeks and finished with a dab of cream to the mouth of my anus, pushing her finger just a little way in.

Gavin coughed, and spoke. 'Does that mean, er, we get to bum fuck her?'

'No,' Poppy answered patiently before Sabina could speak. 'She always has her bottom creamed, don't you, Gabby?'

'Yes,' I managed, my voice a weak sigh.

'Watch it,' Sabina warned. 'Right, Gabrielle, nappy time. Lift your bum.'

I gave a miserable nod and did as I was told, lifting my bottom from the bed to allow her to slide the nappy underneath me. As I lowered myself into it and felt the warm, soft towelling on my bare skin, first my back and then my bottom, I had to bite down a sigh. It felt so good, too good, bringing me all the feelings I've come to crave, feeling my hips and bottom encased in soft material, not being able to close my legs properly, knowing I can just let go. They grew stronger still as the nappy was turned up between my thighs, hiding my sex with the towelling bunched thick between my legs. The top came right up to my tummy, almost to my ribs, and Sabina had to wrap the edges around and tie them off before she could put the pins in.

'Up you get, and go and look at yourself in the mirror.' She laughed as she closed the second pin.

She wasn't the only one laughing as I rolled myself off the bed and scampered red faced across to a wardrobe, the whole outer door of which was a mirror. Gavin was in fits; Jeff sniggered, and even Monty was trying to hold back his amusement. I could see why too. The thing was huge, with a great puff of material between my legs and over my bottom, with the huge knots at either side like rabbit ears in grotesque, comic exaggeration. I was still struggling not to smile because, however ridiculous it looked, it was still intensely babyish.

Instead, I hung my head, looking at my feet as I stood there for all to see, nude but for my absurd nappy, and after they'd all made a thorough inspection of my newly shaved pussy and bottom crease. Sabina stepped towards me, first to touch my nappy where it swelled out over my bottom, then to place a single finger under my chin and lift my head, forcing me to look her in the eyes. 'Well?' she said. 'I hope you're sorry now.'

I nodded.

She went on. 'I'm sure you are, but not nearly as sorry as you're going to be. Come here.'

She took my hand, and there was nothing I could do as she led me to the bed and sat down, quite clearly intending to put me across her knee and spank me.

I was stammering as I spoke, thinking of how much it had hurt before, and the fuss I'd made. 'Not now, please, Sabina, not now!'

'I'll spank you when I please, young lady!' she answered.

'No, it's not that,' I blustered as I was drawn down into position. 'I'll scream, and everybody'll hear! You know I can't help it!'

It didn't stop her. I was laid across her lap, the huge puff of my nappy seat stuck up in the air and towards the three men. Only when she'd taken me firmly around the waist and pulled the rear of my nappy open to expose my cheeks, helpless and ready for punishment, did she speak.

'Do you really think it matters if the other guests hear you squalling?' she asked. 'What are they going to think? That some brat's getting her bottom warmed before bedtime? Big deal.'

'No, really, Sabina – Mistress,' I begged. 'I couldn't bear it, not if everyone knew I have to take spankings, not like this –'

'They won't see you, silly,' she interrupted, 'although I suppose it might be fun to do you in the dining room, in front of everybody. Now do stop fussing. I just want you to have a nice blushing bum to keep you warm until after dinner, that's all, and, if there's one squeak out of you, your panties are going in your mouth, like before.'

'That's a point,' Poppy put in. 'What did you do with my panties, Gabby?'

'I – I left them in the bunker where Sabina tied me up, sorry,' I admitted as Sabina made a further adjustment to my nappy, pulling it so far aside that just about the whole of my bottom was sticking out bare behind.

'You did, did you!? Right, use this, Sabina.'

'What?' I asked, craning around, and to my horror she was holding out a wooden hairbrush. 'No! Not that! Please, no, Sabina! They were ruined anyway. Ow!'

I'd screamed as the hairbrush came down on my bum, a stinging pain far worse then her hand, which was repeated as Sabina set to work, holding me hard around the waist as she spanked, my legs kicking and my arms waving wildly, every bit the spanked brat she wanted, squalling too. Maybe a dozen swats fell, no more, when it stopped.

'Will you shut up, Gabrielle!?' she breathed. 'You are such a big baby! I tell you something, if there's one grown woman in the world who deserves to have to wear nappies, it's you. Now, a dozen more and your bum should be nice and toasty, but do try and be quiet.'

'I do!' I wailed. 'I can't help it! Ow!'

Again the hairbrush fell, again, and again, picking up a rhythm on my bare, smarting bottom. I went straight into my pathetic, uncontrolled little dance of pain, my limbs waving, my bottom jiggling, my hair flying, and bawling all the while. My display set Poppy and the boys laughing immediately, which only made me worse, Sabina's squalling little brat, punished in my nappy. I got extra too, maybe fifty in all, and by the time Sabina finished I had tears running down my face and was sobbing badly. I crawled off her lap to inspect myself in the mirror, pushing the sides of my nappy apart to show my smarting cheeks. My flesh was bright red, and I was looking seriously sorry for myself, tear streaked, with my face almost as flushed as my bum.

'There, and let that be a lesson to you,' Sabina said evenly. 'Now I think we'd better go down.'

We went down to a restaurant grander still than the one in Ambonnay, where I felt distinctly out of place in my jeans and angora jumper, although the other choices, my torn red dress or my tiny leather shorts and bra top, would have been worse. A shopping trip into Dijon was definitely called for, first thing. For the time being, I was more worried about the fact that I was sitting on a hot bottom, and that both Sabina and Poppy were clearly intent on putting me through my paces.

Spanking me to keep me warm really worked, as did knowing what my companions had just seen. All through the meal, even with a succession of courses every bit as brilliant as the night before, I could think of very little but how it had felt to be upended across Sabina's knee and beaten with a hairbrush while they laughed at me. Even being shaved and put in my ridiculous nappy was easier to cope with, and I hadn't even been allowed to come.

Gavin, who earns a substantial wage as a money broker, seemed determined to impress, insisting on covering the wine bill and ordering Meursault,

Volnay and a magnum of Fixin, all First Growths, and the last from the vineyard outside our window. Glasses of Muscat followed with our dessert, then Cognac, leaving me pleasantly drunk as well as horny, and also tired.

There is no condition so sexually susceptible as that combination, for me anyway. Nothing seems to matter but sensual pleasure, like waking in the night after sharing a bottle in the evening, in Poppy's arms, and a nappy, safe and secure in the warm, and just letting my pee run, or whatever I need.

I still knew, faintly, that I ought to be a little reserved in front of Sabina. Yet she loved being cruel to me, and perhaps was ready to accept my complete surrender, to learn what it can mean to have complete physical control over me, beyond mere sadism. When we trooped upstairs the boys wanted to come in with us, hoping for sex, but she sent them to bed. I felt that was wrong, as they were part of it, but I wanted to be hers, and said nothing.

Within the bedroom, she purposefully locked the door and showed us the key, smiling. She took our hands, and we were led into the bedroom, Sabina very cool and in charge despite the trembling I'd felt in her fingers. The three chairs were still there, and she sat down in the most comfortable.

'Get naked, both of you,' she ordered, folding her hands in her lap.

I began to strip, thinking of my warm bottom and wondering if I could expect further punishment as I peeled off my shoes and socks, my top, my jeans, my bra, and finally my panties, to leave myself nude. Poppy was bare before me, with just her dress and underwear to take off, and I knelt beside her on the bed, our arms around each other's waist. Being naked felt right, with Sabina fully clothed and Poppy and me completely nude and vulnerable. Sabina's eyes were shining as they moved over our bodies, and her full mouth curved into a wicked smile.

My stomach was tight, my bottom cheeks twitching, imagining spankings and painful bondage and maybe whipping, or being put on the floor and made to lick her boots, or any one of the sadistic skills she might have learnt from David Anthony. When she finally spoke, her words came as a complete surprise.

'What is it you two get up to in bed then? Show me?'

I nodded, a little uncertain as I took Poppy into my arms. What Poppy and I got up to in bed was often very rude indeed, probably far ruder than Sabina could handle. We'd have needed plastic sheets too, and I knew I'd be putting on a show rather than simply being me, even as Poppy's lips touched mine.

Not that it was fake, not at all. As we cuddled together with our eyes closed and our mouths open in a long, wet kiss, my already strong need was rising higher still. Poppy slid a hand down under my bottom, stroking my still warm cheek. I did the same, and as our tongues moved together we were holding each other's bottom, to soothe our bruises. Sabina had punished us both, and now she was watching us caress each other, which was wonderful.

We went over together on to the bed, each with her fingers moving on the other's skin, touching necks and backs and faces, breasts and bellies and legs and arms, but always moving back to each other's bottom, and always kissing. I wanted Sabina to join us, to give us orders, taking away our responsibility as we were made to be ever more intimate, ever dirtier, or maybe to stand over us and pee all over our intertwined bodies, leaving us to come to orgasm together as we squirmed in her piddle.

She simply watched, very still, saying nothing, her full red lips a little parted, her eyes bright. Before long Poppy and I had begun to work on each other's pussy, our fingers pushed in up wet holes to be sucked clean, tongues applied, head to tail, with Poppy's beautiful, full bottom spread in my face as I licked at her sex and tickled her anus. Still Sabina watched, now playing with the hem of her skirt, perhaps a little nervously.

I realised she might never have had full lesbian sex before, for all that she'd spanked us and maybe others. She wanted to see, to learn, maybe. Maybe she was shy, unsure of her own sexuality, but Poppy's tongue was lapping at my pussy and I had to come, and enjoy my lover properly, whatever Sabina thought. My legs came up, wrapped around Poppy's head to pull her firmly into my sex.

She responded immediately, taking my bottom in her hands, two fingers pushing in up my pussy, another at the mouth of my bumhole, tickling, then slipping into my creamy ring, deep in. Penetrated, I buried my face in her sex, licking from her pussy to her bumhole in my eagerness, and I was coming, lost in rapture as my thighs went tight around her head, my twin holes in spasm on her fingers and my tongue pushed just as deep as it would go up into the soft pink star of her anus.

I kept it there as I came, knowing full well Sabina could see but just too high to care. Only when I was done did I relax back, a little shamefaced, and before I could judge Sabina's reaction Poppy had sat up, queening me, her bottom spread full in my face, my nose in her slippery ring and my mouth to her pussy. I licked, eager to please as she wiggled her bottom in my face. Her thighs were wide, well spread, smothering me in warm bottom flesh as she used my face to masturbate on and played with her breasts.

In no time she was coming too, squirming and groaning in ecstasy as I licked as best I could manage, before collapsing sideways on the bed. Poppy wriggled quickly around, and for a moment we held together, trembling in each other's arms with our mouths wide together before we pulled apart to look up at Sabina.

'How's that?' Poppy said happily. 'Would you like some of the same, or something kinky?'

Sabina was staring, her eyes large and moist, her mouth open. Her hand was pressed to her belly. When she spoke, it was to me. 'You – you licked her bottom!'

'It's lovely!' Poppy answered. 'I'll lick yours, if you like, or you can make Gabby do it.'

'Maybe I should,' Sabina answered, trying to sound commanding, but her voice full of uncertainty.

'I would like that,' I admitted, 'and I would like to make you come, very much, however you please.'

'Maybe at your feet?' Poppy suggested. 'Side by side.'

Sabina nodded, far from sure of herself. She was still in her black skirt and jacket, and boots, her nipples stiff beneath her blouse, several inches of golden-brown cleavage showing. I thought of suckling her lovely big breasts, with my bottom still hot from punishment, before being put on my knees to lick her to ecstasy. She nodded her head, and beckoned.

She was shaking, far from sure of herself, but determined to have us as her playthings. Poppy was eager to obey, and I no less so, both scrambling from the bed to crawl to her. I was on my knees, Poppy on all fours, side by side as we came to her feet, two naked girls, kneeling for their Mistress, one rosy behind, the other bruised, awaiting our orders.

Very slowly, Sabina edged up her skirt, to show first the patterned tops of her stockings, and higher, the flesh of her upper thighs, bulging a little, as smooth as cream and golden brown, below the plump, soft swell where tiny, vivid green panties covered her sex. Not really covered, because a good deal of meaty brown pussy flesh was spilling out at either side where they caught between her lips. They were also wet, and as I caught the scent of her sex I simply couldn't stop myself.

She gave a little squeak of pleasure and surprise as I leant forwards, nuzzling her, my nose pressing her panties into the groove of her pussy, right on her clitoris. Poppy giggled, and Sabina's hand found my hair, taking a firm grip to pull me from her sex. Poppy was trying to undo the buttons of Sabina's blouse, and got the same treatment. She spoke first.

'Pretty please, Mistress?'

Sabina hesitated, then let go. 'Oh what the hell, I've fantasised about it enough times.'

Poppy was nuzzling her breasts, and already had one button open. I wanted Sabina too high to stop herself, and pulled her panties aside, to bury my face in her sex. She tasted strong, very feminine, and she was juicy, so juicy two fingers slid in without trouble. Her lips opened a little wider as her pussy filled, she moaned, and I knew she was lost, ours to worship. Already her blouse was open, her breasts bulging up from the tight confines of her bra, then free as Poppy undid the catch.

From the first moment I'd seen the photo of Sabina in my flat, I'd wondered how her breasts would look bare, and how it would feel to smother my face in her chest. She didn't disappoint, each one a heavy globe of plump, soft girl-flesh, round and firm and resilient, topped by a large, black nipple, both rock hard. I had to suckle her, then and there. So did Poppy, the two of us squeezing together as we took Sabina's nipples in our mouth, sucking eagerly at the big teats, two pink piglets fighting for milk.

She giggled, perhaps still nervous, perhaps at our eagerness, but she was sighing as she began to stroke our hair, her eyes now closed and her mouth wide in bliss. Her thighs had come wide too, and my hand was still on her pussy, easing my fingers in and out of her ready, juicy hole as I worked my thumb on her clitoris.

I was in heaven, slick and shaved and naked at Sabina's feet, put in a nappy, my bottom spanked, made to show off with Poppy before I was permitted to crawl on the floor to my Mistress' feet. My spare hand went between my thighs and I was rubbing myself, in rising ecstasy as I played over in my head how she'd treated me, spanking my bottom, gagging me with Poppy's panties, leaving me helpless in collar and cuffs, making me buy my own nappies, and wear one in front of three men, and spanking me again, spanking me with my shaved pussy and bottom flaunted for male amusement, making me strip and perform in the nude for her with my lover, and last, and best, permitting me to crawl on my knees to suckle at her breast as I masturbated her, and myself.

We all came together, perfectly, clutching on to each other, Sabina with her head thrown back in bliss, her hands tight in our hair as she held us to her chest, Poppy and I with our mouths full of nipple and our fingers working our pussies, and hers, all three of us shaking hard and blind with ecstasy for what seemed an age, until finally the grip in my hair slackened and I could slump exhausted into Sabina's lap.

Six

I had thought being shaved and put in a nappy in front of everybody was my punishment. I'd been wrong.

As we gathered in the breakfast room at La Maison des Vignes, I was looking forward to going into Dijon to shop, but not really thinking about anything in particular. It looked like being a blazing hot day, and we took a table on the terrace, sipping coffee as Monty and Jeff bemoaned the food and discussed the English breakfast they would order on the ferry home.

Sabina was the last to come down. Like Poppy and I, she was in need of clothes, and had enthusiastically accepted the idea of a shopping expedition as the three of us sat and talked in bed after playing together. Given what we'd done, that was particularly pleasing, as for me it is very important that I'm treated as an equal once the sex is over. In Sabina's case the difference was close to surreal, one moment stark naked at her feet, in a state of deep servitude, the next discussing French sizes and makes of jeans.

It came as quite a shock when she put down the croissant she'd been eating and looked up at us with an expression I was coming to fear, and love.

'What shall I do with you two then?'

'I thought we were going shopping?' Poppy answered her.

'We are,' Sabina confirmed, 'but that doesn't mean you get off your punishment. It's hard to know what to do with you, Poppy.'

'You could throw her to us?' Monty suggested hopefully.

I was trying to speak, to point out I'd already been punished, but it was difficult with my mouth full of bread and honey.

'I don't think so,' Sabina went on, with a slightly cruel smile for the boys. 'She hasn't been that bad. I'll let you watch, if you're good boys, and maybe you can offer some advice.'

'Sure thing,' Jeff offered, 'we put her in clown gear, with her arse and tits hanging out, and hunt her –'

'No, done up like a pig,' Gavin suggested. 'There must be a joke shop in Dijon, for a snout, and –'

'Better still,' Monty interrupted, 'we look out a dogging spot and give her a spunk supper, make her flash too, and maybe earn remittance on a caning by seeing how many Frenchmen she can suck off, a stroke per cock and –'

Sabina was shaking her head. 'You three are perverted; did anyone ever tell you that?'

'And you're not?' Jeff retorted.

'Never mind me, how about Gabby!?' Poppy broke in. 'It's all her fault!'

'Oh, Gabby is easy. She goes in her nappy.'

'I've been punished!' I managed, swallowing frantically.

'When?' Sabina asked, all innocence.

'Last night!'

'That wasn't your punishment, darling, that was just a dry run.'

'A dry run? But you shaved me, and you – and you made me wear a nappy in front of everyone!'

'And you loved it!' Gavin laughed. 'Dirty bitch!'

'Mind your language!' Sabina snapped. 'No, Gabby, that was not your punishment, not after what you did. You're going in a nappy, sure, but not just with us, in public.'

'In public? But, Sabina –'

'No buts. You do as you're told.'

I didn't answer. I couldn't, but hung my head to hide my emotions at the thought of going out in my nappy, under Sabina's control. It was so arousing it hurt, and so emotionally charged it had me swallowing back tears, which I did not want her to see. Poppy did, and reached out to take my hand.

Sabina spoke again. 'Oh, I'm sorry, Gabrielle, I didn't mean to –'

'I am OK,' I cut her off. 'Do it. I want you to.'

She nodded, perhaps in understanding, perhaps in acceptance.

Poppy quickly changed the subject. 'It's great here, isn't it? I always picture Roissy a bit like this. Imagine if they had dungeons, like they have a breakfast room and a dining room and everything, only so that bad girls can be taken down and punished whenever necessary.'

'Neat,' Jeff agreed, 'but for my money I'd rather see a girl get her knickers pulled down for a spanking in the dining room or somewhere, much more than anything in some fancy dungeon.'

'Yeah, me too,' Monty agreed.

'Where's Roissy?' Sabina queried.

'Roissy, the château in the *Story of O*,' Poppy explained. 'You know.'

Sabina shook her head.

'You must have read *Story of O*!' Poppy retorted. 'It's the original slave training novel!'

'Yeah, and it's male dom,' Jeff pointed out. 'I don't see David Anthony letting her read that. Fucking control freak, that guy.'

'Have you read *Venus in Furs*?' Gavin asked.

'Yes,' Sabina answered immediately. 'David gave it to me for my birthday. He said it explained male sexuality like no other –'

'*Male* sexuality!' Gavin interrupted. 'The fuck it does –'

'He's been feeding you the old men are subs, girls are doms crap?' Jeff queried.

'I –' Sabina began uncertainly, and then sighed. 'Yeah, I suppose so. He says men are the naturally submissive sex anyway, but –'

'Bollocks,' Monty and Jeff chorused.

'So you think women are?' Sabina queried, raising her chin.

'No,' Monty answered with a shrug. 'It's a personal thing. You like to dish it out. Pops and Gabs like to take it. Me, I'm easy.'

'You said it!' Gavin responded, making Jeff, and Sabina, laugh.

Poppy was still holding my hand, and gave me a rueful smile. I was about to be taken out in public in a nappy and they were chatting casually. It was almost too much. They carried on too, as I sat there with my stomach churning in apprehension, arguing SM philosophy, with Sabina rather tentatively putting forward the conventional viewpoint in the face of the boys' different takes on hedonism and Poppy's occasional balancing comment.

For all her naivety, Sabina was no fool, and had already realised that, far from opening her mind, as he had claimed, David Anthony had been grooming her to suit his own purposes. She wasn't best pleased, and the conversation left me feeling a little guilty for my own aspirations, and Poppy's. As we rose from the table I was promising myself I would let her make her own choices, offer, but not push, and avoid expressing one idea as superior to another, also, to do as I was told.

We were staying a second night, so there was no need to pack. In our room I was told to take my jeans and knickers down and stand with my hands on my head. I obeyed, trembling badly as I pushed my clothes to my knees in one corner and awaited instructions. It was a game, maybe, but my emotions were no less strong for that, along with that irreconcilable need to keep my punishment to a minimum while at the same time wanting it as strong as possible.

'Should I wear my dress, do you think?' I asked as Sabina threw the pack of monster nappies on the bed.

'Shut up,' she answered, 'or you'll be going in those little shorts you wore at the club.'

I shut up as ordered, thinking of just how ridiculous I'd look in my tiny leather shorts with the seat and crotch bulging with nappy material and great puffs of towelling sticking out at every hem. My jeans were better, much better.

Not as much as I thought. Sabina told Poppy to put me in the nappy and sat down to watch. Humming happily to herself, Poppy extracted a nappy from the pack and laid it out on the bed, a square of thick, cream towelling big enough to have dried myself with, almost to have sat on on a beach.

'Legs apart,' she ordered, and took two of the big, pink-headed nappy pins between her lips.

I obeyed, opening my legs as far as my lowered panties would permit as she picked up the nappy. She was still humming to herself as she threaded it between my legs and pulled it up, very casually, as if putting me in nappies for public exposure and humiliation were an everyday task. I held still, my hands on my head where I'd been told to put them, while she tugged the nappy firmly up to enclose my pussy and bottom, tied both sides off with huge, floppy knots and fastened the pins to keep the towelling snug around my hips.

'Good girl,' she announced as she closed the second pin, 'now let's see if we can get this lot in your panties.'

She ducked down, to pull up my panties, stretching the waistband wide open to get it around the nappy and letting it snap shut. Before I'd felt snug, and my panties made me snugger still, squashing the soft towelling between my legs and around my bottom and tummy. It felt wonderful, and the reflection looked intensely submissive, with my jeans still down and my panties straining around the nappy material with most of it hanging out at the sides.

Alone, with just Poppy, even with Sabina too, or Monty, I'd have wanted to strip off everything but nappy and panties and give myself over to them completely. With the prospect of having to go out, it was impossible not to think of how ridiculous I looked, and the implications of a grown woman having to wear a nappy in public. Most people wouldn't even be aware it could be sexual and would either think it was some sort of prank or, more likely, that I had to wear it because I couldn't be trusted not to wet myself.

'Now your jeans,' Poppy remarked. 'This is not going to be easy.'

She was right. They were quite tight, not like the ones Sabina was wearing, which seemed to have been painted on to her magnificent bottom, but figure hugging, and fashionably low cut. From the moment Poppy blew her breath out as she tried to get them over the bulging nappy seat I knew I was in trouble. They weren't going to fit, as simple as that. She did manage though, sort of, tugging them up until my pussy was squeezed tight inside a thick wad of compressed nappy flannel. My waistband was roughly level with the top of my bottom cleft, and, while she managed to pull my zip maybe two-thirds of the way up, she simply could not close the button.

Finally she gave up. In the mirror, the whole upper part of the nappy still showed, back and front, also the two big knots at the side, each decorated with a large, pink-headed pin. One glance would be all it took, and from several hundred metres, to know that without any possible doubt I had a nappy on. That was only part of it.

I'd had to borrow a top from Poppy, and while it was quite loose over my breasts, it left a great deal more of my midriff on show than it would have done with her. Before, the effect had been simply girlish, and I can get away with that. Now it seemed not just girlish, but babyish, extraordinarily babyish, with the hem hanging loose under my breasts above where the bare pink swell of my tummy was cupped in nappy material. Her top being lemon yellow didn't help either.

Sabina was trying not to giggle. Poppy wasn't.

'I think we can do without the bra,' she remarked, when she'd managed to get herself under control. 'Arms please, Gabby.'

Her hands went up under my top to unfasten my bra and pull it out of one sleeve. My nipples were hard, making two prominent little bumps in the yellow cotton and adding one more dimension to my look. Poppy nodded as she stepped back, trying to look serious but with the corners of her mouth threatening to twitch up into a smile.

'Cute,' Sabina remarked, 'but maybe we can do better. Have you got any hair bands?'

'Yes, somewhere,' Poppy answered and began to dig in her bag, quickly pulling out a pack of mixed hair bands.

She chose two yellow ones and came back to me. She pulled my hair into bunches at either side and fixed them in place with the bands to leave me more babyish still.

'Very pretty.' She laughed as she stood back to admire her work. 'Hmm ... what else? Shall we let her keep her glasses, or not?'

'Let her keep them,' Sabina answered, 'it adds to the look, and I want her to see other people's reaction.'

They looked very pleased with themselves indeed, especially Poppy. I could still see my reflection, which brought extremely mixed feelings. One thing was not in doubt: I was being punished. Even indoors the mixture of my favourite sexual thing with the absurd would have been as much as I could take. The thought of walking through the hotel was unbearable. I was near to tears.

'I – I cannot go out like this! What about the hotel staff, other guests!?'

'You have to start somewhere,' Sabina pointed out.

'Yes, but – but could I not just go out with a nappy on under my dress? I've done – I mean, that is what Poppy has done to me before.'

'Then you clearly need a little more to make sure you're properly punished,' she chided. 'Now come along.'

At that moment there was a knock on the door. Poppy went to answer it, and to my relief it was the boys and not a chambermaid. The relief was short-lived though, as the three of them trooped into the room and saw me. Gavin laughed. Jeff gave a thoughtful nod. Only Monty spoke up.

'Well kinky! I'd love to give you a good fucking, just like that.'

'Behave, Monty,' Sabina told him. 'OK, let's go.'

'Please – please, wait,' I stammered, 'just a moment, I – I am not sure I can cope, really. It is just the hotel, and –'

'She's a bit shy,' Poppy put in. 'Maybe a coat, just until we're in the car?'

'It is just the hotel,' I protested, wishing my voice wouldn't come out in such a self-pitying whine. 'It would still show under my coat, and I just –'

'No problemo,' Gavin interrupted. 'Leave it to the Razorback boys. Jeff, scout an escape route. Monty, get your coat. I'll be in the back car park, engine running. It's now zero minus ten. Go, go, go.'

He went, and so did I, hustled to the door despite my continued protests. Monty was back in moments, with his blue anorak, which completely swamped me, but must have looked odd to say the least with the heat of the day already building to a level suitable for a minimum of clothes. I got plenty of strange looks as we came downstairs, but not as strange as they would have been, and that knowledge alone was enough to keep me pink with blushes, even once we'd piled into the jeep.

We left the hotel, Monty and Jeff following in the other car, driving down through Fixin to the main road and into Dijon, with my feelings growing stronger with every spin of the wheels. My bladder felt weak, inevitably, but I was determined to hold it, because with no plastic pants to go over the nappy it might soak through, adding one final, terrible detail to my humiliation.

Sabina was simply not that cruel, or not that imaginative. I wasn't sure which, but she seemed more than happy with what she'd done to me, on a high of pure sadistic relish as we made for the centre of the city, never quiet and never still. Poppy was little better, hugging me and giggling and feeling under my coat to touch my nappy and the bulge between my thighs.

I was wondering if I would faint, my feelings were so strong. Half the population of France seemed to be out on the city streets, hundreds of people, of every sort, and I was going to have to parade myself before those hundreds, letting them see, letting them wonder. I'd thought before they'd either think it a prank or that I wet myself. Now I wasn't so sure. My nipples wouldn't go down, and I was convinced my arousal would show in my face, that they'd see, and know.

Gavin parked, by the canal, not too near the busiest streets, to my relief, and Monty pulled up beside us. My heart was in my mouth as I stepped out of the car, my stomach churning, and an awful sick feeling in my throat. Sabina stepped towards me, her face full of cruel glee as she reached out to open my coat. She peeled it down off my shoulders, tugged it away and I was exposed, fully dressed, showing nothing, but making ten times the exhibition of myself I would have done fully nude.

'How – how far do I have to go?' I asked, glancing frantically around.

One man had seen, and looked quickly away.

'Search me,' Sabina said blithely. 'Where are the shops?'

'The shops? But –'

'We're going shopping, aren't we?'

'Like this!?'

'Why not? Come on.'

She slapped my bottom, which I barely felt through the thick nappy, and I was walking forwards, mechanically, my legs weak, trembling hard. Always before I'd done it in skirts, so that people might suspect, might guess, but they could never be sure. Now it was deliberate, and to me it now seemed that nobody could possibly mistake my intention. It was sexual, blatantly sexual.

It seemed to make me a doll, what I'd heard the boys call a fuck dolly, a girl dressed up and made up for one purpose only, to turn men on, and not for some sordid commercial purpose either, but plain and simple, so she could be fucked. Not just fucked though, not the way I was, but made comical first, to take away every last shred of my dignity, to allow men, and women, to enjoy me with no more consideration than had they been masturbating.

I was dizzy with reaction even before I'd crossed the car park. Everybody was staring, everybody; some with sympathy, some with disapproval, some with shock, some with lust. It was all too easy to imagine myself simply bent over the bonnet of a car, my jeans pulled down and the seat of my nappy opened, with Sabina and the boys organising the queue as I was fucked and fucked and fucked.

There was a fence at the edge of the car park, painted vivid green, and I leant against it, sure that my legs were going to give way. I felt drunk, light-headed, as if I wasn't really there at all, but as Poppy came to take my arm I was walking forwards. A man passed, his eyes opening in surprise as he realised what I was wearing, and I simply smiled.

Like being spanked harder than I can take, like being tied up tight and just left, Sabina had taken me beyond the point of pain, beyond the point of rational feeling. I was in a nappy, in public, and it was pure excitement, my arousal the focus of everything around me. We were by a park, a long stretch of green beside the canal, full of sunbathers. Another man was seated on a bench, young and very dark, eyeing the girls from behind his shades. As I passed I lifted my top, flashing my breasts to leave him gaping after us as we passed.

Poppy was next to me, holding my hand, Sabina walking behind, the boys further back. All eyes were on me, and I was enjoying what I'd been made to do, and the reaction of people around me. I wanted more, to peel off my top and go as an adult baby-girl should go, bare chested, because she has nothing to be embarrassed about, no sense of embarrassment even. I wanted my jeans off, to show the world that all I had on was a big, puffy, cream-coloured nappy. I wanted to let go, to wet myself, not deliberately, but when I needed to go, because it didn't matter.

Maybe, just possibly, my top would be a problem. My jeans weren't. I sat down on the next bench along from the dark man, to pull off my shoes.

'Gabby!' Poppy demanded. 'What are you doing?'

'Going in my nappy, as I was told to,' I answered.

'OK,' she replied, doubtful. 'If you want.'

'Hold these,' I told her, and lifted my bottom to push down my jeans and my panties too.

She took them, her face set in a nervous smile. Sabina looked bemused, Gavin and Jeff astonished. Not Monty, who was grinning. I put my shoes back on and stood, stretching in the sunlight, feeling liberated in the way only being naked or in nappies can bring me, but not outdoors, never before.

I was walking on air as I moved on; white shoes, white socks, bare legs, bare tummy, little yellow top, my hair in bunches and, best of all, my middle wrapped in soft, creamy towelling. Everyone was staring, and I wanted them to, but I no longer cared if they disapproved. They were the silly ones, hidebound by their conventions. I was free.

Buying clothes seemed completely pointless. Why bother? I didn't need clothes. An ice-cream was another matter, just what I wanted. There was a stall a little further along, and I stopped, to order a mint chocolate cone. Poppy had to pay, and as she did the man was peering out from his booth, one way down the street and then the other. Monty had his camera out, and was taking photos, and Jeff followed suit, both circling around me as I moved on.

Trickles of green ice-cream were soon running down my chin, the full glare of the sun melting it faster than I could lick. Again came the temptation just to peel my top off and go in nothing but my nappy, and this time I acted on it. After sticking the ice-cream cone down the side of my nappy, I pulled my top up, and off. Poppy was staring as she caught it, and Sabina, with both Monty and Jeff clicking away with their cameras just as fast as they could.

Now people were really staring, wide-eyed, as I walked happily on, not a care in the world, intent only on soaking myself in the glorious sensation of going in public with just my nappy on. One thing remained, one only, and I was going to do it, because if I didn't I'd regret it, and I knew I might never again be able to bring myself to do what I was doing now.

I turned into the park, walking faster. There were fewer people nearby, none really close, but plenty who'd stopped to stare from a distance. Maybe they thought I was modelling, for some strange or avant-garde photographs. Maybe they thought I was protesting, or trying to create a stir. Maybe they thought I'd taken a dare, or made a bet, or was simply mad. Maybe they thought I was a thoroughly bad girl enjoying being all but nude and showing off my new nappy.

Which I was about to wet. I didn't care who saw, or didn't, except for my friends. I wanted them to know, and react. Poppy I could rely on, for a little surprise and a lot of delight. Monty the same, and the ruder the better. Jeff would think it funny, and Gavin rude. Sabina . . . Sabina was going to have to cope. She'd put me in nappies, after all.

I stopped to savour the moment, set my legs a little apart, put my hands behind my head and closed my eyes in sheer bliss as I let go. My beautiful sense of liberty grew stronger still as hot pee gushed out into the thick layers of towelling between my legs. Poppy had realised, and was giggling. I heard Sabina's little gasp of shock, and Monty's crude laugh. They were stood around me, watching as I wet myself, the piddle quickly soaking in around my pussy, my nappy growing steadily fuller, and fatter, to give me that exquisite heavy feeling between my thighs. I could feel more weight as the towelling shifted, the soggy nappy pulling gently at my hips, and I knew it would be swelling too, a bulge growing at back and front, over my bottom and around my pussy.

'You've wet your nappy!' Sabina breathed.

At her words I nearly came. My pussy tightened, in sudden spasm, to squirt out more pee. There was laughter in her voice, but shock too, and disapproval, which I could only imagine as the disapproval of a nurse, my nurse, watching me wet myself and knowing I could have avoided it, angry because she was going to have to clean me up.

'You're going to have to be spanked for that,' she went on, and again my pussy went tight, squeezing out the last of the pee into my now soggy, bulging nappy.

'If – if you think I should be,' I managed, babbling, 'then do it. Do it right now, on a bench, over your knee, and pull my nappy down to show everyone what I've done.'

'Gabrielle!'

'Sorry, Sabina.'

'Come on,' she said firmly, 'back to the car with you, and quickly.'

She took my arm, hustling me forwards, Poppy at the other side. My nappy had burst and I could feel the pee trickling down one leg.

'She's dripping!' Jeff remarked.

'We'd better go,' Gavin insisted, 'before somebody calls the pigs, and then I've got to fuck her. I don't care what anyone says, I've got to fuck her.'

'You'll keep your dirty cock to yourself,' Sabina answered him. 'Come on, Gabby. Put her top on, Poppy.'

They stopped, my top was pulled on over my head and we hurried on, with me still trying to get my arms into the sleeves. I couldn't see what all the fuss was about, because nobody looked like interfering, and I was sure I could nip in among the bushes and bring myself to ecstasy under my fingers as my friends watched. What I really wanted was too much, yes, a hard, public spanking across Sabina's knee, my wet bottom slapped until I was in tears, before she masturbated me from behind.

I had to come, one way or another. I had to come with my wet nappy still on, but I knew it was best to let them take charge. Poppy at least knew what to do with me, but I was praying Sabina could cope as we reached the car park and I was bundled into the back of the jeep, sitting on top of my own clothes. I lay back, closing my eyes once more, as Poppy and Sabina climbed in on either side of me. The jeep started, and we rolled forwards, Gavin heading for the far exit where nobody would have seen.

'You're very bad, Gabrielle!' Sabina stated as we pulled on to the main road.

She meant it, and all I could do was whimper with pleasure as I let my legs come open.

'Incorrigible,' Poppy remarked. 'She needs that spanking, that's what she needs.'

'While she's like this!?' Sabina demanded.

'Not in the car, maybe,' Poppy pointed out, 'but yes, while she's still wet, to make her think about what she's done while she's punished. Meanwhile . . .'

Her hand had gone to my tummy, pressing a little, and lower, on to the fat bulge of soggy nappy material between my thighs. I moaned as I felt the pressure on my pussy, squirming my hips to make it stronger. My bottom and belly were wet with pee, but there was more than that between my pussy lips and bum cheeks: my own juice, warm and slippery where I badly needed a hand, a tongue, a good big cock.

'Not on the seats, Pops,' Gavin remarked from the front.

'Don't worry, you can make her clean it up,' Poppy answered, and she had begun to masturbate me, rubbing the pee-soaked towelling on to my pussy with slow, circular motions. 'Stop it, Gabby, I'm just keeping you warm, that's all. Make for the woods, Gavin.'

I relaxed, lost in a submissive ecstasy tempered only slightly by Sabina's doubts. Gavin, I suppose, must have taken a while to get out of the city and into the hills somewhere up behind where our hotel was. I'd given my trust over completely, and let Poppy and Gavin make the decisions, parking beneath overhanging trees where the road widened and helping me from the car in among dense beeches and chestnuts.

Monty and Jeff had followed, and pushed ahead at Poppy's request, quickly finding a place where a big beech had fallen and lay along the slope, creating a perfect seat for Sabina to punish me. She still looked doubtful, but was doing her best to stay in charge, telling the boys where they could sit to watch and demanding Monty's anorak to protect her lap.

'I hope you're ashamed of yourself?' she asked as she adjusted the anorak.

I shook my head, but hung it too.

'Well, you should be,' she told me. 'Now come on, over you go.'

There was real determination in her eyes as she patted her lap for me to get down. I went, shaking with reaction, and fear too, but I knew I ought to be spanked, that only after my spanking would the punishment be complete and the experience perfect. As I draped myself over her knees, the others were watching: Poppy in front of me to see my face as I was beaten; the boys behind, to get the most intimate view.

Sabina's arm closed around my waist as I steadied myself in spanking position. As I was held tight, and bent over, my wet nappy was sagging badly between my legs with the weight of my own piddle, keeping me very aware of what I'd done.

Sabina gave a single, disapproving click of her tongue, and pulled my nappy seat to the side, exposing one moist pink bottom cheek to the air, and spoke. 'I'll teach you, Gabrielle, I'll really teach you to wet yourself, I'll –'

Her hand came down, hard on my cheek, stinging my wet flesh to wring a scream from my lips and set me kicking. She was so hard, maybe because she really meant it, smacking at my poor bare cheek with all her force and telling me I was a bad girl and deserved what I was getting. I was squealing and kicking, my legs waving wildly behind me and my bunches tossing up and down, too lost in pain to even speak. When it did stop, I was left gasping for air, my skin prickly with sweat, my first tears running from my eyes and my now cool pee trickling down the insides of my legs where the wet nappy had been pulled against my skin.

'Other cheek,' Sabina announced, and my nappy was tugged out of my bottom crease and over, covering my spanked cheek and baring my fresh one.

I braced myself, my lower lip trembling so hard I couldn't shut my mouth, hot tears of frustration welling in my eyes, as Monty spoke, his voice high and full of petulance.

'Come on, Sabina, pull her nappy down. We can't see her cunt this way!'

'Shut up,' Sabina answered. 'She's my girl and I'll spank her how I please . . . and don't be dirty.'

Monty grunted, and I screamed. Sabina's hand had landed on my bottom cheek with all her force and the spanking had begun again, on fresh, cold flesh, wet flesh too, and a wet spanking always hurts so much more. Having it done on one cheek was awful too, her hand landing in the same place over and over, until I was absolutely howling.

She was telling me I was a bad girl again, and should be ashamed, but her words barely registered through the rising delirium of my spanking pain. The boys were laughing too, and cracking jokes about the fuss I was making, with my legs pumping crazily, but I didn't care, lost to shame and indifferent to the appalling indignity of being spanked in front of them, no more than a snotty, snivelling, tear-stained brat, spanked for wetting my nappy, as I should be.

It stopped, both my smacked cheeks now burning, my vision hazy through my tears and because my glasses had fallen off into the leaf mould as I struggled, twin streamers of mucus hanging from my nose and sticky spittle from my lip. Slowly the pain began to be replaced by warmth, only for Sabina to speak again.

'OK, boys, I suppose you deserve a treat.'

My nappy was taken and pulled down with one quick tug, leaving me bare behind, my glossy pink bottom stuck up, naked, my pussy showing, my bumhole, and bitter frustration hit me as the spanking began again, as hard as ever, full across my already hot cheeks. It was so unfair, when I'd been done so hard already, and it sent me straight into a full-blown spanking tantrum, bawling my eyes out, beating my fists on the tree and on Sabina's leg, kicking my legs stupidly in every direction, and squalling pathetically, pleas and insults and squeaks and sobs, all to the sound of the boy's uproarious laughter and crude remarks at the view of my sticky, pee-slick pussy and twitching anus.

'You are such a baby, Gabrielle,' Sabina chided as she finally stopped. 'You really do belong in nappies, you know that, don't you?'

'Yes,' I answered weakly, and slid off her lap as she let go, to sit down in the leaf mould.

Poppy came to cuddle me, holding me tightly as I wiped my eyes and nose on my top, too far gone to care about the mess, or that lifting it showed my tits. Sabina had stood up, and I was expecting her to take her jeans down and make me lick her to ecstasy. I'd have done it, and masturbated as I did it too, on my knees in front of her with my soggy nappy still down at the back and my freshly spanked bottom showing behind. She didn't, but stood looking down on me as she spoke.

'Go on then, I know what you need to do.'

I nodded. Pulling my nappy up behind, high into my crease so my smacked cheeks stuck out the sides,

I set my knees apart, at her feet. Poppy took hold of my top, quickly pulling it up and off to leave me near naked once again, just in shoes, socks and nappy, as I pushed my hand down to my pussy. I was soaking wet, and had begun to rub and let my mind come into focus on my wonderful experience when Monty spoke.

'Hey, what about us?'

'Yeah, I want to fuck her!' Gavin put in.

Jeff added a grunt of agreement even as Sabina answered back. 'You get to look, and count yourselves lucky.'

'No,' I managed, 'let them, Sabina, please? It's only fair.'

I was looking up at her, and her eyes widened in astonishment.

'What – but I thought – I thought you and Poppy? All three of them!?'

All I could do was nod weakly.

She shook her head, and for one awful moment I thought we'd gone too far, before she snapped her fingers, pointing to the beech trunk. 'If that's what you want, you slut, you'd better get over there.'

I nodded again, in gratitude, and crawled forwards as the boys advanced on me with whoops of delight. The tree trunk was broad, and smooth, allowing me to drape myself over it with my bottom lifted behind, the bulging seat of my nappy offered, with my red cheeks sticking out to either side. Monty got to me first, Gavin and Jeff giving way to him, and as his fat hands took hold of my legs I'd let my mouth come open in an obvious invitation to one of the others. Gavin accepted, jumping over the trunk with a crow of pleasure and anticipation.

'I knew I'd get you sucking, sooner or later. Here, cop a mouthful of this!'

He'd come to stand in front of me, and as Monty and Jeff began to fondle my bottom Gavin flopped his cock out, right in my face, chortling with glee. I took him in, sucking cock, eagerly, because they'd handled me properly, and made me their slut.

'I tell you what,' he joked, 'this'll make a good baby-bottle. Suck hard enough and you'll even get some milk.'

He laughed. Poppy giggled. Monty gave an appreciative grunt as he pulled the back of my nappy aside, once more exposing my bottom, only this time not for spanking, but for fucking. Both he and Jeff began to molest me, their hands everywhere, exploring my most intimate details, fingers easing in under the crotch of my nappy and up my hole.

'Fucking soaking!' Jeff declared happily, and a second, fat finger was eased in up my pussy.

'Let the bitch suck!' Gavin complained as my mouth came wide in reaction to being penetrated and his cock slipped free.

I took him in hand and fed him back in, making a slide of my lips so he could control me even as Jeff pushed a third finger in up my sopping hole. Monty was watching, holding my nappy aside and my cheeks apart, to spread out both my sex and my anus.

'I'm going to fist her cunt!' Jeff declared, and I gasped again as he wormed the full mass of his joined fingers in up my sex.

'Don't stretch her too much,' Monty complained. 'Not till we've fucked her.'

'Use her arse, if you want her tight,' Jeff retorted, and screwed the knobbly bulk of his fist in up my hole.

I wasn't ready, not quite, and screamed as my pussy spread to what seemed an impossible load. Gavin gave a grunt of annoyance as his cock slid free of my mouth for the second time, and as my hole spread to accommodate Jeff's fist I was taken firmly by my bunches and my mouth stuffed full of cock.

'That's right, fuck her head!' Monty laughed. 'Come on, Jeff, stop clowning around.'

Jeff gave a reluctant grunt of assent and his fist slid from my pussy hole, which closed with a soft, wet fart. I felt Monty as he got behind me, his cock between my bum cheeks, rubbing in the juice and pee. Jeff called somebody a good girl, and I realised Poppy was helping him with his cock. Sabina I couldn't see, and she was silent, but I knew she was watching, which put the final touch to what was being done to me, because she had given me to them to be used, however they liked, not my choice at all.

Monty was groaning as he rubbed himself erect in my bottom crease, with his hands holding my nappy aside and spreading my cheeks, so his shaft was touching my anus and his balls slapping on my empty sex. I needed fucking, with Gavin's cock now hard in my mouth, and stuck my bottom out. Monty took the hint, his knuckles pushing down between my cheeks, his cock taken in hand, and fed up into my gaping, willing hole.

He gave a long moan as I filled with his meat, and they had begun to row me, back and forth on their cocks, mouth and pussy, two men inside me, as behind me my girlfriend sucked a third hard in readiness, and my Mistress watched. I was stroking Gavin's balls and ringing his erection as he fucked my head, masturbating him into my mouth. I already wanted a mouthful of spunk, and I was going to get it, his groans growing louder, his grip on my bunches tighter, his cock jamming deep into my throat.

And he'd done it, ejaculating right down my neck to set me choking. Most of it came out of my nose, in a great froth of spunk bubbles, all over his cock, as I managed to push him back a little, feeding myself come as Monty in turn grew urgent. My bottom was getting squashed, his bulbous gut crushing my soggy nappy seat against me, to squeeze the pee out, trickling down my bottom crease and one thigh. Gavin pulled back, gave a grunt of distaste at the state of his cock and wiped it in my hair before he stood away.

I gripped the tree, my whole body shaking to Monty's furious thrusts as he grunted and gasped his way towards orgasm. He'd been known to fail to make it, but not this time, finishing with a final rasping explosion of breath, jamming himself as deep up my pussy as he could go, and coming up me, deep up me, his fingers locked in my flesh as my pussy filled, and burst, spunk squashing out of my well-fucked hole, all over his balls.

He'd jammed me halfway over the tree, so my bottom was the highest part of my body, and all I could do was lie there, limp and sore, as he let go of me. My nappy closed over my pussy, the spunk oozing out into my already wet pouch, but only briefly, before I'd once more been exposed, this time with my nappy pulled down to show off the full spread of my bare pink bottom.

Jeff had climbed on to the log, erect cock in hand, his great red, bearded, blurred face grinning down at me as I looked back. His cock pushed between my cheeks, pressing to my bumhole, and I let out a vain squeak of protest at the thought of being buggered, only for it to turn into a long moan as he drove the full bulk of his cock down into my upturned pussy. I was still brimful of Monty's spunk, and it squashed out as I filled. Not that Jeff cared, fucking happily away on top of my bottom, with every thrust pushing me into the hard wood of the tree trunk.

The others were watching, all four, standing in a ring, Poppy and Sabina with their arms around each other, wide-eyed with excitement. Monty was grinning, Gavin's face set in mixed amusement and disgust, his eyes on where Jeff's heavy scrotum was bouncing up and down on my spread pussy as I was fucked. I was going to come too, his thick hair tickling my clitoris with every push, a maddening sensation that would nevertheless get me there, if he just kept it up, if he just fucked me a little harder, if he just fucked me a little deeper.

I came, crying out my ecstasy to the wood as Jeff finished off inside me in a furious crescendo, working my slippery hole and rubbing my clit, on and on, until I was screaming and clutching at the tree trunk, so high I could barely breathe, so well used I thought I'd faint. Not that he cared, enjoying my pussy to the full before pulling out and squeezing the last of his spunk into my bottom crease, to leave me with what Monty so delightfully described as a cream pie on my anus.

When he finally climbed off I stayed just where I was. I couldn't do anything else, too well fucked to even move, never mind being made to parade in my nappy and the hard spanking. I was in a fine state too, my hot red bottom pushed high and wide, with the boys' come still bubbling from my pussy hole into my lowered nappy, which hung heavy between my thighs, my pee still dripping from the bottom, while my face was a mess of Gavin's spunk and my own snot.

It was Poppy who came up behind me, pulling my nappy up, to squash the spunk in my pouch over my pussy and up between my cheeks before climbing up next to me, her legs set astride the tree trunk. She had my glasses, and I put them on, bringing the world back into focus.

'What about me?' she asked. 'And Sabina, or are you going to be selfish?'

I managed to nod my head, and pull myself up a little, willing to do my best, but Sabina spoke before I could.

'Back at the hotel, I think, Poppy. After poor Gabby's had a clean-up.'

Poppy gave a happy shrug and bent forwards to kiss me, indifferent to the mess I was in. She helped me up too, and to clean up, using all the tissues we could muster between us. I'd left the rest of my clothes in the car, and was forced to walk back bare bottomed under Monty's anorak, with just my badly soiled yellow top beneath. My jeans and panties were filthy too, leaving me with no option but to stay in the car when we returned to Dijon.

Poppy went shopping for me, with Sabina, while the boys drank beers at the bar we'd parked outside and teased me about my behaviour. I didn't mind, too tired to worry and too used to them anyway. They, after all, were as bad as me, maybe worse in Monty's case. My only worry was Sabina, who'd been having trouble handling the state I'd got myself into, although she was doing her very best to be cool about it.

When Poppy and Sabina came back they had several large shopping bags marked with the logos of what looked like worthwhile shops. They were laughing and joking together, which could only be a good sign, and as Sabina loaded the bags in the back Poppy went to speak to the boys at their table.

'What did you do?' Gavin joked. 'Grow you own cotton?'

'We've only been a couple of hours,' Poppy protested, 'and you'll be glad we took the time to look around as well. There's a paintball shop, a good one – at least, it looks good to me – in the Rue 13 Juillet. Here's their card.'

She handed it to Jeff, and all three of them bent eagerly forwards.

My bottom gave an involuntary twitch, and I hid a sigh. I didn't protest because I knew it was pointless. I did want to get back to the hotel, though, and spoke up. 'If you're going to go there, could one of you drive the rest of us back first?'

'Sure,' Gavin answered promptly. 'Meet you there, guys.'

Poppy and Sabina climbed into the jeep as Monty and Jeff set off. Gavin followed, grinning happily as he pulled out into the traffic. Poppy and I were in the back, and she was immediately teasing me by trying to make me open Monty's anorak so passers-by might get a flash.

Sabina turned around in her chair. 'You two are an utter disgrace,' she said, and she meant it, for all the nervous laughter in her voice. 'Especially you, Gabrielle. Honestly, wetting yourself, and getting off on it!'

'You're not joking,' Gavin answered her. 'Jeff says she goes the whole way sometimes.'

'No, Gavin,' I managed, but it was too late.

'The whole way?' Sabina demanded. 'How d'you mean the whole way?'

'You know, dumps her load,' Gavin replied, 'in her nappy.'

I groaned, shaking my head.

He went on, making absolutely certain she could be in no doubt whatsoever of his meaning. 'The whole fucking works, and in her knickers too, panty pooping the Yanks call it.'

Poppy was talking too, fast. 'It's a punishment, Sabina, the worst punishment possible, for – for when

169

she's been really, really bad – and me, me too, sometimes.'

'You're a dirty pig, Gabrielle, and you too, Poppy,' Sabina said, and she really meant it.

Seven

Sabina was quiet as we drove back to the hotel. I couldn't think of anything to say, not wanting to try and explain myself in front of Gavin, who'd only make a joke of it, and not intending to make any excuses. Poppy held my hand, and Gavin talked, apparently oblivious, or perhaps trying to defuse the situation, telling us cheerfully about rival makes of paintball guns, protective gear and his favourite tactics.

Back at La Maison des Vignes I went up to our room under cover of Monty's coat, with the girls carrying the shopping bags. Jeff had discovered a back staircase, and we weren't seen at all, which was a relief, as my emotions were simply too raw to cope with anything else. Once we were inside I got straight into the shower, leaving Poppy to attempt to initiate a conversation with Sabina as she investigated the contents of the mini-bar.

By the time I'd finished, and wrapped towels around my hair and around my body they both had drinks in their hands, Champagne cocktails, and were sitting in the window bay, Poppy fiddling with her glass, Sabina staring out over the vineyards and the plain beyond. I pulled up the third of the comfortable chairs, wondering what to say. I couldn't deny it. I couldn't apologise or pretend it was something I'd been made to do, or had a problem with. I couldn't even attempt to persuade her it was a reasonable thing to do, not after the way David Anthony had sought to manipulate her. What I could do was tell the truth and hope she understood.

'You know I am a therapist, don't you, Sabina?'

She nodded.

'I base my ideas on those of Carl Rogers, an American psychologist. He relied on five basic tenets: openness to experience, living for the present, trusting one's own thoughts and feelings, acknowledging one's own freedoms and taking responsibility for one's own actions, and full participation in the world.'

'Including dirtying your own knickers, on purpose?'

'Yes. If it helps you to come to terms with yourself. Why not?'

'Why not!? It's disgusting, Gabrielle!'

'Why? It is taboo, but it does not harm anybody. True, one ought to pop into a shower immediately afterwards, but, like so many things, it is perfectly safe as long as you are sensible.'

'Safe, sane and consensual,' Poppy put in.

'That's what David Anthony used to say,' Sabina answered.

'And it's true,' Poppy went on. 'Why allow your values to be dictated by society? Why not make your own, based on your own moral judgement? How many people would tell you it's wrong to use corporal punishment on other people, even if they like it, even if they beg you for it?'

'Plenty,' Sabina admitted, and I held up a hand before Poppy could start trying to persuade Sabina to try it.

'You have to take sensible precautions, yes,' I admitted, 'and it is not something I would suggest other people do. I do not use it as a therapy, for instance.'

I smiled, and so did she, lifting a little of the weight on me as I went on.

'Although for me it is therapy. After a day's work – and bear in mind that I am constantly taking the weight of other people's problems on my shoulders – there is nothing better than to simply strip naked, put on a nappy and go to bed, and if I wake in the night, or before I sleep, and nature needs to take its course, then what happens, happens. As I do it my stress simply melts away.'

'And it turns you on?'

'It arouses me, yes. Being helpless arouses me, and it is part of the same thing. When you tied me up it was wonderful, and when you spanked me, even though I hate the pain, because I was helpless, unable to control my physical responses.'

Sabina bit her lip. I paused, unsure if it was fair to make her compare her own desires with mine. Poppy had no such reservations.

'It's no different from what you get off on, Sabina. You love punishing us, don't you, and I want you to, more than anything else. I don't fully understand your feelings though. A little yes, but not fully, because for me it's all about misbehaviour, being naughty and being punished for it. I need somebody to punish me, but I wouldn't dream of criticising you for wanting to enjoy my pain, or Gabby's and she does hate it –'

'I'm not criticising,' Sabina interrupted, suddenly defensive.

'It's the same with nappy play,' Poppy went on. 'It makes Gabby feel liberated, but it makes me feel naughty. OK, we've come a bit closer in our feelings since we began going out, but at first we barely understood how the other felt. We still worked together, just like you and me, and you and Gabby. You still like us, don't you?'

'Poppy!' I protested, because what she'd said was pure emotional blackmail.

It was too late anyway. Sabina had stood up.

'Of course I like you. Come here, both of you. Give me a hug.'

I came, what else could I do? Poppy came too, the three of us cuddling together, then kissing, before we broke apart.

Sabina was laughing as she went on. 'OK, I'm sorry, both of you. All I've ever wanted is for people to like me for who I am. You both do, and then the moment it gets a bit heavy for me I freak. Friends, yeah?'

'Friends,' Poppy confirmed, and kissed her again.

I did the same, then went to make myself a drink as Sabina continued to talk, once more explaining how David Anthony had seemed such a breath of fresh air at first, and how disillusioned she'd been to discover he was only telling her part of the story. She also admitted that she'd been starting to have doubts even before France, when they'd been to Morris Rathwell's club. It had been quite obvious that there was a whole range of people indulging many different tastes, and that, while female dominance and male submission were in the majority, it was not something carved in stone. We sipped our drinks as we talked, until at last Gavin's head appeared around the door to suggest we go wine tasting in Fixin village. Sabina drained her cocktail and finished what she'd been saying.

'As it goes, I'm starting to think I prefer girls.'

* * *

Going wine tasting was the best possible thing we could have done. It cleared the air, giving us something else to focus on, and company outside our own group, which had the effect of grounding us. No further mention was made of nappies, let alone filling them, even while tasting the heady, earthy local reds.

I also saw a new side to Gavin Bulmer, who listened with polite and serious attention as I translated what the various growers were saying about their wines. He was also extraordinarily generous, and apparently casually so, not only buying several cases for himself, but also insisting on purchasing examples of our favourites for Poppy, Sabina and myself. I only put my foot down when he offered to pay for a Chambertin at nearly a hundred Euros the bottle, refusing with thanks, only to find he'd included it in the case anyway.

We met Monty and Jeff as we walked towards the next village to the north, where we'd been recommended a grower who had white and rosé as well as the ubiquitous reds. They pulled up, looking well pleased with themselves as they climbed from the car, like two self-satisfied cartoon bears. I was in a loose blue dress Poppy had bought me in Dijon, and Monty's eyes went straight to my middle.

'No, I am not,' I answered, and stuck my tongue out at him. 'We are going tasting in Couchey. Are you coming?'

'Sure,' he answered, 'let me dump the car and we're with you, but you want to see some of the stuff we've got.'

'Maybe after dinner?'

'Like this really cool headgear,' Jeff went on, 'but that's a surprise, and some ace guns –'

'With rapid fire,' Monty added, 'no-jam action –'

'And some cool colours –'

'And kneepads –'

'And these well weird rubber panties –'

'With bunny tails –'

'From a sex shop, not the paintball place –'

'And for Sabina!' Monty finished.

He'd reached into the car, and pulled out like a conjuror producing a rabbit quite simply the most enormous strap-on dildo I could have imagined, at least a foot long, as thick as my wrist, jet black, and sculpted in the form of a grotesque, veiny cock. A monstrous, wrinkly scrotum hung beneath, along with a system of straps in heavy-duty leather. It was for Sabina, in a sense, but it wasn't Sabina it was going in, but me, and Poppy. I could only stare, my pussy twitching, and they went happily on.

'It's great. You put stuff in the bollocks, right –'

'Like egg whites,' Jeff supplied in open glee, 'whipped up with a bit of cream –'

'To make fake spunk,' Monty finished.

'Egg whites whipped up with a bit of cream to make fake spunk?' Poppy echoed, speaking very slowly.

'Or maybe beer, if you want to be bum fucked and got drunk?' Monty suggested.

Poppy shook her head, speechless.

'It would not fit, not up a girl's bottom,' I pointed out. 'Do be sensible, Monty.'

'Yeah,' he insisted, sounding slightly hurt. 'There's this vid they showed us, with these gay guys, and the – what d'you call the guy who takes it?'

'Brave?' Jeff suggested.

'Sponge,' Gavin supplied.

'That's right, the sponge. Well, he –'

'I don't want to know, thank you,' Sabina interrupted. 'That is way too much information.'

'Don't you like it?' Monty queried, now genuinely hurt as a wave of relief flooded over me.

'I love the strap-on,' Sabina answered. 'I just don't want to know about some guy taking it up his arse.'

'Each to his own,' Gavin pointed out.

'Yeah, great,' Sabina answered. 'I just don't want it in my face.'

'It's not meant to go in your face,' Jeff pointed out. 'It's meant to go up Gabs's cunt or Pops's, although I suppose –'

'We understand, Jeff,' I cut him off. 'Put it away, Monty, please?'

He did as he was told, but was looking more pleased with himself than ever as he climbed back into the car and started for the hotel.

The evening was strange. I came back from the tasting a little drunk, despite having done my best to spit, and stayed drunk as we worked our way through yet another enormous dinner. Monty, Jeff and Sabina did anyway, eating huge steaks topped with melted cheese and flamed in brandy, among other things. I was feeling I'd been overdoing it, and the others didn't seem quite so enthusiastic either, going for small amounts of good things rather than wallowing in it.

The thought of the hunt was also making me nervous. I could hardly back out, in the circumstances, with everyone else, including Poppy, so full of enthusiasm, but as they discussed what to do it sounded increasingly terrifying. The basic idea was that Sabina and the boys would hunt Poppy and I through some lonely piece of woodland, with paint-ball guns, and that if we were hit we had to submit to whatever the successful hunter wanted.

I wanted to escape, and listened carefully in the hope of finding some flaw in their tactics. As I nibbled at a piece of Tarte Tatin and watched Monty and Jeff wolf down huge pieces of chocolate cake, a good idea came to me. Gavin was reasonably fit, but neither Monty nor Jeff would be able to catch me running, and probably not Sabina either, especially uphill. As if casually, I suggested the Morvan as a good site, presenting it as a large and lonely forest without bothering to mention that the hills rise to over eight hundred metres in places.

My idea was accepted, and the time set for the next day. I was still nervous, which Poppy noticed, bringing out her mischievous streak. She began to tease me, pointing out that she and Sabina were still on a promise from earlier in the day. Sabina wouldn't react, but the boys did, Monty looking up from his chocolate cake with a beaming smile.

'Yeah, go for it, and give her a good spanking first, to get her warm. I love watching you get it, Gabs, you really react.'

'Me too,' Jeff agreed. 'The way you kick your legs, and shake your hair, like you just can't handle it.'

'I cannot, genuinely,' I pointed out.

'I think she's been spanked quite enough for one day,' Sabina put in, 'and besides, if anything did happen, who says you three get to perve over us?'

'Aw, come on, I want to see!' Monty protested.

'You see what I allow you to see,' Sabina replied, 'and you do what I allow you to do. For now, you can think about what we're getting up to while you're on your own in bed, and save your energy for tomorrow.'

'Somebody,' Gavin remarked, 'is getting a bit too big for her boots.'

'Dead right,' Jeff agreed. 'Perhaps she could do with a good spanking herself?'

'Now that, I'd like to see –' Monty laughed '– and do!'

'You can fucking try it!' Sabina answered him.

'Can I?' Monty retorted. 'Really?'

'No, Monty,' Poppy put in, 'you can't. Don't be such a pig.'

'Aw, shame,' Monty answered, 'that'd be a laugh, that would.'

'Not for you, it wouldn't!' Sabina answered him. 'You'd be the one who ended up on the receiving end. I've taken boys down before, so, like I said, bring it on any time you like.'

'I'm cool,' Gavin answered hastily, while Monty and Jeff exchanged glances.

Sabina went on, now well pleased with herself. 'So, boys, you have a drink or two, or go and fiddle with yourselves, whatever turns you on. We girls need to be alone, for something that's definitely for grown-ups.'

She stood up, and signalled to Poppy and me. We both rose, and she took our arms as we walked from the dining room, putting a mocking wiggle into her walk as we went. Only when we reached the stairs, well out of sight, and hearing, did she burst into giggles. 'Oh, they are funny, aren't they? With their little tongues hanging out of their heads, like they were puppies or something. What a laugh!'

'I'd be a little careful,' Poppy advised.

'Oh crap,' Sabina answered. 'Men are all the same. Give them a little, but never give it all, and you'll have them eating out of your hand. David Anthony was like that. At first he thought I'd be grateful for a lick, 'cause so many guys won't do it, but he needed it so bad I soon had him begging. 'Course he just wanted it all the more.'

'What do you think's happened to him?' Poppy asked.

'Who gives a fuck?' Sabina answered. 'I've got you two, and you are much more fun.'

179

We'd reached the top of the stairs, and as she spoke she smacked our bottoms, just gently, but she kept her hands in place, steering us down the corridor to our room. Inside, she purposefully locked the door and went to turn one of the comfortable chairs around from where we'd left it by the window. I could see she was drunk, a little unsteady, and horny too, with her nipples poking up through her top and her eyes bright with lust and mischief.

Poppy spoke as she sat herself down on Sabina's knee, her eyes fixed on me. 'What shall we do with her then? Make her strip for us? Maybe spank her again, just to keep her in her place? Would you like to watch her lick my bottom?'

Sabina coughed and planted a firm smack to where Poppy's fleshy rear cheeks bulged out over her leg. 'Aren't you forgetting who you are, Poppy? And that you're due a punishment.'

'Me? A punishment?' Poppy answered in very real surprise, which quickly gave way to consternation as Sabina went on.

'Yes, Poppy, a punishment, as we agreed. Now, make me one of those Champagne cocktails from the mini-bar, but, first, strip. You, too, Gabby, I think I'd like you both in the nude this evening.'

Poppy was going to protest, but thought better of it, and rose from Sabina's knee and quickly started to undress instead. I did the same, peeling off my dress and quickly divesting myself of bra and panties, shoes and stockings, to leave myself stark naked. Poppy was still struggling with her bra catch, which seemed to be stuck, and she finally had to wriggle out of it instead, letting her big breasts fall free of the cups as she pulled them up. Her panties followed and she too was naked, running immediately to the mini-bar with her bottom wobbling behind her, the marks of Sabina's caning still clear on her flesh.

'Kneel,' Sabina instructed me, pointing to the floor at her feet.

I got down, feeling ever so slightly pleased with myself at Poppy's obvious discomfort but hanging my head to make sure it didn't show. Just the thought of another of Sabina's spankings had been enough to set my bottom cheeks clenching and my bumhole pulsing weakly between them. She was so hard, and for all it did to me the prospect was still frightening. My flesh was a little bruised too.

'Good girl,' Sabina addressed me. 'I can see obedience comes naturally to you. Come on, Poppy, chop, chop.'

Poppy had opened one of the quarter bottles of Champagne, and was pouring in a miniature of brandy, the golden fluid swirling in the yellow. There was a little tray, and she put it all together before coming to Sabina, on her knees, but still looking a little put out. Sabina took the glass, sipped once, and again, before reaching out to put it down on a table. Poppy had come close to me, so close I could feel the warmth of her body and smell her skin, and her excitement.

Sabina beckoned to her. 'Time you were spanked, and hard, because you've been getting well above yourself, haven't you?'

'Yes, I suppose so,' Poppy mumbled, 'but –'

'No buts,' Sabina cut in. 'Just do as you're told. Come on, over my knee, stick that porky little bum in the air and we'll soon have this over and done with, or maybe not.'

Sabina had moved forwards in the chair, extending her knees to make a spanking lap for Poppy, who crawled obediently over, balancing herself on her hands and toes so that her bottom was the highest part of her body, twin, plump crests of girl-flesh. Smiling, Sabina gave Poppy a little pat, took hold of her firmly around the waist, and laid in, hard.

I'd have screamed the room down. Poppy merely gave a little gasp and closed her eyes in bliss, absorbing everything Sabina was giving. Inevitably Sabina's reaction was to spank harder still, setting Poppy's bottom wobbling like a jelly as her flesh grew slowly pinker. The expression on Sabina's face slowly became more determined too, and her grip tighter, yet still Poppy held her place, her face set in the same, sleepy, contented smile. At last Sabina stopped, to shake her hand, her palm as red as Poppy's bottom.

'Gabrielle, the hairbrush,' she ordered.

It was in the bedroom and I jumped up to get it, not bothering to crawl. I got a swat for my pains, as soon as I'd passed it over, making me squeak. Again Sabina tightened her grip and laid into Poppy's bottom, applying the hairbrush with all her force to the big, rounded cheeks. Finally Poppy reacted, gasping and shaking.

'That's better!' Sabina declared as at last Poppy's thighs began to pump, so that she lost her footing and slumped down over Sabina's lap, her legs cocked half up and a little open.

The spanking grew harder still, and Poppy began to squirm, her pussy now showing fully to me where I'd knelt after getting the hairbrush, moist and ready, just as moist and ready as I'd have been, for all her cool reaction to her punishment. She was kicking too, just a little, and wriggling her bottom in a vain effort to avoid the hard smacks of the hairbrush.

At that Sabina began to play a cruel game, stopping to let Poppy relax, before delivering a sudden, hard salvo of spanks in one spot. Inevitably

Poppy would try to squirm away, only for Sabina to choose a new spot and give it the same treatment. On the fourth go she chose the tuck of Poppy's bottom, where her meaty cheeks turned down to meet her thighs, and right over her bumhole. Poppy went wild, finally broken, one leg kicking out to the side and her hair flying as she shook her head in a desperate effort to dull the pain. At that Sabina stopped.

'There, not so tough after all, are you?'

Poppy gave her head a single, miserable shake and tumbled off Sabina's lap as she was released. I went to cuddle her, her body wet with sweat and shaking as she came into my arms. Our mouths met and we were kissing, as we had before licking Sabina to ecstasy for the first time. I was more than ready to provide the same open show, but stopped as Sabina gave another pointed cough.

'Ahem! Less of that, you sluts. You attend to me, not each other.'

'Yes, Mistress,' Poppy answered promptly as we pulled apart.

'Lick me,' Sabina ordered, and lifted herself in the seat.

She was in loose black trousers, which she pushed down, taking her thong with them, all the way to her ankles, exposing the plump, furry mound of her sex, her lips swollen and showing moist pink flesh between. Her top came up too, and her bra, baring her beautiful dark breasts, each heavy globe of flesh tipped with a hard dark nipple I yearned to take into my mouth.

Poppy and I crawled forwards together, jostling for space between Sabina's open thighs. I knew what I wanted, to suckle, and have my hair stroked, but I was more than willing to do as she told me. Poppy went lower, kissing Sabina's pussy mound, and I was put to the teat, in bliss as I suckled, and thinking of all the things she'd put me through that day.

I wasn't going to play with myself though, not until Sabina had come, both because it felt right to give her pleasure first, and for fear of the hairbrush now lying beside her glass but close to hand if she chose to use it on my bottom. Not that it would be long anyway. Sabina had cradled my head, holding me to her breast, and her other hand was locked in Poppy's hair, keeping her firmly in place as she licked.

Sabina had begun to moan, and I could feel her body starting to tighten against mine. I began to lick, and took her other breast in my hand, stroking the firm, smooth curve and letting my finger bump over the nipple. She was going to come, but went suddenly tense, pulling me back, and Poppy.

'No, not that,' she sighed, 'not my bottom.'

'Pretty please, it's lovely, really,' Poppy answered.

I rocked back on my heels, not wanting to ruin the moment, but unsure what to say. Sabina's thighs were wide open, her pussy too, and glistening with her own juice and Poppy's spittle. Beneath, her firm, smooth cheeks were pushed together, the dark crevice showing just a hint of the tiny lines that led to her anus. She gave a low moan, and suddenly her legs were up, right up, spreading her cheeks to make her bumhole a round, black star, with the centre a knot of flesh, darker still.

'Do it – do it then, you dirty little bitches,' she babbled, 'both of you, if that's what you like, get your tongues up my bum.'

'Go on, Gabby,' Poppy offered, and I'd been taken firmly by the hair. 'Go on, I know you want it, so kissy, kissy.'

She pushed my head forwards, until my mouth was just centimetres away from the dirty black star of

Sabina's anus. I poked out my tongue, hesitating, and touched, flicking at a tiny piece of rubbery flesh, hesitating again, and licking at the star of tiny lines, hesitating again, and lapping at her, my tongue pressed to her anus, to fill my mouth with her earthy taste. She gave a long, deep moan, and I was lost, licking urgently at her bumhole, to get her clean, and to burrow inside, my tongue tip pushing deep as her tight ring opened to the pressure.

'Oh, you filthy little bitch, Gabrielle,' she groaned, and she'd grabbed both of us by the hair, pulling Poppy into her pussy.

I couldn't help myself, my hand already between my thighs as I licked urgently at Sabina's beautiful, tight bottom hole, alternately lapping and sticking my tongue up, my face pushed hard to her glorious bottom, cheek to cheek with Poppy as we gave our Mistress the pleasure of our mouths. She was already moaning, her anal star tightening in long, steady contractions, right on my tongue.

She'd punished me, badly, spanking me until I was in tears and putting me in nappies and making me go in public, giving me to three men for my pussy and mouth to be used, and filled with spunk; she'd made me strip and made me crawl; she'd let me suckle and lick, but best of all, best by far, she'd ordered me to put my tongue to her dirty bottom hole and lick her clean.

We came together, Sabina laid back, her thighs up, in ecstasy as we licked her, me kneeling nude at her feet, reduced to rubbing my own pussy as I tongued her twitching bottom hole. I was still coming when she'd finished too, her bumhole now an open, slippery hollow with my tongue stuck deep in, where I kept it until I'd come right down and could finally collapse in exhausted bliss on the floor.

* * *

Poppy and Sabina and I slept together in the same bed, which wasn't particularly comfortable but seemed the natural thing to do. Sabina was full of energy, and still talking as I drifted into sleep. She was the same in the morning, relaxed and at ease with us, so much so that she was chatting happily about her home life back in England as Poppy applied powder and cream to my bottom.

At breakfast she was worse than ever with the boys, extremely bossy and teasing them by hinting at what we'd done without revealing any details. They were getting increasingly wound up, but could at least content themselves with planning what had come to be called the Bunny Hunt that afternoon. We also had to be out of our rooms by mid-morning and find a suitable hotel for the following night, which kept us busy until lunchtime.

The boys had been poring over a detailed map of the region while Sabina, Poppy and I had been playing the evening before, which had rather spoilt my plan to choose a hilly site where they'd be unable to chase me. They'd identified four possible sites, all reasonably close to the town of Château Chinon, so we drove up, into pleasantly fresh air, with the roads still damp in the shade from rain the night before. Once there, we selected a hotel, L'Auberge des Lapins, a name the boys found extremely funny, funnier even than I'd have expected of their sense of humour. After all, we were only going to be wearing rabbit tails, a bit like old-fashioned bunny-girls.

We had an early lunch and went to explore the sites. The first was a forested area beside a lake, flat and with well-spaced trees, but fortunately far too full of tourists for our purposes. The second would have suited me down to the ground: a long, wooded ridge rising to a rocky peak and apparently completely deserted. I did my best, but they rejected it as too rough, and we moved on to the third.

I knew they were going to choose it even before we'd got out of the cars. The road cut off a small, conical hill in the bend of a river, with no tracks, no buildings save for a shed beside an apparently abandoned radio mast and only a rotting gate with an ancient enamel notice to prevent access. The notice stated that the owners were a broadcast company, and even I had to admit they were unlikely to send anybody out to an abandoned site miles from the nearest town on that particular afternoon.

We parked the cars to make sure nobody else could fit into the space, just to be on the safe side, and the boys began to sort out the gear: their camouflage outfits, paintball guns, the balls themselves, each a distinct colour, goggles and more. Only when it was all laid out did they hand over Poppy and my outfits: cheap army boots, long, thick socks, the ridiculous rubber panties, pink with fluffy white rabbit tails to go above our bottoms, and our headgear, which consisted of pantomime rabbit heads made of fluffy pink and white fur on a cardboard base, with huge blue eyes, whiskers, goofy teeth, and ears two feet long with floppy tips.

'What are those!?' Poppy demanded.

'They're your headgear,' Monty said happily. 'Good, aren't they?'

'No!' Poppy answered. 'Cute, sort of – maybe – just don't you dare take any photos of me like that!'

'How are we supposed to see?' I asked.

Gavin picked one up, his voice completely reasonable, as if demonstrating how one of the paintball guns worked, as he began to speak. 'You look out through the nostrils, and you'll be wearing goggles underneath just to be extra safe, and obviously we'll be aiming for your bums anyway.'

'Obviously,' Poppy sighed. 'OK, Gabby, I suppose we better let the boys have their fun. Any rules, or do we just get shot and then ravished?'

'Bunny Hunt rules are like Pig Sticking rules,' Gavin explained. 'You have to get to a predetermined point, safe ground, and avoid us as best you can on the way. First run, the mast is safe ground, second run, the cars.'

'By the road?' Poppy queried.

'Sure. You'll have the keys.'

'What if we're seen?'

'You get an extra thrill, and so does some French guy. It's safe, though, 'cause you can hear a car coming easy, and wait to make a dash.'

'And if you get us while we're waiting?'

'You take a hit, or you flash your tits at some Frog. All part of the game.'

Poppy nodded thoughtfully. Not a single car had passed since we'd arrived, and it seemed safe enough. His rules made my ideas for escape almost impossible, but not completely. With a deliberately loud sigh I began to undress, taking off my shoes and socks before removing my panties under my dress, so I'd be standing near naked by the road for as little time as possible.

The pink rubber knickers were tight, one size only, fitting snugly over my bottom and pulling up a little between my pussy lips, but more comfortable than I'd expected, while if I hadn't been able to crane back over my shoulder to inspect the fluffy tail sticking out above my bum I wouldn't have known it was there at all. Poppy was less lucky, the knickers impossibly tight over her heavy bottom, with almost the full expanse of her cheeks spilling out to either side behind and the shape of her pussy moulded by the rubber at the front. Her tail looked ridiculous, perhaps more so for her fatter bottom.

With my rubber knickers on I sat down on the back of Monty's car to do my boots and socks. The socks were thick white wool, and came right up to my knees, like the longest school socks, while the boots were a little too big, making me feel clumsy as well as silly. I felt sillier still as I peeled my dress off, leaving me topless, in pink knickers, white socks and boots, as if I was a member of some all-girls sports team whose main reason for existence was the gratification of male humour. Although in a sense I was.

I took my goggles and head before climbing the gate, walking a little way up the track to where I couldn't be seen from the road. Poppy wasn't ready, still fighting a losing battle to make her rubber knickers less indecent. Nor were the others, the boys dressing as if they were about to go into a real battle, and all three simultaneously trying to be the one who got to help Sabina.

She at least looked good, if not in a way I'd pictured her. They'd bought her camouflage trousers, but fashionable rather than functional, loose in the leg, tight over her muscular bottom and cut so low her bright-red thong showed at the back. Her top was equally impractical, again in camouflage, but so short it left her entire midriff bare, and so tight her breasts were left sticking out like a pair of balloons, each topped by a bump where her nipples showed through. She also had a belt angled across her middle for her paintball gun, spare ammunition and the huge strap-on, hung menacingly over her left hip beside her water bottle. Like my own outfit, and Poppy's, it was plainly chosen more for the boys' satisfaction than any practical purpose.

The only sensible piece of equipment they'd given her were the goggles, an expensive, heavy-duty design the same as my own. As Jeff began to clamber over the gate I put mine on, only to discover they wouldn't fit properly over my glasses.

'You'll have to take those off, Gabs,' Gavin stated. 'How well can you see?'

'Not too well,' I admitted, my already considerable sense of insecurity rising as I took them off.

'I'll put them in the car,' he offered, extending a hand, and I passed them across.

Suddenly I seemed to have very little chance of escape indeed. The surrounding wood had become a green blur save for the nearest trees and the grass at my feet, while my confidence had gone through the floor. I was going to get shot, then fucked, or made to suck cock, or have Sabina's monstrous dildo pushed up me, if I could take it. The fucking I could take, but the thought of the paintball hitting me had my stomach tying itself into knots. It hurt, a lot, as I knew only too well, and as I adjusted my goggles I was seriously considering backing out.

I just couldn't do it. Poppy was on edge, giggling and chattering, scared despite her enthusiasm, and I couldn't leave her on her own. I felt I needed to impress Sabina, too, a foolish reaction perhaps, but one I couldn't help. The boys were so full of enthusiasm, as well, which affected me, for all that a real rabbit could hardly be expected to sympathise with the enthusiasm of a fox or a farmer.

All six of us were over the gate, Sabina and the boys checking their gear. Each had their own colour: scarlet for Gavin, a vivid yellow for Fat Jeff, green for Monty and fuschia pink for Sabina, designated by a bandanna, which along with their green clothing reminded me of a children's cartoon, although I couldn't put a name to it. It suited their behaviour though, even Sabina was full of childish glee at the prospect of hunting us down.

'We're game on when you hear a shot,' Gavin informed me, as he came to join Poppy and me, his eyes flicking between our bare chests.

Poppy responded with a nervous nod. I didn't bother, glancing instead to the thick vegetation to either side of the track.

Gavin grinned and signalled to the others. 'Let's go, boys, it's rabbit season!'

'No it's not, it's duck season!' Jeff answered him.

'Rabbit season,' Gavin called back.

'Duck season!'

'Wabbit season!'

'Duck season!'

'Duck season!'

'Rabbit season.'

'OK, Doc, have it your way, it's wabbit season.'

Gavin loped off up the track, laughing, and the others followed, Sabina first, then Monty and Jeff talking together in sniggers and whispers. I watched them go, waiting for them to disappear around the curve of the track before I made a move.

'What shall we do?' Poppy asked.

'Split up, for one thing,' I advised.

'I'd rather stay with you.'

'We will get caught that way, both of us, but, if you want to follow, I am going to run back down the road a little way, to where it goes along the river, follow the river around to the back of the hill and go up that way.'

'Good idea, I'm coming with you.'

'OK, but you go the other way.'

She nodded. We kissed and pulled on our rabbit heads. With no glasses, and only the tiny nostrils to look out of, I could barely see. There was nothing to be done about it though, and I scrambled over the gate as quickly as I could, waited a moment to listen for cars, and ran.

I could picture how I looked, all too well: bare breasted, with half my bum showing around the tiny rubber knickers and my tail bobbing behind me, never mind the rabbit head. As I ran I was sure a tour bus full of pensioners or a convoy of army trucks was bound to choose that exact moment to come down the lonely rural road, but neither did, nor anything else. I made the river just as a distant pop signalled the start of the hunt. There was an ancient barbed-wire fence, which I climbed gingerly across, grateful for my long legs and wondering how Poppy would cope, then hurried down to the bank.

It was not easy. The river was fast and rocky, with overhanging trees and moss-grown banks, slippery from the night's rain. It was also noisy, and I could see the hill only as a vague green bulk to one side. The boys were sure to guard the track, and have the others fan out to cut off anyone going through the foliage, but with luck wouldn't bother about the back. I was still expecting the sting of a paintball on my bare flesh at any moment, but it never came.

My skin was soon prickly with sweat and I was wishing I could just strip off my costume and plunge into the cool water. It would have been amusing to leave them hunting nothing while I relaxed on one of the smooth, sunny flats of rock out in the stream, but it was hardly fair on Poppy. I'd have had it taken out on my bottom too, and after Sabina's spankings I was distinctly tender.

At length I reached the back of the hill, a much steeper slope than the front, broken and rocky, with small trees sticking out at every angle. I began to climb, pulling myself up on branches and trunks, as quietly as possible. I could see the mast above me, just about, then a squat pale shape that could only be the building, with Fat Jeff leaning against it, his great bush of hair and his yellow bandanna unmistakable.

I froze, but his back was to me and I managed to get into the shadow of the building. There was a fence, rusting and broken, allowing me into the little compound around the mast, and I was safe. Feeling extremely pleased with myself, I climbed the concrete steps and pulled myself on to the top of the building, sitting with my feet dangling directly over Jeff's head. He took no notice whatever, until I coughed, and then he almost jumped out of his skin, before turning to look up as if he expected to find a maniac with an axe above him.

'Jesus, shit, Gabrielle! Don't do that! And how did you get there?'

'Why should I tell you?' I answered.

He simply blew his breath out, shaking his head, then made a rather embarrassed check of his paintball gun. I stretched, showing off on purpose, and he was going to say something more when Poppy emerged from the tree, waving happily as she saw me, but not Jeff, who shot her. I actually saw the splash of yellow paint explode on her thigh, and felt a strong twinge of sympathy as she shrieked in pain and surprise, clutching at her leg. Jeff yelled out in triumph, and went into an obscene victory dance, with his great flabby bottom stuck out and his arms waggling, before shambling forwards to grab her by her bunny ears while she was still massaging her thigh. She was hauled after him, into the compound and up the stairs, where he sent her on to the roof with a firm smack of her bottom, and followed.

'I got me a bunny,' he said happily, 'and this looks as good a place as any to skin her and stuff her. Watch this, Gabs.'

He had reached into one of the numerous pockets of his outfit, and produced a pair of nail scissors.

Taking hold of Poppy by her rabbit head, he squeezed the cheeks, to push the mouth forwards, and very carefully cut a hole in the fabric, opening one side of the mouth from the edge to the protruding teeth.

'What are you doing?' Poppy asked, as he let go.

'You'll see,' he said, as he put the scissors back and once more rummaged in his pockets, this time to pull out his tiny digital camera. 'You do the pics, Gabs, only hang on.'

'We said no pictures,' I pointed out, as he took his paintball gun.

He didn't answer at first, but fired three shots in quick succession out over the river, then spoke. 'Aw, come on, Gabs, just for a laugh!'

'Poppy?' I asked.

'It depends what I'm going to have to do!' she replied.

'Nothing heavy,' Jeff replied, 'just suck me off, and maybe take my load in your rabbit face.'

'You're a pervert, you know that?' Poppy answered.

'Sure,' Jeff answered, and peeled down the zip on his combat trousers.

I felt my tummy tighten once more as he flopped out his great fat wrinkly cock and his bulbous hairy scrotum. Poppy's expression was invisible, but I could imagine her feelings, the way her disgust would be bringing out her submission, just as the pain did. Jeff lay back, propping himself on a rusting chimney pipe to make himself comfortable and get his belly out of the way of his cock and balls. Poppy hesitated, then shuffled forwards as Jeff took hold of his already swollen cock, offering it to her.

'OK, you can take photos, but I get to see them first,' she said, and went down, allowing Jeff to feed his cock in at the side of her mouth.

'Cool,' Jeff answered. 'Curl up then, so I can see your tits properly while you suck, and Gabs can get the paint splash in.'

Poppy was already sucking cock and didn't answer, but curled her body so that her breasts showed nicely along with the front of her thigh where he'd hit her. I moved around to take a picture where I could get everything in, and, I had to admit, it did look comic. Because of the way he'd cut the mouth hole, she appeared to be sucking him from the side of her rabbit mouth, as if she was chewing on a fat, pink cigar or munching a carrot.

I took the picture, and more, as his cock grew slowly hard in her mouth. He began to fondle her breasts, holding one chubby pink globe and running his thumb over her nipple until she'd grown hard, and then the other. I knew she'd be getting wet, and so was I, my pussy sticky in my rubber panties just from the scent of sex in the hot summer air.

Once he was hard he took her by the ears again, using them to control her as he fucked her mouth. I moved around, to get a picture of her lying in his lap, his cock in her rabbit mouth, her big bottom cheeks spilling out around her rubber panties. Jeff grinned, and gave me a thumbs up, holding the pose until I'd taken a picture before going back to groping her boobs. I thought he was going to come, but Monty appeared from the mouth of the track, breaking the moment by laughing.

'Shut up, you fat bastard!' Jeff answered him. 'I was just going to spunk!'

Monty approached, grinning, to climb up with us and plant a heavy smack on Poppy's bottom before standing back to watch, and to take photos with his own camera. I could hear Gavin and Sabina's voices behind me as they too arrived, but I didn't look

195

round, concentrating on taking pictures as Jeff whipped his cock out of Poppy's mouth and began to masturbate in her rabbit face, holding her by her long, floppy ears as he tugged furiously.

'Get the money shot, Gabs – get the money shot –'

He finished with a grunt, as spunk erupted from the tip of his cock, all over Poppy's rabbit head, soiling the fluffy pink fur, before he popped it back into her mouth to finish off and make her swallow what was left. Jeff was groaning, his cock jammed deep, Poppy struggling to cope, and left coughing and spitting come when he finally let go of her.

'Nice one!' Gavin announced as he climbed up, followed by Sabina. 'You made it then, Gabs?'

'They came up the back,' Jeff explained, puffing, 'sneaky cows. Gabs was on the fucking roof before I saw her, but, boy, did I get Pops!'

'So I see.' Gavin laughed. 'So, one run and one mark down. That's not good, boys, not good at all.'

'No,' Monty agreed, for the first time allowing his disappointment to show. 'Next time, maybe.'

'Next time, yes,' Gavin replied. 'Be positive. You ready then, girls?'

'Just let me have a drink,' I answered him, and accepted his water bottle, pulling my rabbit head up and draining a good half of it down my throat.

'Hot work, huh?' he remarked as he took it back. 'Second run then, same rules, if the bunnies get to the cars, they're safe.'

'We're safe if it gets dark too,' I insisted.

'Make that six o'clock,' Monty put in. 'I want my dinner.'

'You got it,' he answered. 'Take my keys, Gabs.'

I put them into the top of my sock, Poppy following suit with Monty's. Sabina stayed up with us as the others set off.

'You're going to let me get you,' she told me, 'because, if you don't, it's hairbrush time this evening before dinner, and I don't care how much you squeal, or if the other guests know you've had your botty spanked.'

I answered with a nod, although it was a close run thing whether a paintball hit or full-on public spanking was worse, never mind having people hear. She wagged her finger at me before climbing down, and jogged away down the track after the boys.

'They'll check the back this time,' Poppy said, still trying to wipe spunk from her fur.

'Yes,' I agreed, 'but they might just hang around near the cars, or more likely have one or two there, like they did with Jeff here, or try and rush us here, so we'd better get going.'

'Which way? And are you going to let Sabina get you?'

'No, I'm not. I'd rather take the spanking.'

She nodded and began to climb down. I followed, and moved off to one side, into thick foliage. It was not a good choice, my rabbit ears constantly catching and twigs scratching my skin, but I pushed on, looking for a hiding place. If I could lie low and let the hunters pass, maybe I could get down to the river and run back down the road, coming in behind whoever was guarding the cars. They didn't know I'd dare the road, so it had to be worth a go.

I heard the pop of a paintball and my stomach grew tight once more. There was a patch of gorse ahead, forcing me to go sideways, right towards them, but as I gingerly moved between the spiky plants and a rocky outcrop I discovered the perfect hiding place. The rock stuck out over a hollow, almost deep enough to be called a cave. It was invisible from above, invisible from either side, so unless somebody came along the same narrow, gorse-grown rabbit track I'd used, I was safe.

It was muddy too, so I squatted down on my heels, listening. My feelings were running high, from my apprehension and watching Poppy being made to suck Fat Jeff's cock. After a few minutes I was wondering if I should try to bring myself off, to clear my head and perhaps calm my nerves a little. My squatting position left my rubber knickers pulled tight to my pussy, and I reached down to touch, stroking the contours of my sex. It was tempting, and made it easier to be patient.

I closed my eyes and imagined it had been me, my body curled up on the hard concrete, sucking Jeff's big, ugly cock through the side of my mouth, while the others watched. Unfortunately the scene involved being shot first, and I couldn't focus properly, so switched to the joy of licking Sabina's bottom hole clean, my tongue in the little crevices, her taste in my mouth, exquisite submission as I played with myself on my knees.

The sudden alarm call of a bird sounded, a little way off around the hill and I froze, my fingers still pressed to my clitoris through the rubber of my knickers. Again it sounded, and I saw a black shape move against the sky. Hardly daring to breathe, I waited, expecting one of the hunters to loom up across the cave mouth at any instant. Nothing happened, and again the woods fell silent.

Very slowly, I moved forwards, to peer out through the gorse. At first I could see nothing, but caught a movement among the bushes. It was Monty, his green bandanna and his sheer bulk allowing no confusion, moving stealthily along with his paintball gun at the ready. He was a good fifty metres down the slope, and already past my hiding place. Somebody else would be at the far side of the hill, the others at the cars or coming over the top. All I had to do was wait until he was past and then come out from cover and down to the river.

A minute or so more and Monty had disappeared. I moved forwards, easing the gorse aside, and started down the hill, peering out through the rabbit nostrils to watch my every footstep, and startled a bird from the tree tops, something huge that flapped off with a raucous protest. I froze, scanning for Monty. I didn't find him, but jumped in shock and fear as a green paintball splashed against a tree just centimetres from my face. Panic took me, and I ran, uphill, knowing he wouldn't be able to catch me, even with me near naked.

Another paintball burst against the rock above where I'd hidden, as Monty called a triumphant view from behind me. I stumbled forwards, pushing branches aside, no longer caring about the scratches but expecting the sharp pain of a paintball at any instant as they burst around me, green dye exploding on mossy wood and rock.

Pink dye too, and I looked up in shock to find Sabina on top of the rocks, aiming down at me with her pretty face made grotesque by her goggles and by her sadistic leer. She pulled the trigger. The ball hit, right between my breasts, spattering my skin with dye and as the pain hit me I was going down, only to leap up with a shriek as Monty got me in the bottom.

I tumbled over, clutching myself front and back and gasping with shock. Both places stung crazily, setting my body shaking and bringing the tears to my eyes, which robbed me of what little vision I had. Curled up on the wet ground, I could only wait, as I heard the approaching crunch of their boots, and Monty's voice as I was taken by my ears.

'Rabbit pie!' Monty pulled me to my knees, the cheeks of my rabbit head were pushed in and he spoke again. 'Hold still.'

I held, shaking with reaction as the mouth of my rabbit head was opened, not cut neatly with scissors the way Fat Jeff had, but burst with something sharp and then ripped wide between his fingers.

'What are you doing?' I heard Sabina ask.

'Getting her ready to suck cock,' Monty explained.

'Ahem!' Sabina coughed. 'And have I given permission?'

'I got her!' Monty protested. 'So she sucks, and more –'

'She sucks if I say so.'

'She sucks –'

'May I have a drink first, please?' I interrupted.

I could just about see a blur of colours through my torn rabbit mouth, as Sabina passed me her bottle. Lifting my rabbit head, I put the bottle to my lips, expecting water, only to end up spluttering red spittle all over my tits as I discovered it was wine. Monty was laughing as Sabina took the bottle back.

'OK, you can have me,' I managed. 'Just be a little gentle, please.'

'Or you've got me to deal with, Monty,' Sabina answered, although I'd really meant her.

The strap-on was bigger by far than Monty's cock, or anyone else's, short of a donkey. I felt very defeated as I heard the rasp of Monty's zip, submissive, but resentful for the two now aching paintball splats on my body, and for what was to be done to me.

Monty took me by the ears again; my head was pulled around and I was fed his cock, stuffed through my rabbit mouth and into my real one. He felt heavy, and rubbery, and tasted of unwashed man, setting me gagging a little. As I sucked, I could hear Sabina, getting her monstrous dildo ready.

'Nice one,' Monty said and laughed suddenly. 'Put some wine in too; she'll be pissed as a fart!'

'Why?' Sabina asked.

' 'Cause the wine goes in through her cunt,' Monty answered. 'It's even quicker up the arse. You've got to watch it, as it goes, 'cause it gets 'em pissed in like seconds.'

Sabina's answer was full of disgust. 'You put wine up a girl's bottom?'

'Yeah,' Monty answered cheerfully. 'It's a laugh, and when it comes out, right, if you've put enough up, it squirts really far, like ten feet, serious!'

'You've done it?' Sabina demanded. 'Who to?'

'Gabs,' Monty answered, 'and Pops, and their friend Tasha. That was a laugh, 'cause I used spray cream, and she squirted in her knickers –'

'Shut up, I don't want to know!'

'Suit yourself.'

He went quiet, to my vast relief, contenting himself with feeding his rapidly growing cock in and out of my lips. My ears were still held firm, but he wasn't forcing me, or pushing it deep, letting my pleasure in the act of sucking a man's cock build. Before he was hard I'd gone on to all fours, allowing Sabina access to my bottom and sex.

I was very wet, which was just as well considering what was about to be put up me, and as the cold, rubbery bulk touched my thigh it set my muscles twitching. She took hold of the waistband of my rubber panties and began to peel them down over my heated, sweaty skin, only for Monty to protest.

'Don't pull 'em down, please! I like the way her little tail bobs as she sucks. Just get her cunt bare, that's all you need.'

201

'Shut up, Monty,' Sabina answered, but she let go of my waistband, letting it snap back against my flesh.

Instead, her fingers dug in under the tuck of my knickers, pulling them aside with some effort. I felt the cool air on my sticky, wet pussy, then firm rubber, cooler still, the bulbous tip of the dildo pressing to my hole, spreading me open, straining me, to leave me gulping on Monty's cock as I filled to the size of a fist.

She began to fuck me, easing the huge dildo in and out as she held my rubber panties aside, so that she could watch my penetration over and over again. Monty was hard, and had begun to toss himself into my mouth, making me think of the way Jeff had spunked in Poppy's ridiculous rabbit face. Now it was my turn, to be thoroughly soiled and made to swallow spunk, but with wine oozing out of my pussy hole too.

I could feel it already, cold around my hole and between my sex lips, as it squeezed out of the dildo. Sabina was having fun, giggling as she fucked me, and rubbing the fat tip between my pussy lips to set my body tightening with pleasure. Only when she pushed it deep did I discover that it vibrated, at a click and a sudden buzz, followed by her sigh of bliss.

'You going to frig off in her?' Monty rasped.

'Shut up –'

Her voice trailed off into a sigh and Monty shut up as ordered, masturbating gently into my mouth as he watched. She had me by the hips, grinding her sex into the base of the dildo to set the vibrations running through my body as well as her own. I was going to come too, my bottom and thighs in slow contraction, my bumhole twitching, my pussy tightening on the fat dildo shaft inside.

Sabina gave a long moan of ecstasy, called me her little bitch, and turned the vibrator off. I was left on the edge, so close, and would have finished myself off under my fingers if Monty hadn't pulled out at that moment.

'My turn,' he announced.

Sabina didn't even answer, but pulled the dildo from my aching pussy one last time, leaving me gaping to the air with wine dribbling from my hole. I fanny farted as I closed, and Monty laughed even as he was scrambling around. Once more my rubber knickers were pulled aside and he quickly pushed his cock up, deep in, and once more I was being fucked.

I'd thought Sabina had moved away, but before Monty had even got his rhythm up I'd been taken by the ears again and the dildo fed into my torn mouth. Wine squirted out as she squeezed the ball sac and I struggled to swallow. Plenty had gone up my pussy too, and I could feel myself growing dizzy with drink as well as sex, and taste myself on the dildo. Again I thought Monty would spunk. Again I was going to come, only for him to pull out and slide his erection into the sweaty groove between my bottom cheeks.

'Guess where this is going!' He chuckled, and pressed his cock head to my bottom hole.

I couldn't answer, my jaw agape on the thick, rubbery dildo shaft, but Sabina spoke for me. 'No.'

'Give it a rest,' Monty answered, and pushed.

My bumhole was creamy, as always, and juicy too, from my excitement and the sweat made by being in tight rubber panties, while his cock was slippery from my pussy. I began to spread immediately, with my eyes popping and my fingers scrabbling in the dirt as he started to go in, my ring wide on his helmet, and more, the head of his cock inside me, my straining bumhole open around the neck. He grunted and pushed harder, making my cheeks bulge as my rectum began to bloat out with cock.

'You dirty bastard!' Sabina swore as my slippery anal ring pushed in to the pressure and the bulb of Monty's cock pushed deep up into my gut. 'What do you have to do that for?'

'It's nice,' Monty groaned, 'nice and tight, and there's nothing she likes better than one up her dirt box, eh, Gabs?'

'You are fucking gross, Monty!' Sabina snapped, as I shook my head on the dildo in a futile effort to deny what he'd said.

I was still sucking wine from Sabina's dildo as Monty forced the rest of his cock slowly up my bumhole. He did it slowly, inch by inch, holding my cheeks wide with his thumbs so he could watch my straining, buggered ring pull in and out on his shaft. Twice he spat between my cheeks, and once slid two fingers up my pussy to pull out some more juice.

Sabina had given up, and said nothing, watching me get my bottom fucked. Only when he was right up, with his fat belly resting on my upturned cheeks and his balls pressed to my empty sex did she pull out of my mouth, to leave me grunting and gasping my way through my buggering. With the full bulk of his erection swelling out my rectum, my need to come returned, stronger than before. I reached back, to find my pussy, wet and vacant, and to touch where his shaft was stuck in my bottom hole. It felt good, too good to stop, and I ignored Sabina's little gasp of shock as I began to rub myself.

'That's my girl,' Monty growled. 'You frig your cunt, like that. Watch her come, Sabina. I'm going to cream pie her arsehole –'

He finished with a grunt, buggering me harder. I had found my rhythm on my clitoris, rubbing earnestly as my feelings came together. I was being buggered, on my knees in the mud, a man's cock in my bottom hole, my Mistress watching. They'd hunted me down, shot me, caught me, used me on the dirty forest floor, stuck her dildo and his cock in my every hole: my mouth, my pussy, and now up my bottom, in my dirt box as Monty had said; deep up my dirt box, where he was going to spunk.

My whole body went into violent contractions as I started to come. I felt my bumhole tighten on Monty's cock, in helpless spasm, my legs locked, my bottom squeezed on his lardy belly. He jerked and he was there, squirting his come up my bottom, deep, only to extract the full length of his erection from my pulsing bumhole and tug himself off, filling my gaping, squashy cavity with spunk. I was still in contraction, and could feel his hot, sticky mess oozing and bubbling from my anus, even as I was grabbed by the ears, jerked around, and my open mouth filled with hard, dirty cock, slippery with mess and hot from my own bumhole.

'You filthy fucking pig!' Sabina swore, but Monty merely gave a long, satisfied sigh.

I was still coming, and couldn't help but suck, thoroughly enjoying having his big, slimy cock in my mouth as I came slowly down through a series of little peaks, like mini-orgasms, thinking of how I would look from behind, crawling on the ground, buggered, with my wet pink anal ring wide open and dribbling spunk, with the cock that had just been up my bottom now in my mouth.

All Sabina could see was that he'd pulled his cock out of my bumhole and stuck it in my rabbit head, and she was not happy, calling him every name under the sun and slapping at his back. Monty ignored her, ringing his cock to squeeze the last little bit of spunk into my mouth and then sitting back with a sigh.

'That was good! That was fucking gorgeous! Thanks, Gabs.'

'You are the filthiest, grossest pervert I've ever met, Monty!' Sabina raged. 'In her mouth, after – after –'

'Lighten up,' Monty retorted. 'There's nothing wrong with a bit of bumhole to mouth. You should try it.'

Sabina didn't answer, presumably struck dumb by the sheer outrage of his suggestion. I pulled my rabbit head off, meaning to intervene, but she merely shook her head as she turned to me.

'Are you all right, Gabs?'

'Just about,' I answered. 'Can I have some more wine?'

'I've got brandy,' Monty answered, and passed me a tiny flask from one pocket.

I drank the lot, then some of his water, which left me refreshed if a little dizzy. Sabina was glaring at Monty, but had nothing to say, while he seemed indifferent, washing his cock and balls from the water bottle with his combat trousers and big grey underpants pushed down. He was still messing about when Gavin appeared, closely followed by Fat Jeff, who was carrying Poppy over one shoulder, bum forwards. Her hands were tied behind her back and her bottom marked with a large, scarlet splat, right on the crest of one cheek.

They'd caught her on the other side of the wood, and taken turns with her. Gavin had come between her cheeks after fucking her, so like me her rubber knickers were full of spunk. Leaving the boys to tidy up, Sabina came down to the river with us, where she kept lookout as we stripped off and washed, laughing together in the cool water as we wiped our bottoms.

206

Sabina watched, standing on a rock, a little wry faced but otherwise happy. She kissed us both when we eventually climbed out of the water, and slapped our wet bottoms before uttering a single word, full of feeling. 'Men!'

Eight

My first feeling when I awoke in the L'Auberge des Lapins was one of regret. We still had two days as we drove slowly back across Northern France, but there was a definite feeling that with the bunny hunt we'd reached a turning point. Monty's behaviour in front of Sabina had made her more wary of the men than ever, and more bossy. Again she wouldn't let them play with us in the evening, and made a point of spanking us both so that they could hear through the wall.

We set off quite early, with Monty driving Sabina, Poppy and I, and Gavin and Jeff in the jeep. Sabina had come round a little, in that she'd actually speak to Monty, but was taking every opportunity to exert her authority. Poppy and I did our best to keep the peace, while on the frequently steep and always winding roads of the Morvan most of Monty's attention was needed for driving.

It was beautiful countryside, but slow going, up until Clamecy, where we joined a main road, stopping for lunch just beyond Auxerre. Gavin was keen to buy some Chablis, a small detour, but one that inevitably ended up with us spending most of the afternoon tasting in the village and the boys too drunk to drive on. There was also an excellent hotel, with Michelin stars and a tempting menu, with both a wide range of sea food and local delicacies.

Sabina complained a little, as she'd been hoping to stay in the Champagne country again, but there was nothing she could do, save for once more deny the three men any sexual indulgence after dinner. They were not happy about it, pointing out that they were driving, bearing most of the incidental costs, and that Monty and Jeff at least knew Poppy and I a great deal better than she did. I did my best to mediate, but only succeeded in getting myself called a slut and sent into their room to keep them happy.

'Fucking dignity doms!' Gavin complained immediately. 'She's got no fucking idea!'

'She is inexperienced,' I pointed out. 'I think she is a little scared of you, as well.'

'Bollocks!' he retorted. 'She's not scared of anything, that one!'

'Cool down, Gav,' Jeff advised. 'At least we've got Gabs.'

'That's true,' Gavin admitted. 'Who's first then, or do we give her the old one, two, three; mouth, cunt and arsehole?'

'I am a little sore,' I admitted, 'after the bunny hunt, and because Sabina spanks so hard. Let me suck you.'

'Sure,' Gavin answered. 'How about a spunk facial?'

'If you have to.'

'I think I do, but I'd rather it was Sabina's face – not 'cause you're not pretty, Gabs, but just 'cause she's so up herself.'

'A good spanking's what she needs,' Monty suggested as he came in.

'Yeah,' Jeff agreed, 'I'd love to see her with her knickers pulled down and that big brown arse in the air.'

'Yeah, in your dreams,' Gavin replied wistfully. 'Come on then, Gabs, get your laughing gear round this.'

He sat down on the edge of his bed and pulled out his cock, leaning back on his arms to give me plenty of room. As I went down on my knees I caught the sound of spanking from next door, and for the first time since meeting Sabina was glad I'd been told to service the boys instead of put over her knee. My bottom was bruised and tender, and putting her needs in front of my own was getting a bit much.

Cock sucking was fine, even having my face spunked in. I felt sorry for the boys, Gavin especially, as for some reason he had borne the brunt of Sabina's tongue. As he began to stiffen in my mouth I determined to do my best for him, and took hold of his trousers, indicating that he should rise. He obliged, and I pulled them down, along with the boxer shorts he had on beneath. Monty and Jeff were watching, and squeezing their cocks, so I paused to pull off my dress and push my knickers down behind. I had no bra anyway.

'That's right, tits out, panties down,' Monty sighed appreciatively. 'You know how to please a guy, Gabrielle.'

I didn't answer, because my mouth was full of Gavin's balls, sucking them and rolling them over my tongue as I tugged at his now stiff cock. A little more and he was going to come on my head, while I was feeling hornier by the moment. I wanted to come, eventually, but with the third of them, once I'd really worked myself up. Before then I was determined to be really dirty.

Taking Gavin's thighs, I pulled him a little forwards, to get lower, pushing my tongue between his buttocks to lick at the tight star between. He gave a grunt of appreciation, echoed by Monty.

'Oh, yeah, tongue his arsehole,' Jeff sighed. 'Be a dirty bitch.'

I nodded, and pushed my tongue deeper into the moist crevice of Gavin's anus, licking, and higher, on his balls, and the shaft of his cock, kissing it, sucking on his helmet, taking it deep, pursing my mouth to let him fuck my head.

Which was too much for him. He gasped, reached down, snatched my hair and his cock and he was masturbating into my face with furious energy. My mouth was wide, ready to be filled and made to swallow what he did, but the first gush missed, laying a long, sticky streamer down my face, in my fringe and over my glasses, the last piece hanging from my nose. The second spurt caught me in the face too, and the third, across my cheek and on my other lens, leaving me spattered and half-blind with come as he stuck his cock back in my mouth to have me finish him off and swallow.

'Fucking ace!' he crowed as he finally let go of my hair. 'Thanks, Gabs.'

I managed a weak nod. Both Monty and Jeff already had their cocks out, and I crawled straight to them, earning a slap to my bare bottom from Gavin. Jeff was fully erect and I took him in, sucking eagerly with Gavin's warm, sticky come trickling slowly down my face. He had his balls out, allowing me to kiss and lick at them, playing the slut just as they wanted. Monty had stood up, and pulled my panties down properly.

'Stick it up; let's see your brown-eye,' he asked. 'Yeah, cute. You've got a lovely arsehole, Gabs.'

'Don't bugger me, please,' I asked as he got down behind me. 'You know I can barely take you, and I'm really sore.'

'Relax, I just want to rub in your slit,' he answered.

'Promise. Now stick it up, right up, so my balls smack your cunt.'

I obeyed, pulling my back in to make the best of my bottom, lifted and spread. He settled his cock between my cheeks, rutting on me with his heavy balls slapping against my pussy lips with each push. Jeff was getting urgent too, holding me by the head as he fucked my mouth, deep, and deeper still, to make me gag on his cock. I tried to pull back, choking, but he simply pushed my head down, squeezing his cock deep into my gullet, and coming.

He grunted as I felt his spunk erupt into my throat. My stomach lurched, a mixture of spunk and snot exploded from my nose and I was choking on his erection, dizzy, sick and completely under his control as he gave a couple more deep thrusts down my throat and pulled out to milk what he had left over my glasses and into my hair as I went into a coughing fit.

'That was mean, Jeff.' Gavin spoke from behind me, although there was laughter in his voice.

Still choking, and sure I was going to be sick on the carpet, I scrabbled quickly away for the bathroom, ignoring Monty's protest as he was deprived of my bottom. I could barely see, and it was all I could do to crawl to the loo and cough up my mouthful of spunk into the bowl. It was low down, fortunately, so I could hang my head well down as I snatched for some loo paper to clean myself up.

All I'd succeeded in doing was smearing spunk over my glasses when Monty arrived, gave my bottom a resounding slap, squatted down behind me and drove his erection deep up my pussy with a single hard thrust. My whole body was jammed forwards; the lavatory seat fell on my head, and before I could recover I was being fucked, my hips held in Monty's huge hands, his cock working fast in my pussy, gasping and spitting spunk with my face just an inch over the water in the bowl.

'Watch this!' Monty crowed. 'I'm going to flush her head down the bog!'

Then my face was in it as a great gush of swirling water enveloped my head, blinding me, choking me, in my mouth and up my nose and in my ears, soiling my face and soiling my hair, and all the while with Monty laughing and working his cock inside me. I came up coughing, unable to speak, but trying to rise, but with my head still jammed down the loo by the seat, which he was holding.

'Don't fight it,' he grunted. 'You've been flushed, so keep your head in there till I've spunked. Tell you what, I'll even give you a reach around, how's that?'

I couldn't answer, still spitting loo paper and spunk, but I felt his hand curl under my belly, one fat finger delve between my sex lips, and he began to masturbate me. My face was still half in the water, my hair and skin plastered with spunk and soggy loo paper and my own snot, and I began to fight, kicking and wriggling my bottom and spluttering incoherently in my pathetic efforts to tell him to let go.

He didn't, rubbing my clitoris and fucking me with short, firm jerks, until I just gave in, thinking of myself, kneeling at the lavatory in nothing but knickers and shoes, my head down the bowl, soaking wet with loo water, my face a mess of spunk and lavatory paper, Monty's cock inside me, Jeff and Gavin both laughing somewhere behind as they watched me, fucked and flushed, head down in a lavatory bowl.

I came, surrendered, but still kicking in his grip, and so did he, grunting and wheezing as he pumped me full of spunk, enough to make a great gush of

213

slippery mess explode from my pussy hole and out between my lips. He was rubbing it in as I gasped and shook in orgasm, and at my very peak somebody pulled the chain again, filling my open mouth with dirty loo water.

Sabina was not told what had happened with the boys or, at least, not the filthier details. She couldn't have coped, and we left her in blissful ignorance. I told Poppy after breakfast, to her delight, while my giving in so completely had done wonders for the boys' temper. As we drove north towards Troyes and the autoroute for Calais, the four of us were chatting happily.

We were aiming for the night ferry, so there was no real rush, with the entire day to drive a little over two hundred miles. To keep Sabina happy we left the autoroute before Chalons and drove up the Côte des Blancs, filling what last few crevices remained in the cars with Champagne. Inevitably we spent longer then we'd intended, with every single grower determined to show us his entire range. One even invited us to a lunch of goats' cheese and salad, washed down with his Blancs de Blancs, so that by the time we made for Reims and the next stage of the autoroute it was late afternoon.

There was still no real hurry, Gavin rightly pointing out that even the evening ferries would be packed full of booze cruisers, and he was keen to visit the Chemin des Dames, which he'd never seen. Monty was reading the Michelin, while Jeff and Gavin took photos of each other beside the monument at Cerny, and he discovered an excellent restaurant in Laon, which we simply had to visit.

By the time we got there it was nine o'clock, and by the time we left it had gone midnight. We'd prevailed upon Monty and Gavin not to drink, and set off aiming for the three o'clock ferry, which we just managed to catch. It was even emptier than the one we'd come out on, and we settled down in a ring of comfortably padded seats in a closed bar area, quite alone.

I'd happily have gone to sleep, as I'd been map reading, and Monty and Gavin were tired too. The others weren't, the three of them seated along a bench, Poppy fidgeting and trying to tease Sabina into giving her a spanking, Jeff drinking Champagne from the bottle and egging them on. It was quite appealing to think of Poppy getting it in what was effectively a public place, and I kept an eye open in the hope that Sabina would give in.

'A true dominant,' Poppy was saying, 'would maintain discipline at all times, regardless of circumstances. For instance, if I was to be cheeky right now, maybe complain because you don't always punish me for a reason, then you'd just whip me across your knee and deal with me, to show me you don't need a reason.'

'With a bottom like yours, there's always a reason!' Jeff joked.

'I'll do it in a minute,' Sabina threatened, 'and with your knickers down. That would wipe the smile off your face.'

'Ooo, yes please!' Poppy cooed. 'Right down, so I show from behind, or take them off and stuff them in my mouth like we did to Gabby –'

'Poppy!' Sabina warned, wagging a finger.

'Do it,' Jeff urged. 'I'll hold her down for you, and she can suck my cock while she's spanked.'

'Then mine,' Monty added, opening one lazy eye. 'And keep spanking till we've both spunked.'

'You should be so lucky,' Sabina retorted.

'Aw, pretty please!?' Poppy begged.

'Uh, uh,' Sabina chided. 'If you get it at all, you get it as discipline, which is what you need.'

'Pass her around then,' Jeff suggested. 'I haven't given her a spanking all trip.'

'That's true,' Poppy agreed. 'You can do me, Jeff, if Sabina doesn't want to, and you, Monty, if you like.'

'Oh, I like,' Monty confirmed, 'just you come across my knee –'

'Oh no you don't!' Sabina cut in, as Poppy stood up. 'I decide who gets what around here. I'd have thought you'd have learnt that by now?'

She took Poppy's arm, and pulled her back down on the seat.

'Hey, come on,' Monty protested. 'She's up for it, and I haven't had any fun with her all trip!'

'On the bunny hunt?' Sabina reminded him.

'No, I had Gabs. Jeff and Gav had Pops. Come on, Poppy –'

'No,' Sabina stated flatly. 'She's not being spanked, not by you, not by Jeff, not by anyone.'

'Come on, Sabina!' Poppy pleaded. 'At least a little one, on my skirt.'

Gavin spoke up, not even bothering to open his eyes. 'Thing is, Sabina's jealous.'

'What do you mean jealous?' Sabina demanded.

'Jealous,' Gavin insisted, 'jealous 'cause Pops is getting all the attention and, deep down, you want your own knickers pulling down and –'

'I do not!'

Gavin responded with a sour chuckle.

'I do not!' Sabina insisted.

'Sure,' Gavin responded. 'It's always the same with you dom types, yak, yak, yak all the time, telling everyone what to do, and all the time hoping somebody's man enough to tan your arse, 'cause deep down –'

'That is crap!' Sabina snapped back.

'Oh yeah?' Jeff put in. 'Why did you say we could try it then, if not 'cause you were hoping one of us would?'

'To teach you a fucking lesson, fat boy, that's why!' Sabina stormed.

'Fat boy?' Jeff queried.

'Just spank her, Jeff,' Gavin advised. 'You can tell she's after it.'

'Fucking right!' Sabina swore back. 'Now just you listen –'

'Yeah, yeah, whatever,' Gavin broke in lazily.

'What do you mean, fat boy?' Jeff insisted. 'That's not very nice.'

'Well, if the shoe fits –' Sabina began, her voice full of confidence and mockery, which broke to a squeal of surprise and rage as Jeff reached out, grabbed her by the back of her neck and hauled her down across his knees with one easy movement. Before she could even react, her loose skirt had been turned up, exposing her broad, honey-gold bottom, with nothing but a brilliant-green thong to guard her modesty.

'Jeff, no!' I managed, shocked awake, but too late.

Sabina screamed. Sabina kicked. Sabina scratched. None of it did her any good whatsoever. She couldn't get up and Jeff wouldn't let go. Sabina got spanked.

There was a brief fight for her panties, Sabina screaming in outrage as Jeff took hold to pull them down. She clutched back to grab them, just in time, and they were fighting over them, both hauling hard on the disputed scrap of green cotton, until they tore and Sabina's voice was filled with fresh outrage as her bottom came fully bare, with the plump, black lips of her sex showing behind.

With Sabina bare, Jeff laid in, his face set in determination, his huge hand rising and falling to the chubby golden bottom cheeks to make them bounce and spread, showing off her sex and the black star of her anus. Poppy was clinging to his arm and begging him to stop, as was I, but Monty and Gavin were laughing uproariously and egging him on.

She was really fighting, at first, making it impossible to get close, with her legs kicking wildly around, and her arms too, as she lashed back in a futile effort to hit Jeff, making her big bottom wobble like a chocolate blancmange as she was spanked. Poppy got thrown off and was forced to scramble out of the way, but at that instant Sabina stopped fighting and burst into tears.

At that Jeff stopped, and let go. Sabina fell off his lap, sprawling on the ground, but jumped up on the instant, and fled, streaming tears with her skirt still up over her bare bottom, and her torn panties flapping around one ankle. She managed to tug her skirt down quickly enough, only to tread on her panties and go headlong on the floor, once more exhibiting her bare bottom, only this time to an astonished seaman who had come to investigate the noise.

'What's happening?' he demanded, pop-eyed as Sabina scrambled up, for one instant in a pose that showed the full spread of her smacked bottom, with her anus a dark brown star between wide-spread cheeks.

She was already past him, running for the door, with Poppy behind her.

I had to answer him. 'Just a minor argument,' I assured him, raising my hands in a placatory gesture.

'But –' he responded, pointing to where Sabina and Poppy had now disappeared.

218

'Do not worry,' I insisted, bending to retrieve what was left of her knickers. 'She was messing about with – with her boyfriend, that is all.'

He nodded, staring doubtfully at the torn panties in my hand. I shrugged and smiled.

'Yeah, well, keep it down, OK?' he advised.

'Of course, sorry.'

He left, and I was about to follow when Fat Jeff lumbered up beside me.

'Shit! I'm sorry, Gabs – I was just having a laugh, yeah? I thought she wanted it, I really did. She's been bratting us all the time, hasn't she, and –'

'Sometimes you have to understand –' I began hotly, and stopped. 'Never mind. I am going to find her. You stay here.'

He gave a worried nod. 'Tell her I was just mucking around, yeah?'

I shook my head in despair and left.

By the time I managed to find Sabina, she had calmed down a bit. Not completely though, by any means, and despite Poppy's best efforts she was not ready to accept an apology from Jeff, nor to have anything to do with the boys at all.

I'd found them on the observation deck, where they had gone because Sabina needed some fresh air and hadn't wanted anyone to see her crying. We were already close to Dover, with the chalk cliffs lit orange by the lights of the port, and close enough to make out details on the dockside.

By the time the announcement was made for us to return to our vehicles Sabina's words were still coming out in sobs, and it was obviously hopeless to get them to make up. I had every sympathy with her too, and eventually agreed to fetch our passports and her bags. Poppy stayed by her, and with most of the ferry passengers streaming towards the car decks there was no time to do more than explain briefly to Monty what was happening.

I took our handbags, passports and as much of our gear as I could carry, leaving the rest to be dropped off at my flat in due course. By the time I'd lugged it all back up to the passenger decks and found the correct embarkation point we were in dock, and twenty minutes later we were back on English soil, or tarmac anyway, waiting to get through customs.

Monty knew not to wait for us, as it was only going to make matters worse, and to my relief he'd paid attention. I was less than happy about having to get back to London by train, but kept my feelings to myself, supporting Sabina as she cursed Jeff, Monty, Gavin, David Anthony, her father, and men in general. Only on the train did exhaustion finally get the better of her, and me.

I was woken by Poppy shaking me as we pulled into Victoria, and found myself extremely glad my flat was so close. Sabina came with us, a decision that seemed automatic. We bought milk in the station, and as soon as we were indoors all three of us collapsed into bed. I put her into my normal bedroom, but didn't even bother to close the door to the other one. After all, she knew.

I woke up again late in the afternoon, with the sunlight coming in through my rear window already tinged golden. The entire trip through France already seemed distant, as if it had happened a long time ago, or even in a dream. Poppy was there though, as ever, fast asleep with her thumb in her mouth, which brought a smile to mine. It seemed pointless to wake her, or Sabina, so I made coffee and tried to start making some sense of the mess I'd made of my appointments.

Both my answering machine and email box were full, some messages important, most not, or not very. The only one that caught my immediate attention was from Lyle Ranglin, demanding to know if I was back and what was going on. I needed to think, and to talk to Sabina, before I answered him, so I marked it as priority and moved on.

Poppy woke next, and Sabina last, staggering through to flop herself down on my couch and accept a cup of coffee. She looked dishevelled and tired, with her hair in disarray and nothing on but her top and a fresh pair of panties. After taking her first sip of coffee she spoke.

'What the fuck am I going to do about my dad, Gabrielle?'

'He left a message,' I told her, 'asking what was going on. I suggest we tell him the truth.'

'The truth! Fuck that!'

'Not the whole truth,' I corrected myself, 'but we have no reason to lie. I will simply say that I met you in France, and that you had already decided David Anthony was a mistake.'

'How do we explain how long we were gone?'

'We have a week to account for, and it is at least possible that your father will learn some of what happened from David Anthony.'

'No way!'

'We must assume it is possible, that way we are able to stick to the truth, or at least an approximation of the truth. You came with us on the Monday night, and because our drivers were intending to remain for a week, on a wine tour, or visiting battlefields perhaps, which is again the truth, we were unable to return easily. I also thought it best you took a complete break.'

'OK, that sounds good. So what, I just go home, get shouted at a bit, given a lecture and a hug and it's

221

all back to the way it was before? I don't want that. Dad wants me to do things his way, and he won't give an inch. He wants me to marry a boxer, or a footballer maybe, whatever, but what he calls a real man, and become a sort of baby farm. I don't want that. I don't know what I want, but not that. I'm too young!'

'It is natural for your father to have aspirations for you, and yet he must also accept that you are an individual, with your own aspirations.'

'You've met my dad, yeah? His way is the *only* way, that's how he sees it. If I disagree I'm just being awkward, or immature.'

'His principal concern was that the path you had chosen with David Anthony would lead you into those areas he has escaped through his success. Specifically, he mentioned drink, drugs and prostitution.'

'The fucking hypocrite! He drinks like a fucking fish, and he takes coke, and he uses girls – I'm sure he does!'

'He sees these things as faults, perhaps as faults in himself, or perhaps as something over which he has control, but to which he does not want you exposed.'

'Like I can't handle it! And it's bollocks anyway! There's more drink and drugs up west than in the roughest fucking pub in Hackney! He just wants to control me, that's what it is.'

'Presumably, yes, although his fears are understandable in the context of his life.'

She made a face. 'So what do I do?'

Poppy came out of the kitchen, holding a bowl of cereal in one hand and a spoon in the other. 'Move in with us for a bit,' she suggested, 'while you look for your own place.'

'I can't afford my own place,' Sabina answered. 'I'm just out of college, aren't I.'

'I had been going to suggest that you and your father attend joint guidance sessions,' I put in. 'Not with me, as that would be unethical, but I can make recommendations.'

'Sod that,' Sabina answered. 'It would just be the counsellor and my dad telling me how I ought to behave. If it was with you, Gabby, yeah, sure, and afterwards I can take it out on your bum!'

She laughed, and I smiled, despite an instinctive tightening of my bottom cheeks. It was the first time she'd mentioned spanking since Jeff had done it to her, and fortunately the experience didn't seem to have affected her adversely, or so I thought until she spoke again.

'He'd never budge, not an inch, and if he found out I've gone lesbian –'

'You have?' Poppy queried.

'Well, yeah,' Sabina responded, sounding surprised and a little hurt. 'What have we been doing all week?'

'Being dirty,' Poppy said happily. 'Fun, isn't it? That doesn't make you a lesbian.'

'No? What does it make me then?'

I raised a hand to stop Poppy answering before I spoke. 'Human sexuality is too complex to be pigeon-holed so easily. The conventional terms, straight, gay, lesbian and so forth, are simplistic, nothing more than convenient boxes into which society can put people. In practice, each individual's sexuality is unique, and also dynamic, changing with experience and with your hormones. Your sexuality is developing, and I imagine you have undergone a great deal of change in the last week, including, and personally I hope so, a broader appreciation of same-sex encounters. That doesn't make you a lesbian; it makes you yourself.'

'Yeah, I get what you're saying, but I really don't think I'm into men any more.'

223

'If that is how you feel, then so be it. Express yourself, but do not allow yourself to be put in a straightjacket of terminology, or put under pressure to conform to what other people see as your type. David Anthony, for instance, was wrong to attempt to steer you towards his own personal beliefs of female dominant and male submission. Speaking of that, I myself feel guilty that Poppy and I may have seemed to be steering you in much the same way.'

'Don't be, that's the way I want to go. I love playing with you two, but – but, yeah, thanks. You do get a bit heavy – dirty.'

'I follow my own sexuality, within a framework of my own morality.'

'So, what, you're going to stay a few nights?' Poppy asked.

Sabina laughed. 'What, so you can corrupt me a bit more?'

'Yes,' Poppy answered casually. 'Gabby always makes such a big deal out of everything, but you're going to be in charge, so I don't see the problem. I'd like you to be our nurse, if you're up for it.'

'How do you mean?'

'Take charge of us, completely. Just think, you can spank us if we're naughty, and we don't get any say in it.'

'What about the other stuff, nappies and that?'

'I'd like that,' Poppy admitted, 'but it would be up to you. You deal with us as you like.'

'Poppy –' I began.

'No, that's fair,' Sabina cut in. 'Give a bit, take a bit, like what I really want to do to you, Gabby, is give you the cane. I mean, don't take this the wrong way, but you're so posh, and so fucking slim, and – and perfect! You look like you just stepped out of some advert, and I want you grovelling on the floor, with your neat little arse well whipped up. Sorry, but it just turns me on.'

I nodded rather weakly, my stomach tight and my bum cheeks clenching as she went on.

'I know it's cruel, but I can't help it. And the way you get in such a paddy when you're spanked. I love that.'

'You think of me as "posh",' I replied, hastily trying to draw the subject away from my behaviour when being punished. 'What would your father's reaction be to your associating with me?'

'Are you kidding? He'd love it! Fuck me, you don't even swear!'

'Then perhaps that is the solution. You are very welcome to stay here, and hopefully your father will consider it a step in the right direction.'

'It would get him off your back for a bit, anyhow,' Poppy put in.

'Thanks,' Sabina answered. 'I really appreciate that, and – you know, if you want to play – play dirty?'

She left it in the air, but we all knew the answer. Poppy ducked down to give Sabina a rather milky kiss before putting the bowl to her mouth and draining what was left down her throat.

'Your behaviour isn't so good, though, is it, Miss Poppy?' Sabina joked.

'She had a very strict Mistress,' I explained, 'and she still reacts against it.'

'Yes,' Poppy confirmed, 'rules and rules and rules, with the cane for the slightest infraction. What I just did would have got me maybe four dozen strokes, including on the backs of my thighs.'

'Ouch!' Sabina responded. 'No wonder you can take a lot.'

'I can take a lot,' Poppy answered, 'so long as I'm treated nicely, and given a cuddle when it's over.'

Sabina nodded.

'Anna crossed the line,' I added, 'between accepting what Poppy wanted to give and taking it anyway.'

'I've still got a lot to learn, I can see,' Sabina answered.

'You'll be OK,' Poppy answered, 'as long as you remember you're not perfect yourself. A lot of doms fall into that trap.'

Sabina gave her an arch look, but Poppy was already in the kitchen.

I heard the faint pop of the fridge door being opened and, after a pause, her voice again. 'There's fuck all to eat. Shall we go out?'

We went to a pizzeria, Sabina's choice, washing down our food with two bottles of Italian red wine, which left me both drunk and tired. They both wanted chocolate pudding, and I had a slice to keep them company, leaving me almost as full as after our meal in Champagne. Back at the flat it was all I could do to make it to the couch, and I'd have gladly gone straight to bed again, but Sabina had other ideas, as did Poppy.

Our conversation had been growing increasingly intimate as we grew steadily drunk, and Poppy had been explaining about our special bedroom. They went in together as I sat down to relax, Sabina giggling over the changing station and investigating the drawers. I could hear them speaking, and was feeling a little embarrassed, a little expectant, hoping and scared at the same time, thinking of how it would feel to be nursed by Sabina, and to be caned.

'Right, Miss, bedtime for you,' she announced, and stepped from the door. In her hands she had my blue baby-doll, see-through, too short to even cover my tummy completely, and complete with frilly knickers.

She also had a nappy, a pink disposable with yellow teddy bears. 'Clothes off,' she ordered. 'Come along.'

I began to undress, my fingers shaking as I undid my jeans and pushed them down, removed my shoes and socks, peeled off my top and bra.

She watched, and as I hooked my thumbs into the waistband of my panties she spoke again. 'Come along, Miss Gabby, off they come. It's not as if I haven't seen everything you've got to show long before now.'

Poppy appeared at her side, smiling as I quickly pushed my panties down and off, to stand up nude. 'She needs shaving,' Poppy remarked, 'and a spanking before bed.'

Sabina turned on her. 'Don't you go giving yourself airs, Miss Poppy, or you'll be the one over my knee. You can get your clothes off too, fetch the shaving gear, and then into the bedroom with both of you.'

I went trotting in as Poppy left, and stood in front of Sabina, feeling exquisitely vulnerable in the nude. It was just a little cool, and I couldn't help thinking of the cane, which made my flesh prickle into goosebumps. She pointed to the changing table.

'You first, Miss Gabrielle, up you get.'

She patted the plastic mat on top and I climbed quickly up, then lay down with my knees high. Poppy reappeared with the shaving things and passed them to Sabina, then began to undress, hurriedly.

Sabina put down the bar of soap Poppy had brought, took the guard off the razor and wiggled it in the hot water before speaking to me again. 'Come on, what are you waiting for, there's nothing to be shy about, is there?'

'I – I'm not shy, Nurse – *Bobonne*, it's just that soap stings. There's cream in –'

227

'Getting a little hoity-toity, are we?' she chided. 'Good old-fashioned soap not good enough, is it? Perhaps a smacked botty would change that attitude?'

'No, I'm sorry.'

'You may well be, my girl. Now roll up.'

I rolled my legs up, holding them wide, with my pussy open to her, and my bottom too, nothing hidden, because it didn't matter what I showed. I had no modesty, nothing that needed covering, not from her. She put her hand in the basin of hot water, working up a lather on the bar of soap before slapping it on to my pussy mound, quite rough. I couldn't help but sigh as the warm, slippery bar pushed between my lips, pressing down between.

'Naughty, naughty, Miss Gabrielle,' she chided. 'We'll have none of that.'

'She likes to be frigged off before you put her nappy on,' Poppy remarked casually from behind Sabina as she pulled off her knickers.

Sabina turned on her. 'What did you just say?'

Poppy didn't answer, her mouth pursed in concern at Sabina's tone.

'I will not tolerate such language!' Sabina snapped, stepping towards Poppy. 'Open your mouth, wide.'

Poppy obeyed, puzzled, and then in very real consternation as Sabina pushed the bar of soap into her mouth, twisting it around inside as she went on. 'I will not tolerate bad language, Miss Poppy, but as this is your first offence I will content myself with just washing your mouth out with soap. Now stay like that, and think on your manners.'

Sabina stepped away, leaving Poppy with her eyes bulging and her mouth a little open, with the bar of soap visible inside, bubbles coming out around her lips, and a truly comic expression on her face. I forced myself not to laugh, which I was sure would only get me in trouble. Sabina turned back to me, ignoring Poppy as she began to rub my soap-smeared pussy, and lower, between my cheeks and on to my spread anus. A moment later both holes had begun to sting, and between my lips, making me grimace, of which Sabina took not the slightest notice.

'Hold still,' she instructed, lifting the razor from the water, 'and we'll soon have you nice and clean, the way a young lady ought to be.'

She applied the razor, scraping away my stubble as I held my legs up and open, completely exposed, biting my lip as the stinging pain of the soap increased. The stinging, and her fingers, were having an effect, making my pussy swell and tickle, to bring me the urge to have something pushed up myself, a cock or her huge strap-on dildo.

My need grew worse as I was shaved, the razor working smoothly over my bulging pussy mound, on my sex lips and between my bottom cheeks, to quickly leave me spick and span, and very, very aroused. I held still, sure any demonstration of my feelings would get me spanked, although my entire pussy was stinging crazily and felt swollen and sore.

Only when Sabina had sponged me down did the pain start to die, but not my arousal, with the soft flannel brushing my clitoris and the mouth of my sex. When she wiped my bottom I had to bite my lip to hold back a moan, and again as she burrowed the flannel up my pussy to clean me out inside. Clean, a towel was rubbed between my legs, again bringing me so high I had to bite my lip, before a little powder was applied, shaken over my pussy and between my bum cheeks, then patted in. Last came the cream, but not the way Poppy did it, rubbing a tiny bit in around my anal star. Instead Sabina put the nozzle to my bumhole and squeezed, extruding a worm of cream into my anus and leaving the end hanging from the hole, cold on my skin.

I was already so excited a few deft touches would have made me come, but as she took the pull-up nappy she'd chosen from the drawer and put it on over my feet I couldn't help but sigh, in sheer bliss. Sabina chose to ignore me, and pulled the nappy up. The material felt soft and squashy against my legs, delightful, but not as delightful as the way it felt when it was right up, hugging my hips and bottom and pussy, puffy and fresh, to make me want to stretch and squirm and wriggle in sheer pleasure.

'Behave,' Sabina instructed, lifting a warning finger. 'There we are then, all done. Into your night clothes then, while I deal with Miss Poppy.'

Poppy was still standing there, bubbles frothing slowly from her mouth, not daring to move.

Sabina turned, beckoning to her. 'Come on, my girl, up you get.'

Poppy's cheeks bulged and she pointed to her mouth. Sabina shook her head and reached out to take the soap bar from Poppy's mouth. Poppy didn't move, just wiping her mouth with the expression of disgust on her face stronger than ever. At last she spoke. 'I – I don't shave,' she said. 'I prefer to be hairy.'

Sabina gave a single, impatient tut and stepped forwards, grabbed Poppy by the hair and dragged her squealing across the changing station to apply a dozen hard swats to her bare bottom. Then, before Poppy could recover herself, she had been lifted bodily on to the changing station and her legs hauled apart, spreading the bushy black tangle of her pubic hair to the room.

'Let that be a lesson to you, my girl,' Sabina snapped. 'I stand no nonsense.'

Poppy didn't respond, and kept her legs wide as the soap was slapped on and rubbed vigorously in over her sex and between her cheeks, Sabina even pushing one slippery finger in up her bumhole. It made Poppy gasp, and with my now shaved pussy still stinging a little from the soap, I felt for her.

I was sure the soap tasted foul too, and, not wanting my own mouth washed out, I hastened to dress, pulled on my blue frillies over my nappy to leave them bulging both back and front, and slipped into the top, which hid nothing. Dressed, I went to sit on the bed, watching as Poppy's thick growth of pussy fur was lathered and shaved off, slowly, but thoroughly.

She was left quite bare, her pussy as pink and smooth as my own, also as swollen and moist, her wet flesh showing between her powdery lips. Her bumhole had been powdered too, and creamed, with a little plug of sticky white showing at the centre. She needed to come, I could see, but Sabina simply stood back and began to put the shaving things away.

'Down you get,' she said when Poppy failed to move. 'Come along.'

Poppy got down, reluctantly, and went to fetch herself a baby-doll, like my own, but pink. She quickly climbed into it, facing away, with her chubby bottom bulging in a pair of layered nylon frillies just like the ones I had on, and with no nappy underneath, showing her bare flesh, her boobs too, straining out the front with her erect nipples pushing the fabric into twin humps. Sabina finished tidying up and came to stand over us as Poppy sat down beside me, her hands on her hips.

'Into bed, both of you,' she ordered, 'and stay there. Any nonsense, one word of talking, you get your botties smacked, and if I even suspect you're being rude with each other there'll be hell to pay. Is that clear?'

'Yes, Nurse,' Poppy answered, and I quickly nodded agreement.

'Good,' Sabina answered and walked to the door, then turned as she reached it to watch until Poppy and I had scrambled into bed, before turning the light out.

Sabina left the door open a tiny crack, and I could still hear her as she moved away from it. We waited, silent, until we heard the click of the coffee machine, before coming into each other's arms, neither able to resist. Our mouths joined and we were kissing, tongues entwined, my hands on Poppy's back and lower, to feel the meaty swell of her bottom in her frillies as she squeezed my nappy seat and stroked at my breasts.

I had to come, urgently, and so did she, consequences or no consequences. We'd get spanked, maybe caned, but that only added a thrill of apprehension as we cuddled together, our mouths never once breaking apart as we stroked each other, pulling our nighties up and our frillies down, rubbing on each other's thighs, teasing each other's nipples, tickling each other's bottom, and at last slipping eager fingers on to wet, receptive pussies.

Poppy's hands were down my nappy, front and back, doing wonderful things to me. I had her too, but I was close, and wanted to cuddle as I was brought off. She understood, rubbing harder and kissing with rising passion. A finger slipped in up my creamy bottom hole, another into my pussy and I was being held, nightie up, frillies down, rubbed off in my nappy.

I came, choking off my natural cry against Poppy's mouth, my body jerking in her arms, and melting,

232

completely, given over to pleasure, and whatever she wanted of me as my own ecstasy faded. What she wanted was her bum in my face, and she got it, clambering on top of me as I lay panting gently in the afterglow of my orgasm. Her frillies were already well down, her bottom bare as she mounted my face, smothering me in plump, girlish flesh, the tip of my nose in her bumhole, squashing out cream.

She began to wriggle in my face, smearing cream over my nose and lips as I struggled to lick her newly shaved flesh. One hand had gone to her pussy, and I knew the other would be on her breasts, bouncing them and rubbing her nipples as she masturbated. I did my best to lick her bottom, trying to ignore the slippery, bitter-tasting cream as she squirmed herself in my face. Her bumhole began to pulse on my tongue and she was there.

As light flooded the room, revealing the plump swell of Poppy's bottom cheeks over my face, Sabina spoke. 'You disgusting little –'

It was too late. Poppy was coming, squirming her bottom in my face and jiggling her breasts, gasping and wriggling, with her fingers working furiously on her clitoris and my tongue still deep up her creamy bottom hole. The next instant she'd been unseated, jerked off the bed to sprawl on the floor, face down. She squealed in shock, and then in pain as the big wooden bath-brush Sabina had brought in smacked down on her bottom.

Squirming, squealing and kicking, Poppy was beaten, at least twenty hard smacks of the huge brush applied to her meaty bottom cheeks as she was held firmly down on the carpet. I could only stare, knowing full well it was my turn next, and that what made Poppy squeak would make me absolutely howl. It was real fear, and when Sabina finally let go of

Poppy to leave her sobbing on the floor I was babbling entreaties and holding my hands up, right on the edge of using the stop word we'd agreed on.

I didn't need it. To my amazement Sabina merely reached out and instead of taking a grip in my hair began to stroke me, her tone soothing as she spoke. 'Oh you poor thing! Did she sit on your face, did she? Did she make you lick her bottom? She did, didn't she, the bad, bad girl. Well, I think we both know what to do about that, don't we?'

My response was a nod, astonished that I wasn't having the bath-brush applied to my bottom. Sabina stood to push her bottom out, her big cheeks straining out the seat of her blue jeans, and then bare as she pushed them down, knickers and all, her big golden bottom a little open to hint at her pussy lips and the fleshy black knot of her anus. Craning back, she looked down on Poppy.

'Well, Miss Poppy,' Sabina said, quiet but firm, 'as you seem to think it's funny to make another girl lick your bottom hole, perhaps you'll find it funny when you have to lick mine. Come on.'

Poppy was already on her knees, craning her neck up to press her face between Sabina's bottom cheeks, and licking. I was full of envy as I watched, wishing it was me with my tongue up our Nurse's bottom hole. Sabina had closed her eyes, in ecstasy as Poppy's tongue wriggled on her anus, and she wasn't the only one.

Kneeling, with her smacked bottom stuck out behind and her frillies right down, Poppy had one hand between her legs and the other between her cheeks. She was masturbating, rubbing her pussy and stroking her hot, red cheeks as she licked the anus of the woman who'd beaten her. It took her just moments, and perhaps she'd never really come down at all since she'd been pulled off my face. Even when it was over she continued to lick, but Sabina pulled away, speaking as she turned around.

'You're a dirty piece of work, aren't you, Poppy? Imagine masturbating because you're made to lick my bottom. It's supposed to be a punishment, you slut!'

'Sorry, Nurse,' Poppy said quietly. 'I'll remind myself: I must not frig off while I'm licking Nurse's bottom.'

She was laughing under her breath, and Sabina immediately reached down, grabbing Poppy by the hair to pull her into a kneeling position across the bed and apply another dozen hard swats of the bath-brush. Poppy was gasping and shaking by the time it was done, and scuttled quickly back into bed as soon as she was released.

I could feel the heat of her bottom on my thigh, and kept very still as Sabina looked down at us, speaking. 'Any more trouble out of either of you, and it's the cane. Got that?'

We nodded. She turned and left. I lay back, my head full of visions of Poppy's bottom bouncing to the hard smacks, and of her pretty face pushed in between Sabina's gloriously big golden bottom cheeks. It would soon be me, if not one night, then the next, because we had our nurse, my *Bobonne*, Sabina, so beautiful and so thorough, so stern, too stern maybe.

I didn't care. She could cane me, if she felt she ought to, but I needed her attention, and my arousal, while the wine I'd drunk was making me brave. My thighs came up and open. I closed my eyes, just lightly, as Poppy spoke, a whisper. 'What are you doing, Gabby?'

'Peeing in my nappy. Hold me.'

Her arms came around me immediately, holding me tight as I let go, warm pee squirting out into my nappy, to run down my pussy lips and into my sex, to wet my bumhole and to soak in, making the soft, puffy material swell and bulge between my legs and under my bottom. I was sighing as it came out, in bliss as I wet myself and my nappy grew slowly fatter and heavier. There was plenty, nearly a bottle's worth, enough to let me play with it, holding back and letting a little more squirt out, pretending I was doing it in clean knickers and deliberately letting go. Soon the nappy was a great, fat, squashy bulge between my thighs and my bottom was encased in warm, moist material, a feeling I could easily have come over, but that wasn't what I wanted.

'Call her,' I sighed. 'Tell her what I've done.'

Poppy giggled and called out. 'Nurse! Nurse! Gabrielle's wet!'

My stomach tightened. I was going to be caned, and when I'd been caned . . .

The door opened, Sabina standing framed against the light from behind, rolling her sleeves up her arms. I swallowed hard, and Poppy was clinging on to me as the light came on.

Sabina stepped forwards, her top now pushed up to bare her arms. 'Out!' she ordered, jerking her thumb towards the living room.

I climbed out, trembling badly, my soggy nappy heavy on my hips as I stood up, the telltale bulge around my bum and over my pussy making what I'd done in it unmistakable. Sabina shook her head.

'I'd only just put you in that, Gabrielle! Right, into the bathroom!'

She reached out, grabbing me by the hand and towing me behind her to the bathroom, with Poppy following rather timidly behind. My nappy was so squashy it had begun to leak, pee trickling into my frillies, down my legs and dripping on the floor.

'Into the bath, now!' Sabina ordered, and left.

I climbed in quickly, to stand, touching my nappy to feel the way my pee made it bulge at the back and front, and wishing it didn't have to hurt quite so much to get where I wanted to go. It was going to, though, a lot. Sabina came back, clutching in her hand the long brown cane I used on Poppy and shaking her head.

'I warned you, Miss Gabrielle, and now you're going to learn that I mean what I say.'

'I could not help it!' I wailed. 'Not hard, please!'

'Shut up,' she snapped, reaching out.

My frillies were yanked down sharply, the tabs at my hips jerked open. My nappy fell down, under the sheer weight of my pee, taking my frillies with it, to land on the bottom of the bath with a squashy noise. My bottom was bare and wet, my cheeks moist with my own piddle, which was going to make the punishment hurt even more.

'Bend down!' Sabina ordered. 'Touch your toes.'

I bent, pushing my bottom out, my hands clutched to my ankles, my hair dangling in the bath, where a yellow trickle had begun to run from my soiled nappy. My body was shaking hard and I felt physically sick, but I held my pose as Sabina stepped back, tapped the cane across my flaunted bottom cheeks, lifted it and brought it down.

The smack of wood on my bottom flesh echoed around the bathroom in time with my scream. I felt as if somebody had branded me, the cane leaving a line of fire across my cheeks, to set me jumping up and down, clutching my bottom and whimpering in my pain.

Sabina drew a sigh. 'What a fuss over nothing, Gabrielle. You really are a big baby, aren't you?'

237

'Yes!'

'Well, we can't have you screaming like that, can we?' she went on. 'Here, put these in your mouth, maybe it'll shut you up.'

She reached down into the bath, to pick up my pee-soaked nylon frillies, which had fallen off when I went into my dance. They were dripping, and the consternation on my face was very real as I opened my mouth. She took no notice, cramming them right in, until only a tiny bit of blue frill was sticking out between my lips and I'd twice been forced to swallow the piddle squeezing out of them.

'Get back in position,' she ordered after wiping her hand in my hair. 'You get six.'

I gave a feeble nod and once more gripped my ankles, my hair now trailing in my pee and more dripping from around my mouth. Again Sabina stood back; again she measured up her stroke against my out-thrust bottom, and again she brought it down, as hard as before. Again I immediately went into my pathetic little pain dance, completely unable to control myself, splashing in my pee as I trod up and down, and shaking my head to spatter my legs and the sides of the bath.

'Better,' Sabina remarked, although I thought I'd been as bad as before, 'quiet anyway. Come on now, stick it out again.'

As I obeyed, I was wondering how any woman, ever, could possibly offer her bottom for the cane, but I did it, getting in the same undignified pose for Sabina to take her mark on my bare wet cheeks, lift and give me my third, right under the tuck of my bum, to send me jumping up and down and chewing on my mouthful of pee-soaked panties.

'Three,' she stated, and her pleasure had begun to show in her voice. 'Just three more, you great baby.'

I'd started to cry, the tears rolling from my eyes as I got back into position. My bottom stung terribly, all three cuts hot and raw, making my shivering apprehension worse as I thought how I'd feel with six cuts laid across my skin. As Sabina aimed, my vision was going hazy, and when it hit tears sprayed from my eyes and I was treading in my piddle again, only this time I slipped on my nappy, almost lost my balance completely and ended up in the bath, kneeling.

'Stay like that,' Sabina ordered as I made to rise. 'You're showing your fanny, and I reckon that's good for you.'

She was right, my cheeks flared to show me off from the rear, my pussy and my bottom hole too, slippery with juice and cream. It was right for me to be made to show, everyone says so, and, if I was kneeling in my own pee too, I had nobody to blame but myself. I stuck it out, biting my lip as the cane tapped on my bottom, closing my eyes, and screaming so hard I spat my frillies out as the cane lashed down, across the backs of my thighs, once, a second time, and a third, a seventh stroke, to leave me face down in the bath, one leg twitching uncontrollably, my whole bottom on fire, writhing in my own piddle as she stood back, laughing.

'That's how I like to see you, Gabrielle!' she crowed. 'That's how I've wanted to see you from the day we met, and now – now I'm going to piss on you.'

'Please,' I answered, all I could manage, as her hands went to the button of her jeans.

I stayed face down, wanting it on my hot bottom, which was lifted a little by the soggy remains of my nappy, and craning back to watch her. Her jeans came down, and off, her shoes and socks with them, then her thong, and she was climbing on to the bath to stand on the sides, her legs wide, her richly furred pussy pushed out, her sex lips held wide to show the wet pink crease between, her pee hole opening to squirt hot, yellow piddle all over my back and in my hair, between my legs and on my burning bottom, up my pussy hole, as I stuck my hips up, and I was masturbating in it, wriggling under her as she urinated on me, my clitoris burning, her pee squirting back out from my brimful pussy hole as I went into contraction, screaming her name and begging her to do it in my face as I went into climax.

I got it, right in my open mouth, gulping and swallowing as I rubbed feverishly at my pussy and squirmed my naked body in the hot pool of urine I was lying in. She was laughing as she did it, thoroughly enjoying the way she was soiling me, and that made it all the better as I writhed in her mess and my own, coming again and again, until at last I could bear it no more and collapsed, with the last of Sabina's piss still trickling out over my well-beaten bottom.

'Good,' she stated, as she shook herself dry, 'now clean yourself up, and then you can lick me out.'

She went to sit down on the toilet, wiping her pussy as I reached for the taps with trembling fingers. I turned the cold full on, splashing myself with chilly water then sticking my head underneath to wash the pee from me hair. Poppy retrieved my ruined nappy and soiled panties, also Sabina's lower clothes. I wanted to lick, badly, and come again while I did it, in the nude at her feet, which now seemed completely appropriate.

'Shall I put her in a fresh nappy?' Poppy asked, as I climbed from the bath.

'No,' Sabina answered her. 'I think it's about time she was toilet trained. Where are those rubber knickers?'

'In her bag,' Poppy answered.

'Put her in them. In future, she has to wear them every time she wets herself, all evening.'

'And if she messes herself?' Poppy asked.

Sabina hesitated, then answered. 'Fair enough, as long as you clean her up, and she has to wear the bunny head as well, when we get it back. She gets a good spanking too – no, the cane. That way we'll have her trained in no time.'

My mouth had come a little open as I took the towel from Poppy, thinking of how I'd look, made to go around my own flat in nothing but pink rubber panties with a bunny-girl tail and the ridiculous head. It didn't matter, not even with the caning. She would cane me anyway, and spank me, and punish me in any way she pleased. I was going to be nursed, properly, allowed to behave as an adult baby-girl should, and, if that meant punishment, that too was her right.

I was dry by the time Poppy came back with the rubber panties, except for my hair, which I gave a quick rub with a towel. She gave the panties to me, both she and Sabina watching as I pulled them up, snug around my bottom, holding my cheeks in, covering me, yet making my rear view infinitely more embarrassing than had I been bare. To be nude is free, to be toilet trained in rubber bunny-girl knickers is humiliating, but also exquisite. I'd never understood before, not before Poppy, and others, had taught me, and I was deeply grateful to them all as I got down on my knees.

Sabina had finished with the toilet, but was still sat on it. I was snivelling a little as I shuffled towards her on my knees, and she ruffled my hair as I reached her.

'Now you can say sorry,' she stated, 'and you always will, after every punishment.'

As she'd spoken, she had pulled up her top and bra, letting her round golden breasts fall free. I was taken by the hair, gently this time, and pulled in, my face smothered in the resilient, velvet smooth flesh of her cleavage. She held me like that, letting me rub my face between the plump pillows of her breasts, before moving me to a nipple so I could suckle.

I was in heaven as I took her large, dark teat in, feeding on her as she stroked my head and back. My hands went down to feel the swell of my pussy lips beneath the tight rubber of my panties, and behind, to touch the taut double bulge over my bottom cheeks. I knew I could do it, if I wanted to, to fill my rubber panties with a fat, central bulge between my cheeks. If I did I'd be punished: spanked, caned and made to go in rubber knickers and the ridiculous rabbit head. I'd also get to suckle her, and kiss her bottom hole, and lick her pussy, comforted for my pain.

She took my head again, moving me to her other breast, but this time holding the full globe of girl-flesh out to my mouth. As I took her teat in to suckle I tightened my tummy, pushing a little, to send a thrill of pleasure through me as my bumhole opened slightly to the load within me. I was still uncertain, but my feelings were rising as I stroked myself through my panties, tempting me to do it and to take the consequences.

'Now your favourite thing, you bad girl,' Sabina breathed, as she detached me from her breast.

My thighs slid a little further apart as she rose, stretching the rubber tighter still over my bottom and pussy. She was smiling down at me, and twisted back to watch as she put her hands against the wall and stuck her bottom out, making a perfect globe of warm honey-brown flesh, deeply divided to show the chubby swell of her sex, moist and pink at the centre, and her bumhole, a jet black star with little pieces of my white loo paper caught here and there in the tiny crevices and blocking the central hole.

'Lick me clean,' she ordered, 'properly, right in my arsehole.'

I didn't hesitate, pushing my face between her heavy cheeks to lick eagerly at her anus. She moaned in pleasure as her earthy, acrid taste filled my mouth, and I was rubbing my pussy just as hard as I could. I could even feel the bits of loo paper in my mouth, but that was just fine. I wanted to lick her bottom hole more than anything else; she had a right to make me and, if she happened to be dirty, that was just my bad luck.

Again she moaned, and gave a little shiver, her fleshy bottom wobbling in my face as I pushed deep up, to clean right in, as deep as I could go, utterly in thrall to her, and close to orgasm, wanting to come while I performed that dirtiest, most intimate service for her, using my tongue to wipe her bottom.

'I think I'm probably clean now, Miss Gabby!' She laughed, and reached back to pull my face from between her cheeks.

I was left gasping, saliva running down my chin, dizzy with pleasure, with the scent and taste of her. Poppy came behind me to press something to my lips as Sabina sat back on the loo, brandy, which I gulped down eagerly, holding just a little in my mouth. In front of me, Sabina was poised on the edge of the loo seat, her thighs wide open, her pussy running juice, bumhole just showing, wet with my saliva.

'OK, you dirty little bitch,' she drawled, 'take me there, and yourself, but I come first.'

Her hand reached out to pull me in and I began to lick, her sex lips, between her bum cheeks, in her bumhole, up her pussy, on her clitoris lapping eagerly in my drunken excitement, enjoying her sex as I knelt with my rubber-clad bottom stuck well out, my cheeks hot from caning, my bumhole a little distended, teasing myself as I licked her, and wondering if I really dared fill my bunny knickers in front of her.

She was holding my head between her thighs, firmly, her grip maybe stronger than I could break. Not that I wanted to, but it felt nice to be under the control of a woman big and strong enough to dominate me physically, to lift me in her arms or across her shoulder, to spank me when I needed to be spanked, to make me lick her when she needed to be licked. Now I was doing it, and she was going to come, right under my tongue, in my face, as I knelt, willing and obedient, grovelling on my bathroom floor in my rubber panties.

Her grip in my hair grew tighter, her thighs squeezed around my head, her breathing grew deep, urgent, and she was coming, with a low moan of ecstasy as I lapped hard on her clitoris, firm and even. She was calling me her doll, her plaything, and a dirty little bitch, again and again, delighting in my submission to her, and my complete obedience. Another groan, a last babble of words, and she was done.

'Bitch – dirty little bitch, Gabrielle, little dirt toy – now get your head where it belongs, and you can come too.'

She pushed me lower, pressing my mouth between her bottom cheeks to make me lick her anus again. My tongue went up, deep up, her hole now wet and slippery with my saliva and distended against my lips. She was rubbing my face on her pussy too, using me to masturbate with, as if I really was just a sex toy. Maybe she was still coming, and I was going to, because I had to, and because she'd told me too, and with my panties full.

I reached back to hold my bottom as I pushed, letting my bumhole spread, this time right open, extruding a heavy piece of dirt into my bunny knickers, and I was doing it. Poppy gave a delighted giggle as she realised, and I was gasping out my ecstasy between Sabina's bottom cheeks, my mouth full of her taste as my bunny knickers began to swell behind. I could feel my bulge, growing in my hand, the gentle valley between my cheeks pressing out into a fat, bulbous mass. Again I pushed, and felt it grow a little more, making a lumpy dome in the seat of my bunny knickers, to leave no doubt whatsoever in anyone's mind of what I'd done, including Sabina's.

'You haven't?' she gasped. 'Oh, you have! You filthy little slut, Gabrielle, you dirt bitch, you pig, you filthy pig, you –'

She broke off with a grunt, her fingers locked hard in my hair and she was coming again, using my nose to rub herself off and I struggled to lick at her open bumhole. I had it all out, the full weight of what had been in my rectum now in my panties, a heavy, solid ball, bulging between my cheeks and pushing out the tight rubber behind. Now I could come.

The rubber was pulled tight between my sex lips, and as I began to rub the motion made my load wobble in my knickers, the perfect sensation, keeping me firmly in mind of what I'd done, with Sabina still coming in my face as I licked and sucked at her bottom hole. Poppy came behind me, and began to spank the exposed part of my bottom, telling me off for being so dirty in between giggles for what I'd done, and how I looked, with my fingers working my pussy and the huge bulge in my bunny knickers wobbling to the motion of my frigging. Suddenly I was there, in perfect ecstasy, the climax not just of hours but days, stripped and beaten and pissed on, made to lick my darling Nurse's bottom clean, made to lick her to orgasm, and permitted to come myself, grovelling on the floor in my soiled, bulging bunny knickers as I fed from her bumhole.

The first thing that came into my head when I woke up was that I had my Nurse. The second was that it was Monday morning and that I had a million and one things to do. It had been nearly three o'clock by the time we'd cleaned up and sorted ourselves out, with Sabina needing a lot of reassurance as the three of us sat and drank brandy. We'd ended up hugging and kissing, and would have all gone to bed together had there been room.

I felt weak, tired and my head ached a little, but I also felt wonderful. After so long, so much effort, I finally had my Nurse, and not just for me, but for Poppy too. Sabina was rather sterner than I'd anticipated, in fact, a lot sterner, but the thought of being under her discipline was undeniably arousing as well as frightening. Frightening, yes, but I still felt completely safe. Underneath her dominance, and her very real cruelty, she looked up to me.

Only one thing remained, to assure her father that he no longer needed to be concerned, and that wasn't going to be difficult. It was true, after all. Poppy and I drank moderately, never took drugs to speak of and had nothing whatsoever to do with prostitution. The fact that Poppy and I would be under her discipline was neither here nor there. She was grown up, and her sex life was none of his business.

I was still a little taken aback when the buzzer went at ten to nine and on answering it I heard his voice, demanding to be let up. Poppy was in her baby-doll top and no knickers, eating cereal, Sabina stark naked in the bathroom. I hustled both of them into the special bedroom and locked them in, composing myself as I opened the door. He walked in, as tall and powerful as ever, coming straight to the point as he spoke.

'So you are back. I'd hoped to hear from you before now.'

'We had one or two delays,' I replied confidently, 'but I am pleased to be able to report that your daughter no longer has any interest in David Anthony.'

NEXUS NEW BOOKS

To be published in August 2005

THE INDECENCIES OF ISABELLE
Penny Birch writing as Cruella

By her second year at Oxford, and at great cost to her personal dignity, Isabelle Colraine has managed to gather a group of like-minded women around her, women with a taste for the sexual domination of their fellow female students. She imagines that she can set aside those she's tangled with on the way up, including her dirty-minded scout Stan Tierney, but he, and several other men no less depraved, have other ideas.

£6.99   ISBN 0 352 33989 6

SCARLET VICE
Aishling Morgan

Beautiful, voluptuous and supposedly innocent, K'Tai is also too headstrong for her own good. Obliged to flee her village in a hurry in order to avoid the application of a switch to her curvaceous bottom, she finds herself in a far worse situation, at the mercy of lascivious slavers, cruel priests and sadistic nuns, each determined to inflict ever more severe punishments and indignities upon her.

£6.99   ISBN 0 352 33988 8

TIE AND TEASE
Penny Birch

Penny Birch is playing the fox in a bizarre hunting game. But all does not go according to plan, and she's found by a total stranger, Beth, who's naturally concerned at the state of her. After spending an awkward afternoon explaining herself, Penny becomes determined to seduce Beth, an innocent in all the ways of bizarre naughtiness. Penny's continued efforts get her into more and more difficulty, frequently punished and humiliated, even put on a roasting spit, until even she is wondering if she can take any more.

£6.99 ISBN 0 352 33987 X

If you would like more information about Nexus titles, please visit our website at www.nexus-books.co.uk, or send a stamped addressed envelope to:

Nexus, Thames Wharf Studios,
Rainville Road, London W6 9HA